A Government Agency

"We're putting you in the brothel business, Gaines. I'll teach you the ropes, bring you in slowly so you get used to it. After a couple of months you'll take over the day-to-day, under me, of course. It's a tricky job and sensitive. We're after anybody who's got access now or might get some access in the future. It'll be pivotal in our dealings with the Japanese. With the hold we get on them, we'll be able to subvert those dirty tricks they use to upset the trade balance. Who knows what else we'll dredge up?

"Oh yeah, and we're also preparing a room for you here," he went on. "But for now you'll stay at a hotel down the street." Leamer continued to smile broadly. "We're expecting a lot from you, Gaines. You might even enjoy the perks."

"A disturbingly memorable account of a man's search for his soul set against the background of international intrigue."
Booklist

OPERATION FANTASY PLAN

PETER GILBOY

AVON BOOKS  NEW YORK

AVON BOOKS, INC.
1350 Avenue of the Americas
New York, New York 10019

Published in hardcover by William Morrow and Company, Inc.; for information address Permissions Department, William Morrow and Company,
Inc., 1350 Avenue of the Americas, New York, New York 10019.

First Avon Books Printing: July 1998

AVON TRADEMARK REG. U.S. PAT. OFF. AND IN OTHER COUNTRIES, MARCA REGIS-
TRADA, HECHO EN U.S.A.

Printed in the U.S.A.

WCD   10 9 8 7 6 5 4 3 2 1

*This book is dedicated
to my son Preston,
who loves secrets
as much as I do.*

PART
I

We had fed the heart on fantasies,
the heart's grown brutal from the
fare.

—WILLIAM BUTLER YEATS

1

PETER GAINES

It is not easy to introduce myself. It is even harder to explain why I took the road that I did.

A psychiatrist would say that my life was determined in its formative years and that I am simply the result of my upbringing. But that would be wrong. I am responsible for the things I have done and the many things I have left undone. And I am determined to confront my failings head-on rather than make excuses for them.

I can tell you that as a young man I was absolutely mystified about which way to go in my life. The only thing I knew for sure was that I loved puzzles and mysteries and that I was especially fascinated by secrets. Like many boys, I often took the long way home—through back alleys and backyards, stopping to eavesdrop on wives and listen to old winos in their cardboard dens—and I always lied to my parents about where I had been. From as early as I can remember there seemed to be a clandestine fellow inside me who delighted in deceptions and was ready to choose a devious way even when a straight one was easier. That is the path I ultimately chose.

The story I will tell here is about some of the choices I made. My intention is not to manufacture disguises but

3

finally to remove them. The only exception is the name
I will give you, Peter Gaines. Everything else is factual
and straight.

Before I begin, I should tell you that less than a month
ago I was dismissed from a certain government organization. It is the same organization that nearly everyone
agrees is indispensable to our national security, yet too
secretive, too deceitful, and generally out of control. And
I assure you that it *is* out of control. Even the paper push-
ers back at headquarters: I know they see themselves as
upright citizens who park in their assigned stalls, arrive at
their desks on time, and tuck their children in at night,
but they are part of it all. And the many agent handlers
in the field who think they are doing the best job they can.
They are part of it too. I do not blame them completely. I
know all the arguments that make it seem as if there is
no black and white, no right and wrong. For me too the
world had become a vast blanket of gray, where I used
lesser evils to overcome greater ones. I had no idea how
far that thinking would eventually lead me.

But regardless of what I disclose here and what people I've worked with may think of me after they've read
this, I want to make it clear that it is not my intention
to betray any personal secrets or to break our special
confidences. What I will disclose is mostly against myself and a particular operation I tolerated. Its code name
was Fantasy Plan, and at one point it included a seventeen-year-old girl named Songkha Chattkatavong. I
called her Song.

The first time I saw her, my life changed in a second.
Just to think of her now, and I see it over again in my
mind.

*"This new girl's unique," Leamer said to me. "She's
unused and insolent, a real fighter," he added with delight. "We got plans for her. She's a special order for
someone we've targeted. She'll get us invaluable access."*
The next day on the monitor I watched him bring Song-

kha into the interview room. Dressed in dark peasant
clothes, her body was slender, and there was a deep shine
of black hair that fell below her shoulders in front and
back. But she was barely a woman at all, her breasts
still maturing.

There was a jump in reality, a skip on a record, and I
thought of my sister, Beth, when she was younger and
just developing. Yes, it was sixteen-year-old Beth standing there with that same look of hurt. Or was it shy
Wendy Morris, who lived next door to me when I was
growing up? Or Rachel Adams, who sat behind me in
math class and slipped me notes with little red hearts
on them?

I wanted to get up and adjust the picture or change the
channel or just make it all go away by turning off the
monitor. I closed my eyes and reopened them, but she
was still there with that same look: Beth, Wendy, Rachel,
Songkha. Each of them at the fine line between girl and
woman.

I shrank back. Nausea rippled through me.

Leamer gazed up at the camera and smiled at me
through the monitor, a see-what-I-mean smile. "Tomorrow
she's all yours," he said to me. "Be sure to get what
we need."

And now, for the sake of the record, as well as for my
own memory, I have to untangle what happened. It is a
report of madness and dreams and of my own deeds,
which now seem incomprehensible to me. I need to lay
out these deeds and look at them clearly because events
have shown me how inventive memory can be, how we
twist the truth to suit our desires and justify what we have
done. But there is no justification for how obsessed I became with Song.

In spite of the urgency that Operation Fantasy Plan be
widely known, by necessity I must explain the beginning,
or this story will make no sense to you at all. Because of
an injury to my hands, I must dictate this report rather

than write it. It all began in Monterey, California, at the Branscomb Institute for International Business. I was much younger then, eighteen years younger. But I can still remember the lecturer's first words: "The name of the game is and always has been A-C-C-E-S-S."

2

THE BRANSCOMB INSTITUTE

The year was 1979. It was early February. Jimmy Carter was still president. The shah had not yet fled Iran, and the embassy had not yet been stormed and all the hostages taken. Brezhnev was still in power, and despite his smiles and reassurances to the President, the Soviet Army was preparing to invade Afghanistan. The Berlin Wall was still up. Mao was dead. Japan was reeling from political scandals and was fearful over the world's oil supplies. Wars in Africa; terrible rumblings in South America; Guatemala and Nicaragua were on fire. The world was not a quiet place at all, and it was going to get worse.

On that first day I filed into the lecture hall with the other new men, about twenty-five of us, and took a seat at the far end of a row. The speaker was already waiting at the podium. He was a round, ruddy-faced man in his late fifties, with a baggy neck that spilled over his collar and a salesmanlike smile. Already taught to observe everything, I noted his manicured hands, the black wing-tipped shoes polished to perfection, and his paisley tie and gray suit. The entire scene could have passed for a corporate sales meeting.

When we were seated, he closed the curtains overlooking Monterey Bay, then moved back to the podium and cleared his throat.

"The name of the game is and always has been A-C-C-E-S-S," he said. He looked back at us as if that statement were the sum total of his message. Later I realized that it was.

I glanced around the lecture hall. The new men were various ages—twenties to late forties—and an assortment of sizes and shapes, but all of us were sitting straight and alert, most of us in shirtsleeves and ties like regular business students. All men. A men's club. No women allowed.

Judging by the speaker's age, I figured he was from the old school. At our introductory training back at headquarters, we were warned that the men from the old school were more clever than we ever would be. They had cut their teeth with "Wild Bill" Donovan at the Office of Strategic Services and later under Truman with the Central Intelligence Group, the forerunner of the present Organization.

The speaker smiled cryptically, and his baggy throat jiggled as he swallowed. Then he made his second pronouncement. "The world is not what it seems," he said softly. Of course I had understood that even as a boy; there is so much hidden beneath the surface in everyone, including myself. "All spies are liars," he went on. "Do not ever forget that."

I didn't take it personally. We were being trained as agent handlers, and an agent handler is not a spy. Not exactly. Our job is to recruit foreigners to spy for us. Persuade or even coerce them to work against their countries and then "handle" them as our agents.

The speaker cleared his throat again and tapped the microphone on his lapel. Finally he introduced himself.

"I am Mr. Haycock, the senior sales representative for IBM Office Systems."

There was an uproar of laughter around the room. He studied us with a mixture of bemusement and scorn. The laughter quickly died.

"For the next fifteen months you will have none of

the usual distractions of the world. You will be able to concentrate. For the most part you will not be separated from the other students at this business school. But they will not know the real purpose of your studies. First, you will continue your agent handler training that began at headquarters. And second, you will be trained in the simplest way to gain access to foreign countries today: business. As you know, business is the bread of the world, a universal food. It is as welcomed as the dollar itself because it is nearly synonymous with the dollar. And business means *access*. Access to technologies. Access to militaries. Access to governments.'' He shrugged dramatically and smiled again. ''So, we are businessmen. That is how we get in to recruit our agents. And that is how we get out.''

Mr. Haycock stepped from behind the podium and casually approached the edge of the stage. He dabbed his forehead with a crumpled handkerchief as he surveyed us with a skeptical eye. His gaze seemed to penetrate each of us individually, but I thought it lingered on me a bit longer than the others. Perhaps he had a special assignment for me.

Then he continued on, proudly explaining how the present refinements of intelligence far surpassed the import-export covers of the old days. The Organization's companies were no longer shady fly-by-night outfits but worldwide corporations—many with names we all know—corporations with their own research and development departments and masterful marketing strategies, producing a wide range of everyday products from TVs to running shoes, dress shirts to refrigerators.

''It is all so very tidy,'' he told us. ''The managers, the factory workers, and ninety-eight percent of the staff are unwittingly involved. But within each corporation there are special individuals—agent handlers like yourselves who are also trained as businessmen—whose real function is the Work.'' For a moment Haycock's stern expression twitched to a smile. ''We even manage to make a respectable profit, gentlemen. But don't worry. Since we are upstanding Americans, we always pay our corporate taxes back home."

Laughter rippled across the room.

"Some people rave about the new high-tech spying gadgets—lasers, computers, satellites. But there will never be a substitute for human intelligence. And that means human *access*. Those technology people with their satellites and computers are always on the outside trying to peek in. But we are already on the inside."

A smile spread across his face. "Not just inside their militaries and businesses. Sometimes we are even inside their minds."

I thought that was an odd statement and thought it curious as well that he would take such delight in it. A hand sprang up on my right. I looked over to seen an earnest and serious-looking fellow in his mid-twenties, with round glasses and blondish hair. He waited until Haycock stopped smiling, then interrupted his next sentence.

"Excuse me, sir, but what do you mean, we are inside their minds?"

Haycock smiled strangely and faced him directly. "Your name?"

"Vaal, sir."

"Brush up on your history, Mr. Vaal. Nothing's changed since the days of the Romans or the Phoenicians or the ancient Chinese. We are spotters. And when we spot someone with access to targeted information, we determine their personal vulnerabilities. Then we recruit them to spy for us by exploiting their friendship or their patriotism or anything else. We learn what makes them tick, Mr. Vaal. We get inside their minds and find out where they're weak."

"And what if they don't have a weakness, sir?"

"Then they have a price."

"Isn't that the same as a weakness, sir?"

The smile strained on Haycock's face. "Mr. Vaal, this isn't a philosophy class. The point is that everyone is vulnerable. Everyone. And when we find that weakness, we've got them by the balls. Lesson learned, Mr. Vaal?"

"Yes, sir," he answered concedingly.

"And after we've got them by the balls, we train them well, dispatch them to specific targets or plant them inside, and then collect the information. We simply harvest the fruits of our labors."

With a wave of his hand Haycock indicated the conversation was over. He paced in front of us for a few moments, then continued, telling us that after we had finished our business training, some of us would be joining the Organization's own companies. The rest of us would begin as brokers or junior executives, moles planted inside Exxon, Sony, NEC, Corona, and other corporations. The Organization would send out our résumés for us. And companies would seek us out because of our multifluencies, our social graces, and our business acumen. Some of us might even be assigned to the so-called illegitimate operations, such as producing counterfeit designer clothing or dealing weapons. But all this, he assured us, was in the service of A-C-C-E-S-S. Over the years we would find ourselves in many places—Rome, Barcelona, Marseilles, Seoul, Taichung, Bangkok. We would be joining a handful of "businessmen" who were already spread out across the globe, secretly doing the Work.

"We are the protectors of millions of people who have little idea that we are the ones who keep their world safe. The burden lies on our shoulders. It is not pretty work, but it is necessary and always toward a good end."

I watched Haycock's eyes narrow to a squint as he waited for other questions. We offered none.

"If you are wondering when your first assignment begins, consider that it already has. There will be secure areas here at the Branscomb Institute where our specific work and training can be discussed freely. Beyond those places—with absolutely no exceptions—you will live your life as a business student concerned with international affairs. In addition to the real Work, you must excel in public finance, marketing management, environmental economics, and all the rest of it. It goes without saying that it will profit you to cultivate business acquaintances among the regular students here.

"And of course you will be polygraphed at two-month intervals. We do not apologize for that. It is one of the prices for what we do. Everyone is vulnerable, and our little polygraph checkups discourage any possible straying."

He cleared his throat. "Gentlemen, you are here because of your language abilities, your aptitudes, and of course your patriotism. If that last point sounds corny to you or in any way embarrasses you, then you are in the wrong place. Get out now."

My eyes involuntarily glanced toward Vaal, the student who had asked the questions. He was staring straight ahead with total attention. Haycock waited a long, dramatic minute before his face softened again to a salesmanlike smile. He stretched out his arms as if embracing us all. "On behalf of our staff here, I welcome you all to the Branscomb Institute for International Business."

I remember filing out a side door with the others and observing how the stream of us converged with the regular students on the sunny Branscomb campus. In seconds we blended in. I made my way past the Spanish-style library and through a courtyard surrounded by classrooms, then down a path through a eucalyptus grove in the direction of the parking lot. I felt light and happy. After four years of accounting at Ohio State and then another four years trying to find a grain of satisfaction with the international investment firm of Wilson, Wycoff, and Lowell, I had tossed it all in and applied to the Organization. After a dozen interviews and probably a hundred background checks I was finally accepted.

Now my future seemed wide open and exciting, offering me everything I wanted. I would be someone special, someone more than an ordinary commuter, more than the workaday accountant my father was. I would not have to sit in a cubicle with a calculator and spreadsheet and stand in line for a paycheck and drive the same route home every night to the same two-story house. I would take risks. I might even become a hero of some sort. I would travel the globe to places I'd only read about, experience the wonderful textures of different societies, the chatters of many languages, the waves of exotic smells in foreign marketplaces. And I would do it all inside the mysterious Organization, inside the inscrutable profession of secrets.

A voice spoke up from behind me. "I guess I'm going to be a businessman after all. And I thought I had escaped that rut." I turned to see that fellow from the lecture, Vaal, smiling as he approached me.

"You were pointed out to me," he announced, still smiling. "I'm Vaal. We're going to be roommates, or should I say apartment-mates?" He thrust out his hand, eager to take mine.

"Peter Gaines," I replied, surprised at his iron grip.

Vaal was interesting looking. His high forehead and round-rimmed glasses gave him an intellectual look, and behind the glasses his eyes were genial and bright and unusually blue, the bluest eyes I had ever seen. But despite the intellectual look, Vaal was muscular in a sinewy and athletic way, a combination of weightlifter and marathon runner. He was a few years younger than I, twenty-three or twenty-four. Maybe right out of college. His cheeks were smooth, and his chin was square, the kind of jaw you see on an aftershave commercial.

"You had guts going up against Haycock," I said.

His blue eyes shone with laughter as he imitated Haycock. " 'Get everyone by the balls, Mr. Vaal. Lesson learned, Mr. Vaal?' " He laughed and shook his head.

"And do you have a first name, Mr. Vaal?"

"Steven," he answered, but dismissed it with a wave. "I never use it. Just call me Vaal."

We headed down a tree-lined path that led through an open area of the Branscomb campus. Strands of blond hair fell across his forehead, and with a motion of his head he tossed them back. His walk was brisk and boyish, his whole air friendly and upbeat. "I have to admit," he went on, "it's all pretty clever and tidy. American businesses are everywhere, and we'll be in the middle of it all. A chance to make a real difference in the world."

Mindful of the restrictions on our discussions, even under the trees on the open Branscomb campus, I merely nodded. We reached the parking lot, and he leaned toward me as if sharing a secret. "I could never stand the business stuff I grew up with. You know, stocks and bonds, corporate meetings. All for money, with no thought for ordinary people." He shook his head. "It's not just narrow and immoral. That corporate wheel is nothing but chloroform. It'll put you to sleep, and you won't even know it."

Chloroform. With one word Steven Vaal gave a name to my greatest fear. I did not want to go through life like my father, stuck in a cubicle and in a deadening routine.

"Yes, it's going to be so different," I said. "No cubicles or chloroform for us."

Vaal smiled kindly. "Be careful, Peter. The Organization will have its own kind of cubicles, its own kind of chloroform. Don't be naive, or you'll get swallowed alive."

"I know that," I said quickly, surprised by his directness.

"But there is a change in the world," he went on, switching the subject, "and we'll be part of it. We made some mistakes in the last ten years. Vietnam was a disaster but we can be the good guys again, and the world will look up to us. There are values and ideals larger than any one country, Peter." He smiled thoughtfully. "Access is what it's all about. We're going to make sure this cold war doesn't turn into a hot one. Maybe we'll even put the other side out of *business* altogether. Now that's a worthwhile venture, don't you think?"

"Absolutely."

"What're your languages, Peter?"

"Oh, my mother was a Russian immigrant, and my father is second-generation German, so I had those as a boy. And I picked up Chinese in my studies. Still struggling with Japanese, though."

He nodded approvingly. "You were lucky to grow up with languages circling around you."

"What are yours?"

"Russian mostly, but with a lot of work in Chinese and Japanese. Maybe that's why they roomed us together. I grew up in an English-only family, though." He raised his blond eyebrows and adjusted his round glasses, feigning a supercilious look. "Mainline Boston, you know. Proper English only. Old money, that's what's important. Lets you know who you *really* are. Polo ponies and knife-creased pants and monogrammed sweaters for lounging around. Ta-ta." Vaal laughed again and fell back into his casual self. "More chloroform is what it is. But I escaped before they got me on the operating table."

I laughed. His openness and zeal delighted me. We understood each other. He had tossed it all in too, to be something more than an ordinary citizen. I liked him, and I felt as if I might have a real friend in the world, someone who understood what I understood: that life is not to be lived with your arms at your sides in a mindless pursuit of the good life. The future was coming into focus, and Vaal and I would be in the thick of things. We would make a difference.

Vaal motioned to a sporty red convertible. "Follow me to the apartment!" he commanded like a cavalry officer ready to lead the charge. Then he took my hand again with his powerful grip and looked me straight in the eye. "I'm really happy to know you, Mr. Peter Gaines. The Branscomb Institute is just the beginning for us. You and I are in for some exciting and rewarding careers!"

3

EIGHTEEN YEARS

*T*hat was how it began. And overall it was an exciting and rewarding career. But the Work was not what I had imagined it would be. At times my life was tedious. At times it was outright frightening. Always it was lonely and precarious and threatening, taking strange twists and turns. One of those strange turns is that now I am recalled to headquarters in Virginia and find myself standing in front of a dark walnut desk. The man on the other side is wearing a tie with little gray penguins on it.

"You do understand, don't you?" he asks me. His tone is casual, as if the topic is the weather.

"I understand," I tell him.

"It's nothing personal, Mr. Gaines."

"I understand," I say again.

And I do understand. Eighteen years since the Branscomb Institute, and now I am out. "Retired" is what they want to call it, though without pension or commendation. Without a watch or personalized fountain pen set. No desk to clean out. And no transitional help to my next position, which can only be what, in department store sales? Just three or four passports to turn in, along with other strands of documentation that establish me firmly as this person or that.

If I pressed them for a reason why, they would claim downsizing because of congressional cuts. But I know I am being dismissed because of something else, something no one will say out loud. I don't know exactly what it is, but I sense this sudden and nonchalant dismissal has something to do with the Fantasy Plan. Maybe even with the girl I met there, Song.

The section chief, whose name is Thayer, leafs through my personnel folder as I stand in front of his desk. Thayer looks up. "Jesus, Gaines. I don't know how you blended in all that time. What are you, six feet four?"

"Six-two and an eighth," I say. I point to the folder in his hands. "I'm sure it's all in there."

"Well, I don't know how you made it with us so long. You guys from the old school must've really been something."

Ironic. Now I'm from the old school. I nod vaguely and watch as Thayer goes back to flipping pages. The worn folder is two inches thick. In large letters it says "Peter Gaines, A.H. CE-2216, 79." The letters A.H. stand for "agent handler." CE means "contract employee," and the numbers following it are my code designation. The number 79 refers to my first year of employment. Eighteen years. But it doesn't count for much.

It's the first time I have met Thayer face-to-face. He is one of those frail desk types you find everywhere from Kmart to the White House: early thirties, cropped blond hair, a pale indoor complexion, and a frozen half smile that he must have perfected in a mirror. He shrugs lightly to indicate that he is powerless in this matter, that the buck stops somewhere else.

"I understand," I tell him again.

It is strange, but although my "retirement" is unexplained and is handled with all the etiquette of an abrupt firing, I feel an immense relief. It is time. It is past time. I know the Work has changed me. In those moments when I stop to assess the damage, I see that a certain heaviness has overtaken me, a growing depression over the years. Perhaps it isn't just the Work. Maybe every middle-aged person experiences such a letdown. But as I stand in front of the section chief's desk I cannot remember the last time I really laughed out loud.

As I wait for Thayer's final good-bye, I consider something else, something so trivial now. Despite all those years with the Organization, they never offered me a permanent position. I served in nine countries in all and did my job well, but I was never allowed inside that circle of career professionals in the Work. As a mere contract employee I was always second class, hired for two years at a time, sometimes three. Many times I've imagined Vaal and the others from the Branscomb Institute going about their careers, rising through the ranks, becoming marketing managers, vice-presidents, or getting pulled into headquarters and becoming division officers or maybe even higher.

Now, with no permanent GS rating, I am out, plain and simple. They don't even ask me to fill out my final report. They are careful to remind me that the Wall has been down for some time, as if I had no part in it all. Eastern Europe is now West, and West is East. China too is gradually transforming itself since its old leadership is finally dying off. The MIAs are forgotten again. Vietnam will probably be an ally soon. Even the Japanese are cooperating some of the time. I had a hand in that too.

I watch Thayer check off some boxes and then turn to a pocket section at the rear of the file. He opens it and examines something.

"It says here you're on Prozac."

"No."

"It's not true?"

"That's right, it's not true."

"Says here you got some from a local doctor in Bangkok."

"What it says there is wrong."

Thayer doesn't believe me. "So you're going to be okay out there, Mr. Gaines?"

"Just great."

As he jots something in my folder, I consider the irony that they recalled me from halfway around the world to give me the pink slip here in Arlington. A hundred other places would have been more appropriate. In my East Berlin apartment, where I spent two years buried in electronic equipment, isolated, living the world in my head. Or in that hovel outside Kabul, where I spent years alone except when the darkly shrouded Afghans came for their instructions. Or in Bangkok, where a year ago the Organization put me in charge of the Fantasy Plan and then after only three weeks replaced me, citing "certain developments," and transferred me to a desk job in Bulgaria.

Now they are giving me the pink slip here, at home base, the one place that has never been my home. Actually the slip is not pink. Actually there isn't even a slip. Just a handshake and a nod of thanks from a thirty-two-year-old desk officer with little penguins on his tie.

Thayer puts the folder down. "You can pick up your back pay at Finance on the second floor," he says, "on your way out. It's over eight thousand dollars, I believe. It'll be in cash. No taxes, of course. It's all yours. And then our relationship with you will be severed."

He looks down and brushes at his tie as if he's found a speck on one of the penguins. "I'm sorry it has to be like this, Gaines. But with all the political and technological changes in the world . . . well, there are younger men, better trained in the newest methods. It's just best for everyone this way."

"I understand," I tell him. But I know the real methods haven't changed, not in two thousand years. And I know that there aren't younger men who are better trained.

Thayer looks up and blinks, his pleasant half smile still in place. Maybe he knows about the Fantasy Plan. But even if he did, he wouldn't tell me why I was transferred after only three weeks or what the Fantasy Plan had discovered that they could not trust me with.

Thayer points to my open folder. "It says that your father passed away recently, but you didn't make it to the funeral?"

"I wasn't notified until after. They had no way of reaching me."

"But your mother's still alive, in Ohio."

I nod.

He flips his hand casually. "And your sister, Beth, too, I see. You haven't seen either of them in ages, have you? And you have a birthday in a few days, Gaines. I'm sure they'd both like to see you."

I just look at him.

Thayer's voice tightens. "You do remember the restrictions on foreign travel for the next five years."

I don't answer.

"Anyway, you have to stay stateside. Foreign travel is too sensitive. So, will you abide by the agreement?"

"I signed it," I tell him.

Thayer smiles approvingly. Without getting up, he extends a hand over a stack of papers. "Thank you for your service," he says.

The words are so perfunctory and his hand is held out with such little care that I do not reach for it. I slip my hands into my jacket pockets. He shrugs, then flops the folder into the out tray, and spins his swivel chair around to his computer monitor. The only noise is the office clatter that seeps through the closed door. Eighteen years, and it is unceremoniously over.

After a moment Thayer glances over his shoulder and raises his eyebrows at me as if to inquire if there is something else. Without turning in his chair, he compresses his lips and nods once more. "Thank you, Mr. Gaines," he says. "You may go."

I stand a moment longer, staring at the back of his white collar where the little penguins are tucked neatly underneath.

Then I turn and I go.

4

A NEW START

My heels thud on the tile floor as I pass the security checkpoints along the long corridor. I am amazed at how calm I am, how effortlessly I move. I feel a huge relief as I push my hand against the double glass doors and step outside. The first thing I realize is that I will be using my real name again. It has been a long time.

I amble slowly through the parklike grounds and out through the wrought-iron gate with stone pillars. I stand at the curb of the four-lane street, with nowhere to go but the cheap apartment I had just rented for the week. The traffic passes easily, and I see that the late-morning sky is bright and blue except for a wash of clouds from the east. The Virginia air is brisk, the sort of morning that could be either the last day of fall or the first day of spring. It is in fact the first day of spring.

As I stand at the curb with the mammoth building behind me, the everyday world seems like a lost paradise. I feel as if I am finally getting my breath after a long time underwater, finally breaking the surface to feel cool air on my face and gulping it into my lungs. Already some of the heaviness and bitterness lift from inside me.

Yes, my retirement will be okay. Now I understand

what my father used to tell me, even in our last conversation, when I called home a year and a half ago. "One day I'll be gone," he said, his tired voice bouncing off a satellite to reach me halfway around the world. "I will be gone, and everything will go on just the same—the good and the bad, the bad and the good. In the end I will have changed nothing."

That is how I feel too. I am halfway through my forties, and I know too much about the world to pretend that I have made a difference. The world is not a fairer and better place. There is still more cruelty out there than one mind can comprehend. But now I can let the international events go on without me. I will disengage my mind from anything of consequence. I will return to that other universe, the wonderment of the ordinary life I had abandoned, the small and quiet universe, uncluttered by important events. Yes, I will see my mother and my sister, Beth, again. I have kept in touch—a present, a letter, or a card whenever I could—but it has been nearly six years since I held my mother's spotted and fragile hands, stepped through the smells of her kitchen at dinnertime, and sat with her aging cat on my knee as the afternoon light streamed in through the living-room window.

Now I will live in her world, working a forty-hour week and looking my co-workers in the eye. I will reside in one place and have letters arrive in my own name. I'll buy a Winnebago and take vacations across this vast country that I know the least. I'll see Mount Rushmore and Cooperstown. I'll stand in bluegrass for the first time. I'll find a major-league park on Saturdays and sun myself in the bleachers.

The irony of course is that the life I now desire is the same life I once fled from, the same life from which so many Americans still seek to escape. In their minds they would gladly exchange their ordinary days for a little international excitement. They have seen too many movies and from their seats experienced every kind of thrill and danger. They leave the theater brushing off the popcorn, exhilarated and amazed at themselves.

But as I think back over these eighteen years, I was rarely amazed with myself or my adventures. The Work meant putting aside nearly everyone in my life and then, without the advantages of a movie script, leaving my hotel in Berlin or Tokyo, or my apartment in Rome, and making the drop, or meeting the man, or recruiting the hill tribesman or the professor. There was no background music the time a Chinese agent of mine stole the documents that helped fourteen dissidents escape from Beijing. No credits rolled after a German agent of mine placed a microphone in the bedroom of an East German minister. There was no applause when I passed the rocket launchers to the Afghan fighters. And no drumroll was needed for tension the time I killed a man in Kyoto. The tension was already there, pounding in my ears like twin hearts.

That was only two years ago. And now that I have told you I killed someone, you will think that I am different from you. You will think that I am a vicious man. But I am not. Killing under most circumstances is a despicable act. It goes against everything civilized and human, every ideal we fight for. But the world is in chaos. It is a fragile and desperate place, whose survival is at best precarious. And sometimes drastic measures are necessary as a last resort. I tell you I killed only that one man. It was under specific orders. I knew it was absolutely necessary. Unlike in the movies, I vomited before I left my apartment, and afterward I was ill for weeks.

But even that event seems distant to me now as I stand at the four-lane street in front of headquarters. My new life is like a picture book, and I am a child watching it all, waiting for the page to turn. I hear a muffled loudspeaker and see a tourist bus creeping along the curb. Heads are out the windows, and outstretched arms point cameras at the headquarters building through the trees. A female guide speaks into a microphone, giving the dimensions and age of the central building. I catch part of a joke, about how one of the passengers on the bus is probably a spy with a recorder. The passengers roar.

The bus rolls directly in front of me, yet no one seems

to notice. Their eyes slide right by, searching the grounds for any glimpse of a spy. I am just another pedestrian, tall with rugged features, wearing squarish glasses, and on this morning with a heavy shadow of a beard. I am skilled at looking ordinary. I am accomplished at being a nonentity. My silver-streaked brown hair is combed to the side as usual and is a bit shaggy as usual, hanging loosely over my ears and over the stems of my dark-rimmed glasses. The bus moves slowly, the tourists pointing past me with their bright jackets and thick watches. The bus picks up speed and moves on to its next destination.

Then a piece of my past comes back with no warning, rushing into my thoughts as it has a thousand times over the last year. Since my transfer from the Fantasy Plan and reassignment to Bulgaria, I have not so much been thinking of Song as possessed by her. Even in my sleep I see the details of her face, and where and how it all happened. The world sets a path of temptations before us, and I have not always been able to walk with steadiness. What happened there seems impossible to me now. It was only after I was removed from the Fantasy Plan that I realized how foolish my efforts had been. I thought I could rescue her. I thought I could beat the system. But its labyrinth of deceptions and lies is endless. I should have just walked out with her. I should have taken her away when it was possible. But I didn't.

Where a moment before I felt some peace in my new life, now my depression returns, a weight in every cell of my body. As I stand at the curb in front of headquarters, the world seems to slow like a worn carousel. A voice whispers inside my head, objective and stern: *Leave her alone. Let go of her. You cannot swim upstream and undo the past. You cannot fix the world.*

I agree with my father. The world will always go on as before. It is beyond repair. Yet for nearly a year there has been a struggle within me, one part of me trying to camouflage Song from my thoughts and the other part needing to remember her.

A revulsion rises within me every time I recall what I

permitted to happen. And now it is clear to me that I cannot go forward with my new life. I cannot work a forty-hour week and look my co-workers in the eye. I cannot visit Mount Rushmore and Cooperstown or stand in bluegrass, or sun myself peacefully at a ballpark. I must return to the Fantasy Plan and find Song so that I can look her in the eye and ask her to forgive me. I will make her see things my way. I will explain that at first I was guilty only of being there, that it began with a concern for nations and events and the confusions of high-level politics, and that I was made to believe in the importance of it all. It was not all my fault that she lost her innocence. She will believe me. Then I will stand with her against the others, and do what I should have done eleven months ago. I will lead her out of there, and put her life back together. And yes, the world will go on as before, but with one less particle of evil in it.

I look up and down the street. The carousel picks up speed again, and everything bustles more vividly than before. But this ordinary world and all the allures of its everyday routines will have to wait. Even my mother and my sister, Beth, will have to wait.

The traffic breaks. The spring air is brisk, and the sun feels warm on my shoulders. I step from the curb with my hands in the pockets of my windbreaker and with the immense building behind me. With wide strides I cross the four lanes to the number twenty-three bus approaching the corner. I board and sit by the window, urgent with purpose again. Already I am starting to plan. Nothing will stop me.

5

THE FANTASY PLAN

I think at this point I need to tell you something about the Fantasy Plan. The premise is simple enough. In principle it is no different from other access-oriented plans I worked with. But the Fantasy Plan takes deception and bribery to new depths. I promise you that I did not originate it, and I knew nothing about it before my arrival in Bangkok. I was involved for only three weeks, but it remains the lowest part of my career.

On my first day in Bangkok I was led to the second floor of the American Embassy, to the office of the Organization's section chief for the area, a man they called Harry Leamer. He was a large and lumpy man, with a shiny forehead where his hair used to be and a sagging jaw that made him appear slightly oafish. His body filled the wide chair as he worked on a cigarette and breathed noisily. Leamer motioned me to a seat on the other side of his desk. He started right in.

"I've heard good things about you, Gaines."

It was just a cordial remark. I knew it meant nothing. I remained silent.

"We want you to join a very special operation," he went on. He took a drag on his cigarette and paused a moment, as if he were about to make a great announcement.

"This is the information age, Gaines, and you know that information means power. Even before the cold war ended, it was obvious that our next rival was the Japanese. Not their military of course—that's laughable—but their corporations and their bureaucracy. So we had to find ways of penetrating their businesses and government."

He waited for some response from me. I just nodded my understanding.

"It says in your records that you spent some time in Japan?"

"Almost two years," I answered. "In Osaka and Kyoto."

"How'd you like it?"

I shrugged. "Cities are cities. But the countryside was beautiful."

"And the people?"

"Polite," I said, not sure where he was going.

"Polite? You know as well as I do how closed that damn society is. They never let an outsider in. It's a racial purity thing. How many mixed marriages you see in Japan?"

"None," I answered.

"That's right. Not even with other Asians, because there'd be mixed offspring, and no mongrels are allowed. One big fucking Japanese gene pool is what they want. It's a kind of supremacy, I tell you. And they're so loyal to their race and their country and whatever fucking corporation they work for that it gives us real headaches getting the access we need. Do you follow me, Gaines?"

"Of course," I said. I was annoyed by his talk but not surprised. It had been pretty standard around the Organization for some time. Someone has to be the enemy, and since the fall of the Soviet Union the Japanese got nominated.

Leamer took a final puff and crushed out his cigarette. "It's no secret we got shoddy intelligence in nonwhite countries. And it's doubly difficult in Japan. So we put our psychological experts on the job, to find out where they are most vulnerable. It really wasn't too tricky. I could have told them. Sex. The great equalizer. The common ground of all races. It's so utterly simple that it's beautiful, isn't it?''

I nodded, uncertainly.

''Back home we've got lots of taboos on sex. The Japanese don't.'' He cracked the seal on another pack of cigarettes. ''To most of them it's just another bodily function, performed in various ways. They're not Christians, so there's never anything immoral about it. Anything goes, if you know what I mean. Not in their own homes, of course. But outside the home the men, they want it all. Wives don't approve, but you know women, they'll look the other way. So the men get what they want: two or three girls at a time, doing it upside down, restraints, a thousand weird fetishes, homosexuality, even doing it with children. And worse, believe me. It's all part of their history. It's probably in their genes by now, and you can't legislate genes, now can you, Gaines? It's just the way they are. Probably why their society came to be so rigid, to contain all those nasty impulses.

''Problem is, the world got smaller on them. And you know how sensitive they are to foreign criticism. We Westerners have a conscience. So they were sort of forced to develop some sex laws that conformed to ours. It wasn't about morality. It was just a public image thing.''

Leamer was gradually coming to the point, and I could see from the look on his face that he thought it was a stroke of genius. Probably his.

''We're planning for the future. And we've devised a way to get inside their corporations and government, to get some of their executives and bureaucrats on our team.'' He took another cigarette from the pack and leaned back. ''Bangkok is already Asia's sex capital. That's one reason why the Japanese are hot to start so many companies here. Cheap labor at lots of levels.'' He grinned. ''Plus, the men enjoy the special recreational time.''

I started to speak, but Leamer motioned me to be silent.

"So we started our own company, called the Fantasy Store. Opened up a little place right here in Bangkok. Think of it as a little therapy for their quirks. We began four years ago by hiring the best professional gals we could find from a lot of places—Italy, France, Thailand, of course, even the U.S., those big California girls with cheerleader breasts. The Japs love 'em. No blacks, though, 'cause the Japs think they're inferior. Anyway, the girls are all lovely, tops in the pleasure business, and in it for the money. We make sure they get good incentive pay for particularly quirky performances. We've even hired some good-looking guys. Never can tell what a customer wants. And you know what, Gaines? They go for it all."

Leamer closed his eyes with a long chuckle, as if imagining something in his head. "Sex is still the best bait there is. So we provide them with every delight—natural and unnatural—all the ones that they can't get at home anymore due to the damn laws. Hell, they can't get them anyplace else anymore, not even in Bangkok. And I mean we cater to *whatever* they want. No limits. The sexual vacation of their dreams. If they can imagine it, the girls can do it. We even manage to clear a tidy profit."

He paused to light the cigarette. "You get what I'm saying, don't you, Gaines?"

"Yes, sir."

"We maintain a little library at the Fantasy Store, Gaines. A video library, you see. We film every customer, the complete bedroom performance. Then we catalog it and we save it.

"Our first clients were just typical Japanese tourists, but it didn't take long for word to spread back to the ones we really wanted. Already we've been quite successful. A lot of the guys we have on film will rise through the bureaucracy one day to some kind of leadership. And when they do, we got 'em. In fact we've already trapped a couple of older bureaucrats and three corporate execs with some fairly kinky tastes—bondage and that sort." Leamer waved a hand and reflected a second. "It doesn't matter how high up they are. Some love to be subservient in bed, bowing and scraping, licking the women's feet like fucking slaves.''

I nodded uneasily. Leamer was enjoying the succulent details of his briefing.

''And others need to dominate. Sheer power, going to extremes that—'' He stopped a moment. ''I'll spare you right now. You'll see soon enough. Anyway, we're already making pretty good use of over a dozen of 'em. Got some inside economic leads from the bureaucrats. And from the execs we're getting good info on artificial intelligence, virtual reality, and all that.'' He chuckled. ''Spying and prostitution. We've taken the world's two oldest professions and put them together like never before. All of it under covers, of course.''

He laughed at his own pun and looked at me to see if I was surprised at the operation. There was a sinking feeling in my stomach, but I was careful not to show what I thought or felt. An efficient, hardworking nation becomes our competitor, so we kick them in the groin at every chance. Nothing in the Work surprised me anymore. The name of the game is and always has been A-C-C-E-S-S.

I raised a doubt. ''It doesn't seem very *Japanese* to betray their corporation or their country, for whatever reason.''

Leamer nodded that he understood. ''I wondered the same thing. But we got our best information from their own psychologists. Told us everything we needed to know, and so far they're right. They said the only thing that'll make 'em turn is *haji*.'' He paused, testing me.

''The Japanese word for 'shame,' '' I said.

''Right. Still the most powerful force in Japan. But shame isn't guilt, is it, Gaines? Guilt means you got a conscience, like us, an internal sense of what's right and wrong. But shame comes from public criticism or family judgment. In the past hara-kiri was expected if you failed your duties. Hell, today Japanese kids will jump off buildings if they don't make their grades. Can't face their parents. No Japanese wants to be shamed or rejected. Get it?''

I nod.

"Every one of those guys we've confronted so far with videos of his weird sex habits knows damn well that if we make it public in the West, he'd be shamed and shunned at home. He'd lose his job, and his company would lose face. Advantages would go to competitors, and so on. Some of them are government officials, so there'd be a scandal, which is the Japanese way of getting rid of opponents. Ironically, as long as they work with us to keep their weird behavior private, they're actually protecting their companies and government. Now do you understand?"

"Yes."

"*Haji*. It's power in our hands. And believe me, we've got some good information so far. Even uncovered a small group of fucking extremists inside their government."

"What group?" I say.

"We'll get to that later." Harry Leamer leaned back again with a wide smile. "The point is that it's all yours."

I took a breath. "I beg your pardon?"

"We're putting you in the brothel business, Gaines. I'll teach you the ropes, bring you in slowly so you get used to it. After a couple of months you'll take over the day-to-day, under me, of course. It's a tricky job and sensitive. We're after anybody who's got access now or might get some access in the future. It'll be pivotal in our dealings with the Japanese. With the hold we get on them, we'll be able to subvert those dirty tricks they use to upset the trade balance. Who knows what else we'll dredge up?

"Oh yeah, and we're also preparing a room for you here," he went on. "But for now you'll stay at a hotel down the street." Leamer continued to smile broadly. "We're expecting a lot from you, Gaines. You might even enjoy the perks."

I try to imagine your reaction. You're probably not surprised that your government would do anything to further its own interests, even run a high-class whorehouse. Maybe the whole thing is simply amusing to you, or titillating. Sex and spying have gone together since Delilah, always in the service of A-C-C-E-S-S. In this case the access helps manipulate the economic world, and economics is just about everything. It's what drove the Soviet Union under. It's what's holding other countries back. And it's not just our government that wants the economic edge. We all want it: cheaper stereos and nicer cars, lower mortgage rates, even a measure of national pride.

But for a lot of reasons, I didn't want any part of the Fantasy Plan. I had a visceral repulsion to it all. But I knew better than to raise objections in the Organization. Still, I think Leamer had some doubts about me from the beginning. Perhaps I seemed too hesitant or uncomfortable. Or maybe he sensed my personal instabilities.

Yes, I use the word "instabilities" deliberately because I have always been acquainted with my weaknesses. I don't have to be a psychologist to understand what goes on inside myself. There is a quiet and smiling Peter Gaines, a man who wants the world to be a better place and who has really endeavored to make it so. But I know there is also a Peter Gaines who has irrational thoughts of passion and violence that spring up unexpectedly, pulling his mind in various ways. I can't point to the source of these thoughts. Maybe everyone has them at times; maybe they are left over from the night of our first ages.

No, I haven't always given in to my impulses. A few times over the years were enough. But until my involvement in the Fantasy Plan I did not understand how thin the line is between civilization and savage.

The first time I saw Song her presence lifted my spirits. There was something unusual about her—not just beauty, something else that seemed to emanate from her, something inside her that was spotless and shining on the outside. Nothing hidden about her, no double sides. She was a piece to a different puzzle, a reminder to me that there is a world beyond the Organization and that not everybody has a double life and a mission with a hundred lies.

But the more I saw her, the more confused I became. Part of me wanted to rescue Song's goodness and steal her to safety; yet another part of me so envied her innocence and strength that I wanted to seize her goodness and keep her for myself, and maybe recapture a simplicity I had lost a long time ago.

Leamer must have spotted how mesmerized I was by her. In any event I wasn't at the Fantasy Store very long— just three weeks. Then he transferred me to a dead-end desk assignment in Bulgaria, as far away from Bangkok as he could get me. And now, eleven months later, I am out of the Organization altogether.

But even after all these months I cannot shake off the memories of Song or the tangle of desires that are still knotted inside me. A psychiatrist would advise me to make an appointment for fifty minutes twice a week so I could talk away my confusion. But that would only postpone the real therapy, which is for me to do something or *undo* something; to stop the fantasies about her, and finally rescue her. I know that my return to the Fantasy Store is not the noble act of a good guy in a nasty world. It is as much to salvage myself as it is to save Song.

Now I lean my shoulder against the window of the Arlington Transit bus and peer ahead as we lurch through an intersection, then continue along Wilson Boulevard. Headquarters building is far behind me. The cheap apartment I rented for just a week is a few miles ahead.

I enjoy watching the cars, the people, the shops rolling by, and I feel an odd sense of community with the passengers who shuffle on and off. I blend in nicely with their everyday world. We ride together, but each of us is alone, absorbed in a private distraction.

Part of my own distraction is the reflection of myself in the plate glass window. The transparent image of my face is ghostlike with the city scenes passing behind it. I stare at the damage of nearly two decades. Time, and the solitary nature of the Work, have had their effects on me. My hair is thinner, and I have squint lines. There are grooves under my eyes. But at least there are no extra chins, no blotches or veins. Still, what some people once called a handsome and athletic face now has the weariness of someone who has seen too much and slept too little and played not at all.

The Arlington bus continues on in the direction of my apartment, lurching to a stop every few blocks. On the sidewalk a woman in a snug blue coat walks briskly along, her head down. She hears the bus and races to the corner, waving her arms. The bus brakes, pulls to the curb, and waits.

She gets on. After looking around, she chooses the empty seat beside me. I slide over to give her room. As she settles, I assess her quickly from the side: over forty, medium build, a pretty face with brown eyes, and fairly long blond hair that is pulled back loosely and tied with a frayed red band.

I have the urge to say something to her, something general and polite. If I weren't going back to the Fantasy Store to find Song, if I were going to stay in this world with its ordinary routines and delights, then I would begin my new life right here and now by speaking to her. I might ask her about her day, or if she takes the bus often, or how she likes living in Arlington.

I watch from the corner of my eye as she unbuttons her blue coat and smooths the front of a wrinkled red smock. I could say something to her anyway. There's no harm in a friendly bus ride chat. But the years of reserve and caution hold me back, or maybe it is my natural shyness, which has been intensified by all those years alone. Even if I were to stay, it would still take time for me to get used to this everyday world. It would take time for my humor to return, and with it a natural friendliness, and certainly for my ability to meet and cherish another person on equal terms.

I turn and look out the window again, and then I see in the window's reflection that she glances toward me several times. Now long-ingrained habits take over, and thoughts sweep forward in my mind. As with everyone I've come across by chance over the last eighteen years, I consider the possibility that she is working for the other side. Or maybe she is on our side, trying to find out if I intend to leave the country. Or in this complex and confused world order, maybe she is on one of the many other sides with their own agendas.

No, I am not paranoid. And she does not fool me. I can feel how the roles are reversed now; if she was trained as I was, she will be as charming and personable as I can be at times. She will be ready to be my friend, not through compliments and flattery but by liking the things I like as she slowly tries to move into my life, eventually sharing her secrets—all of them invented—until I take her into my confidence and share my secrets with her.

Or is all of this just a trick of my mind, a fear that the Organization is watching me?

I wait to see if she says something to me, initiates contact with a clever opening. But she is silent as the bus makes its way down Wilson Boulevard. At times my shoulder jostles hers from the sway of the ride, and I catch the faint scent of her perfume. Then in the window I see her look toward me for a long time. I wait for her to speak.

A block later she does.

6

PENNY

"**Y**ou just moved into my apartment building," she says.

It is an innocent enough opening line. Her voice is barely audible above the whining sounds of the bus. I look over at her. She seems embarrassed, pulling at the front of her smock.

"I beg your pardon," I say.

"You just moved in," she repeats as softly as before.

I have no recollection of ever having seen her.

"I've seen you," she says, chewing on a small piece of gum, "but you probably didn't notice me."

"No, no, I've seen you too. How are you?" I give her a pleasant smile.

"Fine. You on a lunch break?"

I nod.

She nods too and looks away. She seems tired, as if she is already worn out by her day or maybe worn out by her life. But she is interesting-looking, pretty to a degree, earthy and sensual. I glance down at the red and black name tag on her smock. I can't make out either her name or the company's, but under the tag her breasts are uplifted and nice. She has worked hard to hold her figure. Her tied-back hair strays in places, and now she tucks it in self-consciously, then touches her face as if she's afraid her makeup has disappeared.

I have seen that look before: a woman made fragile by the world's harshness, a woman past her prime and now relying on creams and aerobics and depending on the tabloids for the truth, a woman striving to make good first impressions and worried about what the world might say.

For eighteen years I've mistrusted every chance encounter and suspected each new person who came across my path. We all were warned from the beginning about paranoia, that it is the enemy of every operative. But we were also taught to systematically project our suspicions on everyone, to develop a kind of controlled paranoia. But I can see now that she is not working for the *other* side, or *our* side or *any* side. I am actually pleased to be singled out by a woman. It seems like a long time. I feel a kind of adolescent excitement at it all, a winging feeling of freedom and possibility.

I look toward the front of the bus, out through the windshield. It is ironic that I could so glibly recruit a hundred foreigners to spy on their own countries but now be at a loss for words to establish a passing conversation with this stranger.

The bus approaches our stop, and she stands and reaches over me to pull the cord. Her gum snaps between her front teeth. "What kind of work you do?" she says.

I can smell peppermint on her breath. "Actually I'm out looking for work," I say.

She has a teasing smile. "You should shave then. You'd have a better chance." Her smile widens momentarily, then fades. Fearing she's overstepped, she quickly adds, "I'm sorry you're out of work, mister."

I smile and ask if she has any other suggestions.

She shakes her head, then inspects me again and leans closer as if sharing a secret with a chum. "Maybe I'd get some new glasses if I was you. Those rims hide your nice brown eyes." She smiles fully, and one of her eyebrows goes up. "You'd look a lot better in some aviator type.

Those are too old-like, you know, and you're not so old, I don't think."

Such a direct way of speaking, like a waitress who cuts right through the crap. Her eyes seem lively. If I weren't going back to Bangkok, to the Fantasy Store, I might invite her for a walk or to a show. Yes, I truly think I would.

I exit the bus first in order to help her off. We step down into an older part of town, a predominantly white area with a lower-middle-class grayness about it. Pedestrians move along the sidewalks with their heads down, occasionally glancing into windows of the worn shops with apartment rooms overhead.

I pause to zip up my windbreaker. She stops beside me and adjusts the shoulder strap on her bag. Even in low heels she is tall for a woman, five feet eight or nine. I adjust my glasses and ask if we can walk back to our apartment building together.

She smiles with a sense of relief. "My name's Penny," she says as we step off. "Penny O'Hara. Like in Scarlett O'Hara, you know?"

"Not personally," I quip, wanting to be funny but sounding stupid. I want to retract it.

"Like in the movie," she explains earnestly.

I smile inwardly. She is still a small-town girl. "Yes, yes, of course," I say. I look toward her, and in the hard sunlight I see flakes of makeup at the corners of her eyes.

"Listen," she says after a few steps, "I wouldn't have said anything to you on the bus if I hadn't already seen you before. You know that?"

"Yes, I understand."

"But since we're sort of neighbors and all, I mean, it doesn't hurt to say something, you know."

I put up a hand to show her that I understand perfectly. Then I realize I haven't introduced myself.

"I'm Peter Gaines."

"A very nice name," she replies quietly, and puts out her hand. I take it.

"Do you go by Pete?"

"Peter is better. What about you? Is Penny short for Penelope?"

"No, it's just Penny. The family joke is that's how much money my mother paid the doctor when I was born."

She smiles as she says it, but it's a hurt smile.

"Penny is also short for Penelope," I say, "who was the wife of a great Greek warrior."

"I didn't know that," she answers with a thoughtful gaze.

"What do you do, Ms. O'Hara?"

"Penny. I'm a checker. You know, at a market."

"Acme?"

"I wish. I'm just at a mini-market. We're nonunion." She pulls back her coat to reveal the name tag on the slope of her breasts: "Penny." "Food, gas, milk, and awful burgers that someone made the night before. And we get robbed twice a year. I was there for one of them." She shrugs a shoulder as if it were nothing. "I work the rough shift—four A.M. to eleven. But I'm off now. Am I talking too much?"

"No," I say.

We walk in silence, passing a small Greek restaurant and then a water bed store that is having a gigantic clearance sale. Despite her height, her steps are short and choppy, and I have to slow down for her. I consider that while this Penny O'Hara and I are from the same generation, we are likely from different ends of the earth. Unlike me, she was probably married before, perhaps a couple of times, perhaps to large men in sleeveless T-shirts who didn't treat her well. Perhaps she was homebound for years with children and cats and a console TV. Probably somewhere along the line she got fed up. Or maybe she got dumped for a newer and more streamlined model.

"What kind of work?" she asks suddenly, still chewing on her gum.

I was briefed on my exit legend and was required to sign a statement saying I had memorized the cover and would incorporate it into my permanent life history.

"Freelance consulting. International business of sorts. I worked in Europe some years ago, but for the last ten years I've been mostly with Asian companies training their administrators and negotiators on how to deal with U.S. firms, teaching them American customs, business practices—that sort of thing."

"So you've really been around," she says with admiration in her voice.

"More like around in circles."

"I figured you'd been around 'cause there's something real gentleman-like about you. You know?"

"Thank you."

"What places you been to?"

"You mean exotic places?"

"Yeah."

"Well, Newark." I smile at my little joke. "And I've been to El Paso twice."

She laughs. "Come on. You been to China?"

"Yes."

"Japan?"

"Of course."

"You know some languages?"

"Some."

She shakes her head. "Jeez, you must be really smart."

The agent handler's modus operandi at this point is not what you might think. Instead of being vague or trying to escape the conversation altogether, we are taught to launch enthusiastically into the details of our supposed work, producing a monologue so boring that our listener will never raise the topic again. But I don't want to talk about business. And I don't want to lie anymore. I am tired of lies. Everyone's lies. I tell her the truth.

"Apparently I'm not that good. I haven't been able to get another contract. So I'll do something else now."

I wait to see if there is a follow-up question.

"Any idea what you'll do?"

"Not yet," I say, and realize I have lied. "I mean, I'm thinking of going back one more time."

Her eyes flicker. "To Asia?"

I nod, and my mind reaches out for some soft, beautiful image of Song. But all I can see is Song's stare, seeing me for what I really am. A liar.

"China or Japan?"

My mind returns. "Neither," I say, shaking my head.

"More business? Or pleasure this time?"

Her questions are normal, I guess. And her tone is normal. But I detect a deliberateness. Or is it my imagination?

"Business and pleasure both," I reply evenly.

"Must be a girlfriend," she says, raising her eyebrows in a comical way, as if I am a naughty boy.

I can't help laughing at her expression. "No, just some things to finish," I say, realizing it is almost impossible for me to speak without lying.

We turn at Nineteenth Street and continue into the residential section, a mixed area of dingy one-story houses alongside freshly repainted ones with new lawns and fences. We come to a five-story apartment building, its blocky structure sticking up like a sore among the smaller residences. At the main door she looks at me quizzically. "This isn't exactly a business area for China and Japan."

I smile my agreement, and before I can catch it, another lie comes out. "I'm just checking on some business regulations. And what better place than next door to our Washington bureaucracy?"

She nods. "Well, thanks for walking with me." She gives me a shy look and smiles attractively.

There is something girlish and lovely about Penny O'Hara and at the same time something about her that is hurt, as if she has been confused and flattened by life. But her younger self is still visible in her face, and as I gaze at her now, she looks not so much like a middle-aged woman who wishes she were younger as like a child trying to be an adult. We stand facing each other. There is a kind of vulnerable sensuality about her, an invisible warmth, and I actually tingle. She is not like the people from my past. She is normal. She is the kind of woman I want in my future.

"It was my pleasure," I answer sincerely, and search for something more to say.

"Same here." She doesn't move to go in. "What are you going to do now?"

"I guess I'm going to shave. And maybe buy some new glasses."

We laugh together. I am pleased and realize that my depression has lifted since I've been with her, and I feel some tinge of my long-lost self. I like this Penny O'Hara. She is looking at me more intensely. For an instant I'm afraid she will disappoint me by making an offer for the afternoon.

"Listen," she says, "maybe we could talk some more sometime. Maybe you could come up. Push the button to the fifth floor." She seems ready to give me her apartment number when she shakes her head as if reading my mind. "I don't mean it that way. I just meant—" She looks away and continues more softly. "Oh, never mind. I just meant it would be nice. You're very respectable-like."

"It would be nice to see you again too, Penny."

"Remember, it's O'Hara."

"Like the airport?" I suggest with a grin.

"No, like in the movie!" she says before realizing I am kidding.

"I won't forget."

"Yeah," she says, her voice floating away, unconvinced. She gives me a sad look, then turns and heads toward the elevator on the far side of the building.

I never take elevators. But maybe I should have this time. Maybe I should have been a gentleman and ridden with her to her floor, seen her safely in.

I climb the center stairwell to the third floor and enter my dim one-bedroom apartment. I turn on the overhead light and toss my jacket across the dinette table, then go to the window and stand blankly as I look out onto the street. I realize that I could have married a woman like Penny years ago. I would have children now, two or three of them, and a measure of love and security and maybe even some serenity. I might still be a playful and witty person.

Then through the window I see her again, below on the walkway, marching with longer strides away from the building and quickly turning at the sidewalk and disappearing from view. Now I understand. She has made contact. She has completed her assignment for the day.

No, if she were on assignment, she wouldn't let herself be seen like this. Probably she forgot to go to the store or the pharmacy and just now remembered? Yes, that is it. No, that is not it. She is working the other side, whoever that is. Or for the Organization, keeping tabs on me. I shake my head vigorously to clear it. There aren't always sides. There are some normal people in this world.

I stand at the refrigerator with the door open as questions continue to build. Isn't there something about her that doesn't fit? An indefinable something that my years of experiences are picking up on? Or am I no longer in control of my controlled paranoia?

I search the kitchen drawers for the Arlington phone book to see if she is listed. But even if she's not, that doesn't prove she was planted in the building. Many women don't list their names and numbers. I turn to "O" and look for O'Hara. It is there. "P. C. O'Hara." No address given, but the telephone number has the same prefix as mine. But that doesn't prove anything either. Over eighteen years I had been party to some pretty good deceptions, and doctoring phone books is a relatively simple matter.

It happens automatically. I find myself going into the bathroom. I retrieve a small plastic box of needles and safety pins from the vanity, snap open the box, and push the pins aside until I find a slightly larger and longer object concealed among them; it is the color of graphite, straight and slender with an elbow tip. Then I come to another object, similar but thinner, and a third one, just as long but even more slender than the other two and curved at the end. I slip all three into my shirt pocket.

Next I need a letter. Everything has to be explainable,

and a letter will provide a simple cover for action. I take an envelope and paper from my suitcase, fold the paper into the envelope, and address it to "Ms. Penny O'Hara," giving only the city and street address. I peel a stamp from an old letter, wet it, and press it to the corner of the envelope. If someone questions me, I will simply wave the envelope and say that I got her mail by mistake and am looking for her apartment. I will point out that there is no directory at the front of the building, but someone said she lives on the fifth floor.

It doesn't have to be a strong cover for action. It only has to be plausible and spoken convincingly.

I check her phone number again, then dial. It rings. I lay the receiver on the table. It is very simple. I will climb to the fifth floor and locate the apartment with the ringing telephone.

But as I head for the door, more misgivings come to me. My imagination is out of control. Am I sick and lost and accusing the first normal person I meet? Am I retired from the Work, but my mind still trapped inside it? Another instant, and I shake off the hesitations. I must know if I am the one who is sick or if the world is sick. And if I am to return and find Song, I must know what I am up against, if anything. I must be absolutely sure.

The spring-loaded latch clicks behind me. An elderly man and woman approach me in the hall. I nod politely. They nod back. After they pass, I pat the three slender spikes in my breast pocket. Then, moving casually with the letter in hand, I make my way to the center stairwell.

7

THE INVADER

Doubts continue to switch back and forth in my mind as I climb toward Penny O'Hara's apartment. The stairwell is poorly lighted, and there is a damp smell in the dreary carpets. I feel a familiar sensation, a combination of nerves, alertness, and weariness. No trembling. In all the years of the Work I remember trembling only half a dozen times. The other times it has been like this: keyed up and at the same time overloaded to a kind of fatigue. I reach the top step of the stairway, my hand with the envelope resting on the rail.

Again, I try to see Penny O'Hara as a tricky operative. I cannot imagine it. Then I replay how she gained access to me. A chance meeting on a bus. The same apartment complex. Subtle questions about my plans. Or perhaps they are merely honest questions. Perhaps she has a real interest in me. No, it is too much of a coincidence.

Still, her name was in the phone book. Perhaps she wasn't planted. Perhaps it is all a coincidence, a game in my head. She is just a simple and lonely woman who isn't playing any side. I have been away and out of touch too long. I am over the edge and less capable of rejoining the world than I thought. No. I push those doubts from my mind. I am not paranoid. I know how intricate deceptions can be in order to gain access to someone's life.

The fifth-floor hall looks like my own, a gloomy tunnel with doorways about fifteen feet apart and the lighting fixtures of a cheap hotel. I listen carefully. Everything on the floor seems still. Everything is quiet, except for the soft ringing of a telephone down the corridor to my left.

I head toward the ringing phone, and stop at apartment 545. But the ringing stops, and a man's voice comes through the wall, a muffled conversation about an appointment.

I continue. From the various apartments I hear an assortment of American sounds: a blender, laughter from a television show, the pounding beat of a rap song. I turn a corner, and it is quiet again except for another ringing telephone. Apartment 510. I wait. The ringing continues.

The door is identical to my own, hollow core with a cheap button lock on the inside of the knob—zero security, almost immediate entry. Eight inches above the knob is a spring-loaded self-closing Yale dead bolt made of brass—light to medium security, four to six minutes entry.

The hallway is silent except for the muted ringing. I withdraw the slender spikes from my shirt pocket and insert the longest into the keyhole of the doorknob. One twist, and the button gives on the opposite side. The Yale lock is next, and the longest spike slides in easily as I feel for pressure points. Using the other spikes alternately, and the longest for leverage, I probe the tumblers along the top of the opening. It takes longer than I expected—eight minutes—and I finally wedge the two heaviest spikes into the opening and twist them, pulling back the bolt. With the other hand I turn the knob. The door swings gently open.

Now the ringing is louder. I stand at the threshold scanning for evidence of pressure pads, heat sensors, motion alarms, or anything that looks irregular. I step in and close the door.

The apartment is the basic layout of my own, a squarish living area with a kitchenette to the left behind a counter and a narrow hallway leading to a bathroom and bedroom.

There is a dinette table and chairs in the middle of the room and a couch and end table by the window. I step to the phone on the counter and with my elbows lift the receiver to stop the ringing.

I examine the room again. Unlike my apartment, this one is lived in. It is a permanent home, tidier than my apartment, with a newer carpet, a hanging tapestry of woven yarns, and bright print curtains that coordinate somewhat with the faint rose-colored walls. A woman's presence is evident in every corner. I begin to breathe more easily about who Penny O'Hara is. Still, I must be sure.

There is a wall unit on my right. As I begin to examine it, I am startled by a furry animal on the top shelf, a motionless Siamese cat, paws curled under, staring wide-eyed at me. It quickly blinks and stares again. On the middle shelf are a stereo tuner and a CD rack. On the lower shelf are speakers, self-help books, and coffee table picture books of France, Italy, and the Netherlands.

Noises infiltrate from the street, but in here there are no sounds except my own breathing and the creak of the floor as I go to an end table by the window. There are two brass-framed pictures on top. One is a black-and-white photo of a middle-aged couple with their arms around a girl of about sixteen—a young Penny O'Hara with her hair tied back the way I'd seen it today. Her smile is carefree. Her eyes sparkle with fascination and mischief. The other picture is more recent and in color, not of Penny O'Hara but of a sweet moon-faced girl about nine years old in a ballet costume. Maybe her daughter. Stooping beside the girl with his arm around her is a smiling man in a plaid shirt. The resemblance between the man and the little girl is remarkable.

I slide the end table drawer open: pencils, a tablet, red playing cards.

Sixty seconds have elapsed.

I move quickly to the kitchenette. Half pot of coffee by the stove. In the refrigerator, nonfat everything. In the drawers, silverware and a stack of coupons. Under the sink, the usual. I move down the hall and glance into the bathroom. Pink porcelain sink from the fifties. Pink and lime tiles. Colorful soaps in the shape of seashells. Red toothbrush behind the faucet. Ban roll-on. Scattering of bobby pins.

Two minutes.

The bedroom door is open a crack. I ease the door wider and squint into the dimness. A single window with an opaque curtain, letting in a halo of daylight. I reach my hand in and find the wall dimmer switch, and the room slowly comes to a soft golden glow.

My focus widens, and I take in the rest of the room. It has such a different ambiance from the other rooms, as if it is in motion. Walls of florid flamingo. Perfumes in the air. Queen-size bed centered on one wall with flowered sheets thrown back. A red satin pillow and a *True Confessions* magazine tossed on the floor. A chrome pole lamp extends out at an angle, and a television faces the bed with an open *TV Guide* on top. Sliding mirror doors reflect the whole length of the bed, and a tall mirror above a white bureau is conveniently tilted to catch the bed from another angle. I step inside.

The room is so very private, so strangely silent to my presence, and I feel a sinking sensation within me, a terrible sadness.

Peter Gaines the invader.

Peter Gaines the violator.

I catch myself as I fall back against the wall, a sense of disgust rising in me, as if I am harming something innocent and small. But I gather myself. I am here, and I will continue, mechanically if need be. Two and a half minutes have elapsed, and I need only sixty seconds more.

I move to the white bureau with the tall mirror over it. I am aware of my reflection as I pull open the top drawers. Colored panties, some still with department store tags, laid out in neat stacks. Dark stockings crumpled together. Folded T-shirts. A tangle of red and beige bras. The bottom drawers. Jewelry box. Instamatic camera. Pajama bottoms.

I slide back the mirror doors to find a row of coats, dresses, and hanging slacks. I check the pockets, kick at a pile of laundry on the floor, push back some dresses to see behind the shoes. Vacuum bags and sanitary napkins.

Thirty seconds, and I'll be gone.

The subscription label on *True Confessions* says "Penny O'Hara" and cites this address. I step over the satin pillow and open the drawer of the end table at the side of the bed. Matches. Brass candleholder. Candle burned halfway down. There are also towelettes and a rolled-up tube of contraceptive jelly. I slide everything aside to expose two empty condom wrappers.

There is a tightening sensation in my throat as I look down at the most private drawer of this woman. The utter intrusiveness of my presence.

Peter Gaines the trespasser.

Peter Gaines the interloper.

A dizzying rush of nausea comes over me, and a weighted sadness. She had wanted to know me, had spoken with a sense of possibility between us. She had offered a glimpse of a different world than the one I have known, where the good and the bad are not so complicated, where people are who they say they are and do not play at the truth.

I stagger and sit on the corner of the bed. I gaze at myself in the two mirrors, like two photographs from different angles, each revealing me slouched there, a grown man, normally square-shouldered, now rumpled, unshaven, and perspiring, with eyes that seem darkly set behind my glasses, a man I would not want to meet. I study myself in the mirror above the bureau. I am a dim form, manlike but hollow, just a shape where years before substance used to be. I force myself to look in the other mirror, left, then right, and then at all the other mirrors in my mind, and I am caught between them all, a box of mirrors revealing me inside and out, and I think of the fun house mirrors that distort and deform you, except that I am already distorted and deformed.

A door closes somewhere in the outside corridor, and

someone speaks. Voices trail off. Closing my eyes, I admit that my new life is no different from my old one. Forty-five years old. What have I become? And now the momentum to change my life, to undo something in my past, to find Song and explain myself to her, all that is stalled. A terrible depression sweeps over me.

Another voice: a woman greeting someone in the hall. I look at myself in the mirrors again, and I actually hope she will enter and find me sitting on the corner of her bed, discover me for what I am. A welcomed relief, like a covered and festering wound exposed to the sunlight. The voice again, and then the steps coming closer. But they continue past. Disgusted with myself, I turn away from the slumped images in the mirrors. I stand to leave.

Then I see it. A glass bead—a half marble—protruding from the corner of the speaker of the TV set, aimed at the bed. I recognize it immediately because I used the same type of camera lens in Berlin and in Bangkok, though I never placed them in such a textbook location.

My training takes over, my mind racing. The setup is typical. The room will have a network of crisscrossing ultrasonic beams, determining how many people are in the room. Since the cameras are obviously for sexual entrapment, they probably activate automatically when two or more people enter. That means I might not have been filmed yet.

I scan the room for the accompanying microphone. The overhead light, the mirror above the white bureau, and the mirror doors: Each gives clear access to the bed. But the mirror doors are movable, and the overhead light is too obvious. I go to the bureau. It is farther from the bed, but that poses little difficulty given the technology. I see now that the silvering in the lower corner of the mirror has been scraped away and a small hole drilled. Protruding is the tip of a gray cylinder, half the diameter of a cigarette. Behind the mirror is a small box. There are no threadlike wires going to the floor or to a relay unit. It is a cellular microphone, self-contained, very expensive, and very sophisticated for a simple bedroom surveillance.

I sit on the bed again, with that mental numbness that comes when the mind has no answers. I am dismissed from the Work, yet the game continues, this time against me. Or maybe this is some sort of test or preparation, or maybe I am being mocked. Or it is someone else, not the Organization at all. Whoever it is, I tired of the game long ago. The deceptions, the double deceptions, the triple deceptions. The continual odor of lies. As a child I thought it was fun. But as a professional it became so wearying. I guess what they say is true: You are never out. Somebody is always keeping tabs. She could be working the other side, trying to trap me, trying to recruit me. *They* want access too.

Or the Organization is keeping tabs, seeing how vulnerable I am. Afraid I'll switch sides. Afraid I'll leave the country. And they hoped to lead me into some extreme fantasy with her and then record it all so they could control me by threatening to humiliate me with my family.

I move back toward the living room. The cat is on the floor now, cautiously backing up as I enter. I look around again. The tapestry. The curtains and books. The feminine feel in the room. Even the cat. Almost a perfect deception.

The Yale latch clicks behind me. I go quickly through the dingy corridor, feeling claustrophobic, as if glass bead lenses protrude from every door and tiny microphones are attached to every ceiling fixture.

Back in my apartment I sit by the window. The numbness continues. One brief moment of hope that there might be a normal world somewhere; one brief moment of honesty with another human being, and where did it lead me? To a camera and microphone aimed at her bed. But who are they? What side are they on? There are always sides. I am sick of sides. I want someone to be real and honest and exactly who they claim to be.

A sense of urgency mounts quickly in my mind. My instincts say I should walk right out the door and leave everything behind, go back to Bangkok now. But the experienced part of me needs to know what I'm up against, *has* to know what I'm up against and which side she's on. For now I'll play the waiting game. I'll give her a few hours, till morning at the latest. I know I won't have to go looking for Penny O'Hara. She will find me again.

8

DIRTY LAUNDRY

The evening is long, and there is no visit or call from Penny O'Hara. I awaken early, determined to move ahead with my plans. I will pretend to carry on an ordinary morning, just doing my laundry and maybe going for a walk. Then I will pack the essentials and be gone by noon.

At nine o'clock I walk along the residential sidewalk with two pillowcases of dirty clothes. Out in the fresh air I feel a collision of realities. Everywhere spring insists itself: warm sunlight, the budding maple and dogwood trees. I pass a late-model wine red Thunderbird that I have seen only in magazines. This everyday world hums along. But it is a make-believe world. The real world is made up of urgencies and split-second timing and every side spying on another.

I regard how different my life has been from my father's life and from the lives of the people who brush by me here on the sidewalk. An agent handler's job isn't like anyone else's. We collect facts, secrets, and they are often raw and red, like flanks of meat on bare hooks.

Secrets. Most people are fascinated just by the thought of them. But who could stomach all the real secrets in the world? Our history books are ugly enough as they are. Do we really want to know that for the sake of convenience we abandoned hundreds of our own soldiers in Southeast Asia? Or that the Chinese used one of their own villages on a hillside in Szechwan Province to test a mass biological weapon? And when an Arab-Israeli negotiation unexpectedly breaks down, does it matter if it was over "paragraph 147," as the Washington *Post* reported, or due to the fact that the Syrian foreign minister discovered his daughter in bed with the American negotiator?

Inside the Work secrets can be so revolting that they are spoken of only when essential and only to those with a strict need to know. Compartmentalization is not just for security; it is also a psychological cocoon that protects the agent handler's sanity. He must never have more raw meat hanging on his hook than he can stand to look at at one time.

I have often wondered about the others I started out with at Branscomb. We were each assigned to separate operations, and further contact between us was discouraged. But over the years every now and then I would catch sight of one of them on a street in Europe or in an airport or a restaurant somewhere, each of us careful not to show any recognition of the other, each of us not even knowing if the other was still in the Work.

I especially wondered about Vaal. We had become close over that fifteen months at the institute, working intensely on our language and business studies and enjoying nights out on the town. Neither of us had realized that our friendship would be the first casualty of the Work. When we received our assignments, we weren't even permitted to tell each other where we were going. And we respected that because we respected the Work.

Vaal and I did have a chance to sit down and speak once, about six years ago. Besides that, the only times we glimpsed each other were in chance passings. The first time was three years after Branscomb, in the Prado in Madrid, and he looked so comical in a blond ponytail and a rumpled Pink Floyd T-shirt. Then years later, before the wall came down, I saw him in a U.S. colonel's uniform on a street in Berlin. I almost passed him by, but his deep blue eyes gave him away. It was Vaal. The third time I saw him, he was a businessman sitting in an aisle seat of a Singapore Airways flight. His face was still handsome and angular, and he seemed as muscular as ever. But his blue eyes were tired, his coppery-blond hair was thinning, and the age grooves were deeper.

Each time I saw him my intuition confirmed that like me, he was still an agent handler. We were international puppeteers whose job was to pull off the show by recruiting the right puppets, getting them in their places, setting the stage, and securing the props, all in the service of access.

So that was my job. It was tedious and lonely yet sometimes satisfying and often important. But now to everyone around me I am just a man walking down the sidewalk with two bags of laundry under his arms.

I come to an optometrist store, where a blinking neon sign announces FASHION EYEWEAR and CONTACT LENSES IN ONE HOUR. Remembering Penny O'Huru's comment about my glasses, I set my laundry bags down and stare through the store window at the racks of designer glasses that line three walls. But those new designer frames are all made for someone else. I am what I need to be right now, an intentionally ordinary-looking man who has survived so long by being unremarkable.

I continue down the sidewalk and through a Laundromat door. It is the first time I have been in such a place in more than a decade, and I am startled at its complexity and busyness. Washers chug in rows the length of the room. Oversize dryers spin on two walls. There are odors of detergent and bleach, and wet tracks crisscross the linoleum floor. Down one row a stringy-haired youth in a "Jesus Loves You" T-shirt leans over a washer, reading a Bible. Not far away a woman stands impassively with arms folded, staring at a spinning dryer as if it were a television. By the window an elderly couple sits in plastic chairs, reading magazines and looking out the window at the small parking lot. I am the outsider here, a foreigner to this American scene.

I choose a washer in a far corner, pull out my clothes in fistfuls, and stuff them deep into the machine. Next I contend with a reluctant dollar-bill changer while a fat lady in a sack dress stands impatiently behind me. Then I have to decide which hand-size box of detergent to purchase. Finally I place four quarters in the washing machine slot and push the lever. There are spraying noises, and soon the machine joins the others around it with the same deep chugging sounds.

I feel a degree of satisfaction at having accomplished all this. For years my routine was so much simpler: I set my clothes outside the door each morning, to be whisked away by some unseen mama-san who washed, pressed, carefully folded, and returned everything by evening. Asia. A chauvinist's paradise.

As I lean against the machine, I study the elderly couple by the front window. The woman is looking through a local advertisement sheet while the man examines the hairs on his arms. She nudges him and points to an ad. He looks up, smiles, and nods.

I am struck that such a common relationship still exists in a world from which I have been excluded for too long. I imagine this couple's first embrace half a century ago and their first rush of tender affections. But what has happened since then? Were there many triumphs and disappointments for them? Has he strayed? Has she? Are there unspoken pains remaining between them even now? Is there nevertheless an intimacy and devotion that will endure as long as they do?

I have no relationships like that. I have had no ordinary loves. The Organization preferred and even sanctioned the odd encounter with a prostitute or a bar hostess, those unofficial ambassadors of each city, with their green eye paint, their expensive clothes, and smiles hiding their hostilities. Longer involvements were frowned on because they might compromise the Work or subvert it with other loyalties. The Work came first. Tenderness was impractical. And that was just fine with the male agent handlers I knew. They often boasted about the anonymity of their sexual encounters, how they enjoyed the utter animality of the act and could lose themselves in the sheer sensation of it all.

I will say in my own defense that although my physical desires were often difficult to contain, I had no taste for anonymous liaisons, and over these past eighteen years such casual relationships were infrequent and more to ease the isolation than to satisfy merely physical desires. I longed for simple intimacies, and sometimes traveled long and far without them, going years without being held at all. I realize now that I had built a kind of emotional shell around myself, and in all, only three women were allowed to enter there: Torpakai, Anna, and Song. Of course those relationships were unsanctioned by the Organization and necessarily as clandestine as my operations. Each was untimely, and each was much too brief.

First there was Torpakai, a tall and graceful Afghan actress turned freedom fighter. It was she who put an end to a period of celibacy that had lasted for years because of the solitary and often friendless life in the Work.

Torpakai was a sensuous, dark tower of grace and fortitude, a fireball of wartime passion. I knew Torpakai in '83 and '84, when she would visit my hovel outside Kabul, each month coming a long distance over the hills to receive instructions for her guerrillas and to pass me a list of armaments needed by the fighters. She would arrive, her body hooded and wrapped like a man's, and we would eat first, sitting on the cold dirt floor, the room heated only by the invisible warmth of the black coal stove in the center of the room. The stove clicked with its heating noises, and we drank and spoke of the latest fighting and the terrible casualties.

Much later, when all the business was completed, she would stand and slowly unwind her garments. The mustiness of her clothes mixed with the natural perfume of her body, and she would smile down at me with her melancholy smile, so sad was her universe. And soon our animal sensations of taste, touch, and smell would take over, her fiery tenderness leaving us both delirious, silencing the Afghan war and pushing it so very far away.

Torpakai once told me how every night, before she and the other fighters huddled together to sleep on the cold ground, they would stand in the darkness and shake hands and embrace all around, and say a final good-bye to each other, so unpredictable was the night. And when she was with me, we would kiss and play gently for some time, but as the hour for her departure approached, she would slowly transform into a fighter again. And when we stood outside to say good-bye, her mind was already facing forward and not at all backward to the pleasures of our night before. She would never say, "I'll see you next time," or, "I'll see you again." She would extend her hand like a man, and hug me quickly the way a man would, and say good-bye with the finality of one who has said too many good-byes.

After more than a decade Torpakai has stayed close to me. Right now I see her weather-tanned and beautifully taut face, her high cheekbones, which taper downward as her sleek face narrows to a serious, unsmiling mouth. Sometimes I try to recall Torpakai laughing, but it is not within my memories. There was always a kind of soft sadness about her, except in our most intimate moments. Then, momentarily, she would look away from the travesty that had become her country and be fully a woman again, with a sudden passion, not a lust to kill the Soviets, but a woman's deep lust for a man. But I had no illusions. Although at times her lust was for me, her love was always for Afghanistan.

Torpakai's death was so sudden and violent that I am still not sure that I have fully accepted it. I recall the date and the hour I learned of the attack on her camp. It is one of those black moments that form a private calendar of one's life. No Soviet ground soldiers had been sent in. Everything came from the sky, an inescapable rain of death in the night that decimated her camp. The report said that Torpakai was literally cut in half by a helicopter gunship as she raced toward the anti-aircraft guns.

The next week I went there against orders, trekking in the snow over remote and nameless hills to discover that awful moment preserved on the frozen landscape. Her body was severed at the waist, the two pieces of her separated and fused to the icy earth. Her mangled torso was twisted on its back, one arm sticking oddly upward. I stood over her. The strands of her hair were like black icicle prongs covering her cheeks and forehead. I knelt and broke back the icicle hair, revealing her mouth and a yellow eye partially open, and I could remember with a dreadful precision all the living contours of her, and her sighs and tears, and all her little pleasures. I sat down and took off my gloves. I brushed the snow from her bare hand and tried to warm it, tried to fathom that this was real and not just a dream. I looked around. Twenty or thirty others lay quietly in the frost, a sprinkle of snow over them, their bodies unrecoverable until the spring thaw. Sometimes I imagine Torpakai's remains as if they are still on the ground exactly as I saw her then, but certainly they have long since been scattered by animals.

My memory of Torpakai is always followed by another. I considered her a friend and a love, though I am sure that to her I was only the symbol of a temptation not resisted. It was Ann—Anna, I liked to call her—a cryptographer for the Organization who worked in a confidential section of an American soft-drink company in Beijing. Officially she was a clerk-secretary. Officially I was a senior marketing consultant. Anna was a plain-looking woman, withdrawn and self-constrained, with straight bangs, thick glasses, and a fascination for codes and puzzles, an intellectual woman who could decipher everything but herself. We met soon after I was assigned there, as I stood by her desk waiting for her to finish decoding a message through the computer. She finally turned and looked up shyly, her eyes scanning my face, then glancing away after she handed me the pages. But I could tell from the change in her body, the way she shifted slightly, that her shyness covered something else, that her shyness was her protection, and that beneath it lay a different message. Her tight expression was a cover for pure biology; there was a war of desires within her, the same war that I sometimes felt inside myself.

At first it was not a passionate relationship. There was no sex. We became lunchroom friends, and I learned that her exceptional mind was drawn to the clarity of the Greeks. Then we met secretly at night, sometimes for hours. She kept her distance, sitting up straight in an armchair as she read passages from Chaucer and Donne and Blake as well as from the Greeks. She was especially fond of Plato and liked to read from the *Phaedo,* citing how the wise person abstains from all bodily desires, refusing to be a prisoner who is chained hand and foot to the body. After she read to me, she would serve tea with all the formality of a diplomatic occasion. I just enjoyed being with her. It was a passive love, a weightless thing. Different and undemanding. A comfortable harbor in all the isolation.

One evening, while reading from the *Phaedo* again, she read the same passage over and over. Then she stopped and sighed. She took off her thick glasses, and I'm sure I was no more than a blur to her. She turned out the lamp next to her and rose and stood before me in the dimness. She undressed slowly, and I could see her fingers trembling as she undid each button and snap. Then my own eyes blurred with desire. Naked, she led me into the bedroom. We stood by the bed and kissed for the first time, our hands fumbling over each other. Where before she had been formal and demure, now in our intimacy she was a drowning person holding on for dear life. Plato was forgotten, replaced by an uncontrollable mixture of frenzy and agony, spasms of pleasure, her chin snapping back and forth as if saying no, no, but her voice repeating yes, yes, a shuddering incoherence that left her as frightened of herself as she was satisfied. I understood this well because for me too being alone had become my existence, and in my aloneness I had become acquainted with my physical desires. When we finished, we awakened as if from a confused dream, the savage fever of our insides gone, leaving only the taste and smell and the sight of us together now as embarrassed strangers, prisoners of our bodies, wedded in lust only.

But I looked forward to being with her again, a return to Plato and Donne and Blake, and I was going to give her my copy of Longfellow's poems. But she refused my calls and avoided me whenever possible at work. After some weeks she fled, having requested a transfer to a cryptography section in Seoul. I wrote several times, using the official dispatches, first friendly, then casual notes. I heard from her once and not again. I think she is still in Seoul, poring over ciphers and puzzles and ancient books, rededicated to subduing that other part of herself.

I will tell you about one more love, the one that still consumes my thoughts every day. Sadly I knew her because of the Fantasy Plan. And because of her I learned just how lonely and eroded my life had become.

Songkha was different from Torpakai and Anna. She was neither girl nor woman but poised on the edge between the two, on the brink of womanhood. But I knew she would never taste the sweetness of true love and intimacy.

I saw Song for the first time about a year ago. It was the second day of my assignment with the Fantasy Plan. Before they brought her in, Harry Leamer bragged to me that his men had made a special find, the most beautiful Thai girl he had ever seen, maybe the most beautiful Thai girl anyone had ever seen. She was special bait, Leamer said with a twist of a smile, and he added that he wouldn't mind hanging a piece of her on his own hook. But she was off limits to everyone. She wasn't like the pros, he said. Not like those enthusiastic women I had met the day before, with their long nails and hardened smiles who were flown in from around the world to perform their carnal specialties.

Leamer's words are indelible in my mind. "This new girl's unique," he said to me. "She's unused and insolent, a real fighter. We got plans for her. She's a special order for someone we've targeted. She'll get us invaluable access."

I remember sitting in the tech room of the Fantasy Store that first day, waiting for her to be led into the adjoining room. Leamer had recommended that I watch it all on the monitor to see what first-class "access" looked like in the flesh.

On the screen I saw Leamer bring her in. He entered first and gestured politely for her to follow. She stepped forward and peered inside, then entered. But what I saw on the monitor was a mistake. Yes, this girl was lovely. But she was young, too young. Sixteen or seventeen, not older. And I realized the Fantasy Plan was going further than Leamer had let on. It was branching into the Thai slave trade, buying, renting, maybe even stealing girls from their families.

She looked around the windowless room, the brown walls, the table, the two chairs. Her eyes were wide open, nervous but steady. She did not notice the camera high in the corner, or most likely she did not know what a surveillance camera was or that I was observing her as she stood in her dark peasant clothes, her body slender, with a deep shine of black hair falling below her shoulders. Leamer moved to the table and pulled back a chair, politely offering her a seat. She just stood by the door, looking at him.

I realized that what Leamer had said was wrong. Where he had seen defiance, I saw alertness and poise, and with it a pained expression, the soft look of hurt that someone has when they know they are the object of some cruel and terrible joke.

Leamer was also wrong about something else. She was not unusually beautiful. She had a rather common face, partly a child's face, round and soft. Her mouth was small but full. She had delicately rising folds at the corners of her eyes and naturally tapering eyebrows. I realized that her face was very much like the face in the advertisement to visit Thailand, except that Song's face was more radiant and pure. That was the difference. The girl in the advertisement peered out from the page with a quietly seductive smile that said whatever you wanted it to say, whatever need was in your mind. But Song was different. No seduction. No invitation. Her eyes wide open, studying everything around her. A mixture of alertness and fear and hurt.

I shrank back. Nausea rippled through me at the thought of what the Organization would make her do and that I was expected to authorize the violations of such innocence.

I returned to my hotel to clear my head, and spent the whole night thinking about her. I tried to assure myself that there was some justifiable reason to compromise someone so totally innocent. A special order, Leamer had said. Invaluable access, he had said. But I could not accept it. The word *No!* pounded in my head. I thought about all the things I had done for the Organization, much of it dark yet important, and even necessary; and I realized this was not necessary, that there was a place to draw the line, and this was it. I could not be party to what would happen. It was as simple as that.

A plan quickly formed in my mind. I would have to be careful and strategic, and come to her room late one night when the attendants were sleeping, and whisk her away. They would think she had escaped on her own. I would rent a room and hide her for a week, then hire a driver to take her back to her home in the north. I would give her enough money that her family could repay the Organization and still have more for their needs. No one would even know I was involved. She would be free. She could go on with her life. And I would put this shameful incident behind me and go on with my life.

Early the next morning I hurried back to the Fantasy Store, remembering that Leamer had said she was scheduled at eight o'clock for some kind of in-processing. I went to the rear of the building where the dispensary room and some communal showers were located. The showers were running and I looked inside the room. Two people were there, Songkha and a little Thai man who had been introduced to me the day before as the dispensary doctor. Song stood with her back to me, naked under the shower, steam rising around her. She was taller than most Thai girls and women, and physically strong for a girl so slimly proportioned. I was embarrassed to see her naked, but could not take my eyes away, she was so lovely. The doctor poured a red liquid over her head and hair, and scrubbed at her scalp. The red liquid washed down her shoulders and the curves of her back, then down her legs, finally puddling on the floor.

The doctor saw me from the side. "No lice," he said to me in English. "Clean girl."

With a wide brush he scrubbed at her shoulders and back, then her bottom and legs. Her skin was red from the rubbing. Then he dropped the brush and reached around, soaping her breasts with his fingers. I wanted to vomit. I wanted to smash his face. Song stood frozen as his hands lingered, cupping her and playing. Then he turned his head toward me, a slow grin spreading over his face as if sharing a confidence: two men in the universal club of men.

Song never moved, nor spoke, nor cried. Finally the doctor reached for a towel and turned off the water. I slipped back into the hall unseen. A short time later Song stepped out wearing a hospital gown, the kind that is open in the back with no place to tie it closed. Her long hair was wet and tangled, and she was trying to comb through it with her fingers. She saw me and quickly moved against the wall, covering her back.

"Khoon chur a-rai?" she said nervously. Who are you?

"Phom chur khoon Harmon," I replied, telling her my name was Mr. Harmon, the cover name I used at the Fantasy Store. I waited until the doctor walked by us and into the dispensary room. I'd come here for one reason— to find Song and reassure her that I would help her escape and make certain nothing bad happened to her. I stepped toward her to speak softly, but as I opened my mouth the doctor returned.

"Mr. Harmon," he said, pointing at her with his thumb. "Good quality here, no?" He smiled broadly.

"What happens to her now?" I asked, stepping back.

"Complete checkup," he said, still smiling. "Internal exam. Mr. Leamer wants to make sure she's intact."

He pointed to a silver bracelet on Song's wrist, a simple strand of links, and said something to her so quickly that I couldn't understand.

She shook her head. "*Mai!*" she told him firmly. No!

He grabbed for the bracelet, apparently her last possession, but she covered it with her other hand and struggled against him. Still, he managed to rip it away.

"Let her keep it," I said.

"Sorry, but Mr. Leamer said . . ."

"Give it to me!" I ordered.

He handed it over, and I faced Song. Her eyes were teary now, and she was trying to compose herself, her back still against the wall. I saw again that she was just a child, and I felt a certain kinship to her. She was not like the professional women here, and I realized what atrocities were in store if she stayed. I had to get her alone and explain my plan, and tell her not to be afraid, that in a few days she could be home and safe.

Song thrust out her hand to me, demanding I return the bracelet. I gave it to her and she closed it in her fist.

"*Kawp khoon ka,*" she said. A polite thank-you.

The doctor motioned her toward his room. She bit her lip but didn't move. He reached for her arm, but she pulled away. Then, pinching the hospital gown behind her, she turned and of her own accord stepped cautiously toward the dispensary room. I wanted to stop her. I wanted to stop everything and help her right then. But it was simply too dangerous. For now I had to bide my time.

The next day I waited at the table in the interview room, bracing myself to meet Song face-to-face again. Leamer said the interview was standard procedure for all the women. He would videotape her consent and use it as leverage if she ever refused her duties or claimed she was forced. There were specific questions I had to ask, and Leamer was waiting for the answers that assured she understood the consequences to her family if she did not follow through. But I knew it was a test for me too. Leamer would be watching on the monitor to see how I performed.

The door opened, and someone shoved Songkha inside. I jumped up from my chair to help her, but she stepped back from me and steadied herself. Now she was dressed in a shoulderless white wraparound with gold loop earrings. On her right hand were a number of gold bangles. On her left hand was the silver bracelet she treasured. A simple golden necklace accentuated her long neck. But the costume could not hide the schoolgirl modesty that still belonged to her. I desperately wanted to tell her how I would help her, but again this was neither the time nor the place.

I took a breath. *"Sa-wut-dee,"* I said. A general greeting.

She looked at me, not answering.

"Sa-wut-dee," I repeated softly.

"Sabai dee," she finally answered, saying she was fine. But she looked very tired.

She moved to the other side of the table and sat down, folding her hands and looking at me. I was struck by her soulful black eyes that seemed half sad, half wise. I was struck too by her tranquillity in the face of what she surely knew lay ahead. Even in the harsh artificial light with the makeup they had put on her, she still seemed untouched in every way, not just by men but by the world's confusion. She was beautiful like a child, and with a child's mind, still free from wanting. Maybe the Organization had rented her because they had confused her childlike radiance for a woman's beauty; maybe they had confused her uncorrupted innocence for sexual allurement.

Song fingered her bracelet on her left wrist, and addressed me in her language. "Thank you for letting me keep my bracelet," she said. "It was my mother's."

I started to speak but had difficulty catching my breath.

There was something so unusual about Song. More than just attractive and alluring. She seemed comfortable and familiar, like I had known her before. I couldn't put my finger on what it was, but then I realized that looking at her made me remember a long ago when things were simple for me; a time in my life when good and evil were still unclouded by the complexities of great arguments and international ambiguities, and the world had not yet informed me of its chaos.

Now as I sat across from her, things seemed simple and unclouded again. Right and wrong were identifiable. She was right. The Organization was clearly wrong. For an instant a window in my mind opened, and for the first time in years the world was clear and uncomplicated. I wanted to laugh with relief. This was her world. It was honest and straightforward and clean, with no conflicts, no confusions, no excuses or lies. No gray areas. I wanted to stay in her world with her.

And then the window closed.

I was back in a world of guises and false smiles and tricksters everywhere. And I was part of it all. There was sweat on my palms and across my brow, and I thought of the sweat on Haycock's brow at the Branscomb Institute, and the sweat on Leamer's glossy face. I was one of them; I was a forty-five-year-old man sitting across from a blameless girl, and I was expected to turn her into a whore for the Organization, her life an instrument for *access*.

I felt sick, and I needed to open that window again. Song could open it. I wanted her to open it. I needed to feel free. But the interview. And the camera. It was a matter of strategy and timing. The consequences were serious, not just for her but for me as well if I didn't do this right. She could suffer more than I.

My feet felt suddenly too big under the table. She could not speak English at all, and I did the best I could in my limited Thai. "I am Mr. Harmon," I said, repeating my cover name. "I am in charge here." It was a lie. "For the record, what is your name?"

"I am Songkha Chattkatavong," she answered.

"Do you know why you are here?" I continued in her language.

Song ignored my words and fingered the golden bangles on her right wrist. "Is this real gold?" she asked in Thai.

I barely heard her question, it was so difficult to concentrate. Although Song seemed to be just a girl to me, I was distracted by every part of her. Usually when I sit across from a woman my attention falls on just one attraction and for some time rests there. But with Song it was every attraction: her hair, the delicate nose, her eyelashes, the golden nape of her neck, the soft place of her earlobes where the earrings were fastened, and even the way she pulled in her upper lip after she spoke to me, all of it startling me each second.

"I don't think it's real gold," she said, answering her own question. "Because everything here is false." Then she looked up at me. "But you are different from the others, Mr. Harmon. Why are you here?"

Her words hung in the air. I took a deep breath and tried to continue. "We are both here to help your family," I said.

She closed her eyes for a moment, then opened them. "Yes," she answered.

"Your father raises poppies," I went on. "You know they are illegal. He can go to jail."

"He also raises a hillside of squash," she countered quickly.

"We won't report him," I said. "We are helping you and your family." The words were part of my script, and they tasted like filth in my mouth.

"I am here for two years only," she said firmly.

I nodded. But I knew that financially strapped families that rented out a daughter would still be in need when the contract expired. Or if she was truly effective in gaining special access, the Organization would renegotiate the offer to the family, and the arrangement would continue until she was used up or until she could stand it no more.

But I was not supposed to think of that. I was supposed to stress her obligation to us without revealing the Organization's side of the bargain. I kept my voice controlled, searching for words in her language. "You agreed to come here, didn't you?"

She leaned toward me, and whispered four simple words. *"Chuay phom dai mai?"* Can you help me?

I shook my head slowly and at the same time tried to catch her eyes to signal her that I would help her. She did not see it. I struggled to stay on track. "Your family sent you down from the north to work in the city, isn't that right? They want you to be here."

Her loop earrings swayed. "Yes, but this is not a factory job. You paid my father six hundred baht for me. Now we can build a house and dig a well. I think I am worth two cows and six pigs. What do you think?"

I flinched. The mention of money or of renting her was not to be on the video. She kept her eyes on me. A smile briefly crossed her face. I understood then why they said she was so defiant. Even on the brink of what she knew could only be horror, she was fighting to gain control. She would not back down. But strangely, her eyes were not angry at me, just deep and black, with some kind of understanding behind them. They seemed clear, as if they knew who I was. They saw who I was. Saw that she was better than I. Truer than I. Our roles were reversed. She was in control, daring me to remember a long time ago when I was going to be defiant and fearless and right.

She stared at me, unblinking. "I will survive, Mr. Harmon," she said. "I will leave. I will be free again."

Something inside me began to collapse. I wanted to protest that I was not responsible. That I had not made the arrangements with her family, and that I would undo the wrong. But the interview. The cameras. The consequences.

I took another deep breath and refocused. I wanted to get this over with as quickly as possible. She didn't know this was just a game I was playing for the camera, and that I would tell her my plan later. I continued in her language. "Songkha. You will be going north to Chiang Mai, to an orphanage for training. You will learn some basic English and Japanese and some other things you will need, and then after your training you will return here.''

"You will teach me to be a pleasure girl there.''

"And you agree to that, don't you?''

"My father agrees to that.''

"But you must agree too.''

"My family comes first. So I am here. With you. Now I see that you are just like the others, Mr. Harmon. A rich, false man.''

I cringed inside. She did not realize that I was saying this only because I had to. That I was just a man in the wrong place at the wrong time. I wanted to tell her how that window opened inside me, that I needed her to open it again, and that we could help each other. But there were eyes watching me on the monitor.

"There is training at the orphanage,'' I went on, hurriedly now. "So, you will do what we ask?''

"What do you ask?''

"You know.''

"Then say it, please. Say what you will make me do.''

Her gaze was steady into my eyes. "Please, you say it,'' she said again, forcefully now as if she knew what a terrible challenge it was for me. "Say what you men want.''

The words could not come out. I rose suddenly. She continued in Thai as I backed toward the door. *"Khoon ja bi nai, Harmon?"* she called after me, even louder. Where are you going, Mr. Harmon?

The interview ended as I fled the room.

Around me now are the noises and smells of this Arlington Laundromat. I can feel how distant I am from Torpakai and Anna, how removed they are from my life and how each day they recede further and further. But Song—even here, ten thousand miles away and eleven months later, she is still with me as if she were sitting across from me, the shiny pools of her eyes still defiant, still refusing to look away, still seeing me for what I really am.

Behind me a female voice speaks up in an overly cheerful tone. "Did you remember to separate?"

I turn around. Penny O'Hara stands there, smiling up at me as she holds a laundry basket brimming with the flowered sheets from the bed. Behind the mascara and eye liner her brown eyes are wide open in complete surprise to discover me there.

9

LIES AND TRUTH

Penny O'Hara looks different, prettier than before. Her face is perfectly made up, and her blondish hair is damp, as if she has just got out of the shower, and is wind tossed from the walk. She is wearing beltless jeans and a white cotton pull-over that hugs her breasts. I can see the points of her nipples. She looks inviting and sexual in a reckless kind of way.

"What a coincidence," I say, aware of how cold my voice sounds.

"A nice coincidence, I hope," she answers brightly. The gum snaps in her mouth. "Did you remember to separate darks from lights?"

I listen carefully to her words, trying to catch the slightest hint of a foreign accent. But her voice is midwestern small-town America, perfectly so. I look for anything else, any suggestion of what side she's on. She stands with her feet close together, not apart the way Russian women do. Her head is tilted slightly, but more American than Colombian. The smile. The eye contact. The small ball of gum that switches sides in her mouth. Everything thoroughly American.

She puts her basket down and points to my empty box

of detergent. "I know it says it's safe for all colors, Mr. Gaines, but that doesn't mean all colors at once."

"You're with CI-3," I say.

Her smile fades. "Just a helpful tip," she adds, then reaches past me to adjust the dial on my machine. Her breasts graze my arm. "Use warm for washing, then cold for the rinse." She smiles up at me again.

"CI-3. The Bureau. Special Counterintelligence Section. They want to know if I'm going over to the other side. Are you wired? Are they listening to us right now?"

Her face goes blank, then takes on a confused look, even a little frightened. Whichever side she's on, she's really good.

"I didn't mean to bother you, Mr. Gaines. I really didn't. I'm sorry."

She hurriedly scoops up her basket and steps to the far end of the row, then glances back at me, again with a frightened look. She opens two machine lids and begins separating her clothes by colors.

I approach her and stand close, nearly touching her. I recognize the flowered sheets from her bed. "Who are you with?" I demand.

Her fingers are trembling. "Are you some kind of a weirdo or something?"

"Tell me who you are with!"

She faces me squarely, one knee jutting out. "I'm not with anyone, you asshole," she spouts, her voice rising defensively. "Now leave me the hell alone!"

I can feel the eyes in the room turn toward us, but I focus only on her. I have schooled myself in detecting lies and can usually recognize one immediately. A lie has something stifled about it, something interiorly awkward and lost. But the expression on her face, her tone, even her posture are wholly credible. Now a doubt trickles through my mind, and I race through all the other possibilities: I mistakenly entered someone else's apartment. No, there was a picture of her on the end table and the same sheets in her laundry basket. Then the camera and microphone in the bedroom are just for some kinky pleasure.

No, too expensive. I seek some other explanation, but there is none.

"What's the name of the minimart where you work?"

"None of your business," she snaps, and begins tossing clothes into the two washers again.

"Then explain the devices in your apartment."

She calms for a moment and looks at me searchingly, as if piecing something together in her mind. For the first time the gum lays still in her mouth. "There aren't any devices," she says in a small, bewildered voice. Then her eyes narrow. "You were in my apartment!" she shouts incredulously. "You creep. You went into my apartment! You bastard!"

From the corner of my eye I see the elderly man by the window get to his feet. I turn to him with a smile. "Everything's fine here, sir."

The stringy-haired youth in the "Jesus Loves Me" T-shirt is suddenly at my elbow, a good Samaritan asking if there's a problem he can help with.

"This bastard broke into my apartment!" she erupts, accusing me with her finger.

He backs up, then heads to the phone by the door.

"That was real smart," I say. I inch closer, my voice growing more intense. "What did they tell you about me, Penny O'Hara, or whoever you are? Did they tell you that I'm dangerous and unpredictable and unstable? Maybe they're right. Did they tell you why they never really let me on the team—"

"What were you doing in my apartment?" she demands, cutting me off. She is playing it out to the end. She is really good.

"Here's how it works," I say, leveling my eyes on her. "You were assigned to meet me on a bus, and you did that cleverly. But once I catch on, your assignment is over. You're no longer valuable to the operation. That was all covered in your first lecture of Espionage 101."

Her eyes drop to the linoleum floor. When they come back to me, they have a different look, worried and solemn.

"What devices?" she asks softly.

"A cellular microphone and camera aimed at your bed. Someone went to a lot of trouble to get your sex life on film and maybe me on the matinee."

Her lips pinched tight. "They wouldn't do that," she says, still in a low voice.

"They? Which they? Who are you with?"

She doesn't respond.

I shake my head, not at her but at myself. Eighteen years in the Work, and I had let myself be fooled, wanting to start a new life and wanting to feel attractive to someone again. I should have been prepared the moment I saw her running to the bus. A faint laughter ripples inside me. For some reason it feels good. "Look at you," I say, pointing to her tight pullover shirt and jeans. "Your outfit, the gum, the minimart cover. You're a real scream."

"Thanks a lot, but I'm not one of you operatives or something. I'm an administrative assistant to the deputy of personnel."

"I see. You're a secretary."

"Administrative assistant."

"And what game are we playing?"

No longer needing the gum, she spits it into her hand and tosses it in the direction of a large trash can. Her whole demeanor changes. She seems more erect and confident as she eyes me for a moment. Even her voice is different, the small-town accent gone. "He wanted me to meet you by chance," she says.

"Who? Thayer?"

"No. Mr. DeForest."

"Great! Who the hell is DeForest?"

Her eyes move quickly as if her mind is racing, deciding whether to answer. "He does overseas personnel," she says, still in a low voice, "for operatives like you in Asia. I work for him sometimes when he's in country. Filing and dictation, that sort of thing. The rest of the time I work for Mr. Thayer. But Mr. DeForest asked me into the other room when you were with Mr. Thayer, so I could get a good look at you. He said I should try to find out what your plans are."

"Why?"

She leans over the washer, avoiding my eyes. "He said that you're not supposed to leave the States. You signed an agreement."

"And what did you tell him?"

She bites her lip. "I told him what you said, that you're going back to Asia. But now they want to know where. And when."

"Why would they ask you to do all that if you're just a secretary?"

She turns to me with an angry sneer. "*Just* a secretary," she repeats. "I've heard that a thousand fucking times. And if people aren't saying it, they're always thinking it. Like I'm part of a desk or a chair you walk past on your way to something important."

"Let me rephrase it. Why would they plant an administrative assistant in my apartment building and in the phone book?"

"That's *my* apartment building! I'm in the phone book 'cause I live there, you asshole."

She is lying, of course.

"They told me I had access because you moved in downstairs." Then she glares angrily. "Look, I haven't been all over the world. I've been doing the same thing for eleven years, in three different sections, but the same damn thing all the time. Blinking phones and paperwork and more paperwork. And then they asked me to do something different, Mr. Gaines, and I told them I would. Do you know how many times I've been out of the country, Mr. Gaines? Zero. That's how many times. I barely go fifty miles in a year. You've been places that I've never heard of. So Mr. DeForest said I had the access they needed. He said it wasn't dangerous. And I always wanted to do something exciting."

She glances over my shoulder. I glance around. The stringy-haired kid in the "Jesus Loves Me" T-shirt is hanging up the phone. He gives her a "don't worry" nod.

I look back to O'Hara. "So, what about the devices in your room?"

"I told you there aren't any devices."

"They're setting you up. They're using you in hopes of getting me on film or getting something on me."

"I don't believe it."

For a moment we are eye to eye and everything seems still. Then a question leaps out from a black hole somewhere inside me. "Why did they fire me?"

She shakes her head slowly from side to side. "I saw your records," she answers. "But only once. Everything was good except one operation."

"Which one?"

"It was just a number in a folder. It didn't mean anything to me."

"It's called the Fantasy Plan."

She shrugs, then reaches for her basket again and begins throwing lights and darks into separate machines, a pained expression on her face. She stops and faces me squarely. "You know what, Mr. Gaines? If that's really your name. You have so many others in your folder."

I wait.

"I really did see you at our apartment building—just like I said on the bus—a few days ago when you moved in. Before all this. I didn't even know who you were then, and I really thought it would be nice to meet you."

I shake my head in amusement.

"It's the truth!" she shouts, throwing more laundry into the machines.

There is a police siren somewhere in the distance, and then it is suddenly cut off. "What did they tell you about me?" I say.

She sighs loudly. "To watch out for you. That you were real nice and mannerly on the outside but that inside you were a pro with a hard edge. That's what Mr. Thayer and Mr. DeForest called you, a pro with a hard edge. And they said you were an artist at operations, but that you were kind of weird or something and that you never made it big. Like a street cop who just got old and never got promoted."

I nod at the truth in that.

"And that's all I heard."

I glance around the room again. Eyes are still looking at us. "I know you're not an administrative assistant," I say.

"And you're no artist at operations. You look pretty damn ordinary to me."

Her eyes suddenly catch something through the window, and I turn as a police cruiser wheels into the lot and comes to a jerky stop. As if on command her hands tremble again, and tears appear in her eyes. She seems to be trying to get her breath in huge sobs. She is really good.

She goes into her purse for a handkerchief and blots her mascara. "What are you going to tell them?" she says with a frightened look.

I have had my share of encounters with the police. I faced them a dozen times in Eastern Europe but was arrested only once and held for less than twenty-four hours before the U.S. Embassy persuaded them I was just a careless tourist in the wrong place. In China I was detained twice, four days each time, but eventually released with a hundred apologies after my affiliation with the new Coca-Cola plant was verified. In Japan I was detained just once but immediately released when the police realized I was just a Frigidaire executive at a convention in Tokyo. After all the other international incidents I've managed to survive, this confrontation with an American patrolman seems a simple matter, more absurd than perilous. Still, I feel as if I'm entering one of those uncertain moments that could end up being either incredibly comical or violent, I don't know which.

"What are you going to tell them?" she asks again, an edge of panic in her voice now.

"I'm going to tell them the truth," I answer. "From now on I'm telling only the truth."

A black officer with a round, bald head and a pencil mustache slides out of the car and rolls his shoulders as if releasing a kink. He is about three inches shorter than I am, but twenty years younger and compactly built, with arms made powerful by years of weight lifting in a gym. He steps through the Laundromat door with an unmistakable air of confidence, an aura or attitude that announces he is the only one in the place with a badge and a gun. The eyes of the patrons point us out, and he comes down our row of washers, tight-lipped, fingering his nightstick. His eyes don't leave my hands as he comes closer. He stops five feet away and turns down the radio on his belt. My size concerns him, and he gauges me as possibly one of those half-concealed disasters they warned him about at the academy.

"Good morning," he says in a flat, mandatory greeting. "I'm Officer Williams. We got a problem here?"

There is no script for me to draw on, no cover, no ready-made plan. But none is necessary. I feel oddly exhilarated. I am about to engage in the everyday world of straightforward tacts. I remain silent, curious how Penny O'Hara will hold up. She is wiping the manufactured tears on her face. God, she is good.

"Well, whatta we got here?" he demands.

I gesture to her. "Tell him."

"Tell him what?" she says through a wavering smile.

"Tell him the truth."

"You tell him," she says, fidgeting.

His eyes stay fixed on my hands.

"Okay, Officer Williams," I say. "The truth." I lean back against a washer and fold my arms slowly, showing I am not the dangerous kind. "The truth, sir, is that we both work for the CIA. At least I used to. That's the Central Intelligence Agency. You probably read about us in the papers. But I got laid off, what with all the cutbacks and the changes caused by new technology. I know I look ordinary, but I'm really an artist at operations, though she doesn't believe it. Anyway, she's angry 'cause she's trying to get some information from me about where I'm going to go, and I figured her out—"

Officer Williams holds up a huge palm and smiles. "Let's try her," he says in an overly patient voice.

He turns to Penny O'Hara. "What's the complaint, ma'am?"

She collects herself. "The complaint, sir, is that he doesn't know how to separate—you know, darks from lights, reds from yellows. And I told him to do it, but he's an asshole and doesn't care, not one bit."

The smile stays pasted on Officer Williams's face. He knows the situation. A couple of crazies. Lovers fighting over laundry colors. The country is going to hell in a handbasket.

"The dispatch said he broke into your apartment, ma'am."

She shrugs noncommittally.

Officer Williams goes through the mandatory cop talk he learned at the academy. Did he hurt you, ma'am? No, sir. Do you want to go to a women's center or speak to a female officer? No, sir. You two married or something? No, sir.

"Identification," he announces.

I unfold a piece of paper from my wallet, my temporary driver's license, and hand it to him. "I just got into town," I explain.

"Been spying on the Russians?" he says with a smirk.

"Actually we're pretty good friends with the Russians now. I've been spying on the Japanese."

Officer Williams stiffens, then rolls his shoulders again, flaunting his bulk. He accepts Penny O'Hara's license and studies it, then looks us over skeptically. "Well, you two got it all worked out?"

"Yes, sir," she says.

"I'm not gonna have to come back here, am I, Mr. Gaines? Am I, Ms. DeLaurentis?"

She hooks her arm around my elbow. "Don't worry, Officer. We'll work it out."

Officer Williams hands the IDs back.

"You can stick around," she offers, "and tell us whose clothes come out the best."

"Thanks. I got a few other things." He surveys the room. The other patrons shake their heads or look away. He makes a final note on a pad. A moment later he is out the door.

She faces me with her hand to the side of her head. "Why did you say all that shit?"

"Nice vocabulary." I turn and head back toward my washer.

"Did anyone ever tell you you're rude?" she shouts after me. She follows and grabs my arm, whispering loudly now. "Why did you say all that?"

"Because people don't believe the truth . . . Ms. DeLaurentis."

"I can explain that. O'Hara was my married name."

"Of course."

"DeLaurentis is my maiden name. I went back to it after my divorce."

"I'm so sorry." I continue toward my washer.

"Don't be," she says, following me. "Jimmy O'Hara was a loser. *Is* a loser."

"And your married name is still in the phone book because you didn't bother to change it with the phone company."

"Not yet, but I will."

I stop and face her. "So you're not a cashier at a mini-market but work in personnel for the Organization. And you're not really Penny O'Hara but someone named DeLaurentis."

She has an embarrassed look. "Sorry. I'm not very good at this."

"And is Penny still your first name?"

She draws a breath and exhales deeply. "Yes, but I don't go by Penny. I go by my middle name, Catherine. I never liked Penny 'cause of the jokes when I was a girl, about how a penny was how much my mother paid the doctor for me. Anyway, Catherine is prettier-sounding and more serious."

"Is that Catherine with a *C* or a *K*, or are you still deciding?"

She stares. "It's with a *C*. Penny Catherine De-Laurentis."

I lean over my washer. The spin cycle has already begun.

She looks up at me now, proudly, as if we had been allies in the face of an enemy. "I did pretty well there, didn't I? Maybe I should have been in your part of the business long ago."

"Tell me, Penny Catherine DeLaurentis—"

"Just Catherine."

"—what does it mean if your boss hands you back a letter with the number 95 circled?"

"It means the number should be spelled out in letters, not written as a number."

"What does 'LC' mean in the margin?"

Her eyes roll. "It means I should change a capitalized letter to lowercase."

"What about 'GH'?"

"It doesn't mean anything, Mr. Gaines." Her eyebrows rise, superiorly. "You just made it up."

"Considering where the camera and microphone were aimed, I figured you were an artist at a different kind of operations."

"Christ, you're sick. I'd never do that."

She is lying again. But I'm not even angry. Just tired of it all. Her lies are small and singular compared with all the lies I've told. And her deception is probably insignificant compared with what will happen when I return to the Fantasy Store to find Song.

I turn away again and step outside to the parking lot, into the noonday sun. She steps after me. "They want to know what your plans are," she says.

"Tell them that from now on I'm going to separate—you know, darks from lights, reds from yellows."

Catherine DeLaurentis or whoever she is glares angrily. I smile at the expression on her face. "Let me guess," I say. "I'm a jerk."

"You're a jerk," she confirms and her glare changes to

a half-smile. She shakes her head at me. "You're really going to go up against them, aren't you?" There's a kind of admiration in her voice.

"Why was I fired?" I ask again.

She just looks at me. Maybe she really has no idea what I'm talking about. I study her face for any special indicators, but there is only a bit of anxiety and confusion, as if she wants to help me but can't, or doesn't know anything. Either she is really good, or she is so real that she's not acting at all. I'm not sure anymore.

Shaking her head at me, she turns and goes back inside.

I stand alone in the parking lot with the sun on my face. I try to think. I try to connect the dots. But my thoughts spin around uselessly. I was fired just twenty-four hours ago. Why did they send her to discover what I was doing? Why didn't they just ask me? But of course Thayer did ask me. Which means they aren't sure they can trust me. Which is correct. But though she is good, there is something about her that is amateurish. Surely they knew I would figure her out. Which means they wanted me to figure her out. They want me to feel watched. Which means they want me to be nervous. They want me to experience the same anxiety I felt each day in the Work. They want my controlled paranoia to work overtime, so I am watching myself even when they are not. Which means they want me to feel fear. Which is their main tool. And it's working.

Or perhaps it is too much imagination. It must be standard procedure to check on agent handlers after they leave the Work. It is probably routine. Just routine. Yes, routine.

No, that is wrong. I am somebody's plaything. And my instincts tell me I am facing the onset of a storm I cannot yet see. But I have no answers. All I have is my decision to find Song, and now a renewed determination. And with it, a peculiar sense of the inevitability of the course I have chosen. After being lied to by O'Hara or DeLaurentis or whoever she is, I feel released from every obligation to the Organization. The man who labored on their side no longer exists. The lines that used to define my life have been redrawn, and now someone different is standing on this side of the line. But I'm still not certain who and what that line divides.

10

I empty the pillowcases of clean laundry onto the bed, a tangle of shirts and socks and pant legs, much of it still damp. I had been hoping that somehow everything would be folded or at least smoothly pressed.

I look carefully around the room. Something is different. Or is it my imagination again? No, the bedspread is smoother. Things have been moved, then carefully replaced.

I know precisely where to start. I check the corners of the carpets to see if they've been untacked. I flip the mattress to see if the box spring material has been restapled. The toothpaste tube is pinched tight at the end but no longer factory-sealed. In the living room the chairs are too evenly squared under the table. There are shiny scratch marks on old screws where a chair was disassembled. A razor blade cut in the wallpaper. They were methodical, not even knowing what they were searching for. Or were they looking for a place to hide some kind of device?

The afternoon sun falls through the living-room window and lies in a long strip across the rug. It is the only warmth in the apartment; everything else is cold and oppressive, motionless and empty.

In the kitchen I go to the paper towel dispenser and pull on the roll. After one turn, a photograph falls out, my only remaining tangible connection to Song. The photo was taken the day she arrived at the Fantasy Store. It is a kind of mug shot, a full-face picture as Song stares blankly into the camera.

As I look down at the picture, I recall the day after my interview with Songkha, when Leamer informed me she had already been sent north to the orphanage, days sooner than expected. He added that next I should dedicate my time to learning the operations of the tech room. So I spent the following week with the two technicians as their hidden cameras videotaped Japanese clients romping with the professional women in private encounter rooms. But I could not free my thoughts of Song. Nor could I help her now. I had lost the opportunity. And when I saw the acts performed on the monitors, I was sickened by what would eventually happen to her.

Then, at the end of the week, I discovered by chance that Leamer had lied to me, and that Song had not yet been taken from the Fantasy Store. Just the thought of it now, and I see it again in my mind: I am walking down the second-floor hallway, with encounter rooms on either side, each with a different decor and each with hidden cameras and microphones. I turn a corner and Songkha is leaning against a door with her ear pressed to it. When she sees me her eyes open wide and she rushes away.

"Khoon ja bai nai?" I call out. Where are you going?

Song stops at the stairwell, then backs against the wall as I approach.

"Chom doo thao nun," she says innocently, meaning she is just looking around. She is wearing the same white wraparound as before, the same earrings and necklace.

"They told me you were gone," I continue in her language, realizing that Leamer must have lied because he had seen her effect on me.

"Next week I go," she answers. I strain to translate in my head as she continues. "They said the rains are too heavy in the north. And I was not supposed to leave my room. I think now you will tell them."

"No, I won't, Songkha," I reassure her. "I am not the false man you think."

There are no cameras in the halls, and I want to tell her my plan, how I will hire a driver to take her home, and give her money so her family can repay the Organization and still have enough for what they need. I want her to know that I will help her, but that first she has to trust me.

"I am not really part of this place," I tell her. "I care about you."

She gauges me warily. "I am just a girl. Third daughter. Unlucky number. Why would you care about me?"

"Why did your mother let you go?"

"Mother died when my brother, Dornchai, was born. Now my father has too many stomachs to feed."

Tossing her hair behind her, she turns and starts down the hall.

"Wait!" I say, but she does not wait. I go after her. She passes a closed door where two women are laughing with a man. Songkha pretends not to hear. We pass a door on the other side, and there is the slapping of a hand against what must be fleshy buttocks and a man crying out in pain. Then Japanese words, as he begs for more. Song walks even faster.

"Songkha, stop!" I say forcefully. "I need to talk to you." She faces me with a deliberate look. The sounds continue around us.

"The situation isn't simple," I continue, struggling for the words in Thai. "Men rented you because you are attractive and they want you. But they are strong, and it will be dangerous if I try to convince them you are too young."

Her demeanor softens as she studies me.

"When I was little my grandfather taught me how to fish for *talaysap*. They are beautiful fish, blue and yellow. My grandfather said there is a time when a thing is ready. Then it will offer itself. Sometimes when I fished, I saw

a *talaysap* but it would not come near me. Then I saw
another and it came right away. When I raised my net
under it, it spun around, throwing water on me. It struggled
even when it knew it was its time.''

''I don't want you to struggle. I want to help.''

Song shakes her head as if it is hopeless. She moves
away and peers into an unoccupied room, then steps inside. I follow her, and see that the room is plushly carpeted
in red and mirrored everywhere. Even the ceiling, as well
as the surface of the dresser, is mirror glass. Angles of
reflections are everywhere, and the two of us are reflected
and double-reflected.

Near a big-screen television is a rack of videos. She
walks over and picks out a cassette, frowns as she stares
at the cover, then lets it slip from her hand to the red
carpet. I pick it up. On the cover is a photo of two women
giving pleasure to one man. Embarrassed, I slide it back
into the rack.

Song takes out another video, stares, then throws it to
the carpet. I reach for it, but she pulls on the rack and all
the videos spill over.

''Stop it!'' I say, looking up at where the camera is
hidden, afraid we are being recorded. But the camera
should be turned off since no clients are booked for this
room.

Song opens a dresser drawer, lifts out a blond wig, and
holds it out for me to see, then throws it on the floor.
Then a whip. Then handcuffs. A pile on the floor for me
to see.

''Everything here is false,'' she says, looking directly
at me. ''Don't you see? Everything here is foul.''

Then, like before, I sense a window open somewhere
in my mind. Now I am sure she is the one who opens it,
because I can see what she sees—the true horror of this
room and the pile of implements on the floor, and everything else about the Fantasy Store. And it is clear to me
that, like the *talaysap*, it is not her time.

The window starts to close, and I fight to keep it open.
There is only one way. I will help her, as I had decided

before. I will protect her at any cost, because, when the window is open like this I can see the utter pointlessness of all I have pursued. Not just the pointlessness, the fraud of it too. All the so-called noble causes, all the secret missions, all the affairs of great minds, and all the intrigue have only brought me here to this red, mirrored room to permit someone to rape this village child. I will not sink that low for any kind of access. I will even leave the Organization if I have to.

I feel relief. Relief, because I have decided. Yes, I will risk everything and rescue Song. And in rescuing her, I will rescue myself as well.

Song goes to a corner where the mirrors meet. She faces the mirror, looking at me. She is reflected and double-reflected. Then she reaches for the button on her wrap-around. "Do you want to see me now?" she asks. "Do you want to see what I look like?"

"*Mai!*" I shout. "No. Don't unwrap yourself!"

"What does it matter if it is you or any other false man?"

She slowly unwinds the dress as she stares at me in the mirror. Confused, I step back. My breathing is shallow and irregular. She is playing with me, mocking me. Before, she seemed to be so untouched, as if from some higher place. I thought I was gaining her trust. But maybe she is not so innocent. Maybe she is very sharp, with a clever strategy of her own. I think she has already been told about men, perhaps by her mother or grandmother: how mindless we become once our desires and fantasies are aroused. How we will lie, beg, betray, do anything to have our way. That we are foolish and clumsy beasts who can be controlled by a sideways glance or a smile.

Now she tosses her hair, offering herself to me. Is she telling me that it is her time? I move closer behind her. Suddenly a fantasy flashes through my head—*I am reaching around her and touching her breasts*. An instant, and the thoughts are gone. No, they were not my thoughts at all, they were the thoughts of this place. This awful place. I would never touch her. But I have the urge to run my hands over her hair. I want to hold her. I want to fall into her arms. No, I would only pollute her innocence.

Her eyes continue to stare at me in the mirror. Her shoulders are straight, her back is erect as she continues to unwind the garment. "I will be a whore," she says. "But for two years only. And you will be my whore-keeper."

"Mai!" I shout involuntarily. No! I reach out and take her hand to reassure her. Now I have touched her! I did not mean to. I am surprised at how warm she feels. She tries to pull away, but I grip her hand tighter to reassure her. Her wraparound is now loose and falling, her eyes fixed on me.

"Khoon mai khao jai!" I say loudly. "You don't understand! I will help you!"

I grip her hand tighter and move closer. My leg brushes against her loose gown, and I feel her knee beneath it. A strong surge leaps through me. Perhaps she sees the affection in my eyes because she seems to relax a little, and maybe there is a small smile of relief on her face.

Yes, a small smile. She understands. "It is okay," I tell her. "Everything will be okay."

Then a flood of sensation races through me at a pitch that I am unready for. I look more closely at her now, and I see that she is not sixteen or seventeen as I had thought, but at least eighteen, probably older. Young, but not too young for me. *"Wun ma reun nee,"* I whisper. Day after tomorrow. *"Dee neung sip-ha nah-tee."* Early morning, 1:15. I will find your room and come for you.

Now she knows I will help her escape. She knows that it is friendship, not lust I bring. She turns her head to the side, her eyes open, offering me her cheek. In the mirror I see myself bend toward her, and I am conscious of the perfume they have put on her. As I brush my lips against her skin, a thought races through me. I wonder if there is not some secret yearning inside her. The others saw only a childlike facade, but I can see that she is not a child. She is almost certainly a young woman, unusually mature for her age, someone with feelings and desires, maybe even passions that are still unawakened, passions that are eager to be aroused.

I bend farther and delicately touch my mouth and chin against her neck and then brush my face upward against her hair. Everything tingles inside me, a curious, elated excitement that I feel.

Then I realize I don't have to wait until late at night to escape with her. If we are careful, we can escape now, and no one will know for hours. I watch it all unfold in my mind: *I take her hand and lead her down the stairs and unlock the side door to the city sidewalk. There is sunlight and the air is cool and we are totally free. We rush down the side street and across the footbridge over the small canal, then down an alley, finally stopping to catch our breath. She looks up at me, amazed at my courage, and throws her arms around me, innocently, gratefully. I have saved her from hundreds of men in her future, and now she thanks me, sprinkling my cheeks with small, grateful kisses. Unexpectedly she embraces me closer, pressing herself fully against me, harder. The kisses grow more passionate. There is a heat in her mouth. Something urgent and insisting. She wants me the way I want her. Along with her future I will possess her innocence. I am elated. Everything is good and right. I will have her in every way.*

Then I am not outside anymore. I am in the mirrored room with Song, and she is reflected and double- and triple-reflected—a child, no, a woman, no, a beautiful child. I look around the room, and there are a dozen Songs. And a dozen men who want her, and I am all of them. I must flee. No, she is offering herself to me. No she isn't. My mind seesaws in a perverse excitement that arouses and shames and shocks me.

Song breaks away from me and picks up the wig, then the whip. She holds them out. "Take them," she says in her language. "Use them on me. You know that others will." Her lips twitch in anger. She pulls at her wraparound again, and this time it falls to the floor. I turn away without looking and retreat in horror.

Now I am even more frightened for her, because of my own contradictory emotions. Am I just a middle-aged man who has longed to touch youth again? Am I just a lonely person worn down from years of isolation, seeking some womanly sympathy, some youthful understanding? No, that cannot account for her effect on me. She is causing me to think and behave this way, drawing me to her, with her brazenness and fearlessness. She wants me to take her and possess her for myself.

Then I am clear again, and can see what her power is over me. It is not sexual. Rather, it is because she is one person only. One woman confronting the Organization, confronting the entire system. She is mocking the horror of it all with her own innocence. She is willing to start right now. Alone and naked she will defy each man one by one.

I realize I must be as defiant and fearless as she is. I must do it because I can help her and she can help me. I must rescue her regardless of consequences. I don't care if the Organization knows.

But I freeze.

I do not risk everything. I rush from the room afraid of the Organization. Afraid of myself. Afraid of Song.

Then for days—no, for weeks and months—conflicting desires stay with me, and I cannot shake them. Her naked defiance still excites me. Arouses me. At my age I thought I had grown beyond irrational emotions of that kind. Even now, thousands of miles away in my Arlington kitchen staring at her photo, fantasies continue to play in my mind. I wanted to possess Song's courage. I wanted to possess her in every way. But I did not save her. I left her there. And when I left her, I lost my last bit of ground as a human being.

As I continue to gaze down at the picture of Song, I hear a knock at my apartment door. I hear it, but I am lost in a secret place, a deep place, where just the thought of her still carries me to.

The knocks continue. Not the long, heavy rapping of a man's knuckles but light knocks, quick and urgent. I slip the photo back into its hiding place. Even before I open the door I know who will be standing there.

11

TROJAN HORSE

She seems different again.

Her attractiveness takes me by surprise. In a glimpse I see that her hair is brushed up in a more stylish way and that she is still in jeans, but instead of the tight cotton pullover she is wearing a flannel shirt tied in a knot at the waist, exposing a thin line of skin. Her breasts seem more uplifted. Her Reeboks are brand-new, and the carefully applied makeup gives her a kind of spotlight radiance she didn't have before.

Penny O'Hara or Catherine DeLaurentis, or whoever she is, looks relaxed, different, even inviting. My antenna is already up. Trojan horses are nothing new to me.

"May I come in?" she says. Her tone is a mixture of concern and embarrassment.

"I can't imagine what this is about," I say.

"I checked the bedroom, but you were wrong. There's no microphone or camera. I'm sure of it."

"Then you missed them, or they removed them."

"Or you said it just to turn me against them."

I push on the door to close it, but she steps forward and plants her weight. My patience at its end, I release the door.

"I'll tell you what they know about you," she says quickly, and slides her other foot inside. She goes up on her toes and peers over my shoulder. "Christ, this place is a mess. And you've only been here a few days."

I fold my arms. She folds her arms opposite mine and gives me a sweet little smile, a look of haughty superiority.

"Mr. DeForest asked me to come here. He doesn't want a scene. He's going to keep your mail drop open. And he's going to give you severance after all, six thousand five hundred dollars for each year you worked. But only if you stay in the States. It's a lot of money, Mr. Gaines."

"Tell him I said no, thank you."

"The first check is for a real chunk, if you ask me. Over thirty thousand dollars, Mr. Gaines. It takes me over a year to make that. He said you'll get more after six months, and the rest spread out. But only if you abide by your agreement."

"Does it sound like a bribe to you?"

"It sounds like good money to me. So you won't leave the States?"

I push on the door. "It's been a real pleasure."

She doesn't budge. "He knows where you're going," she says.

"Good for him."

"I've always wanted to see Thailand."

"And I hope you do someday."

"No, I mean I could go with you."

"I know what you mean." I push on the door again.

"Look, if you don't accept his offer, then I'm supposed to tell you something else."

"Why doesn't DeForest tell me?"

"He is, through me." Her voice is serious now, a soft monotone. "They said that they know they can't control you, Mr. Gaines. You can go to the press. You have a lot of knowledge of operations and a lot of options. I'm supposed to tell you that they have options too, and they said you know what those options are."

"What has the Fantasy Plan uncovered?" I say.

She shakes her head. "All I know is they're nervous

about you.'' She can see that I don't believe her. ''Okay, I think they have a brothel somewhere,'' she finally says, biting her lip after saying it. ''Is that it? I hear things.''

''Sex isn't exactly a historical breakthrough.''

''I think they got something big. I don't know. I think they're afraid you'll screw it up.''

I glance at her tight jeans, her shirt tied at the waist, and her uplifted breasts. ''How will they stop me? Kill me? Seduce me? Have they sent you as one of the perks of my retirement?''

She frowns severely. I push on the door again, but she stands her ground like an angry wife.

''What did the operation uncover?'' I ask again. ''And who are you really?''

She straightens her shoulders. ''I don't know what the operation has uncovered. And I've already told you who I am, more than once. The real question is about you. Are you unpredictable and dangerous, like they say?''

''Maybe you should be afraid of me.''

She gives me a cute smile. ''Eek,'' she says. ''I think I can tell what kind of person you are, and I don't think you'd hurt anyone.''

''You're wrong. That was my job.''

''I mean, you wouldn't hurt anyone directly.'' There is a subtle, almost imperceptible change in her voice, as if she wants me to confirm this. ''Did you ever hurt anyone directly?''

I reply honestly, to see her reaction. ''I killed a man once.'' Her mouth tightens. ''It was awful,'' I add.

She nods slowly as she looks at me. For a moment I think she is going to reach up and remove my glasses and gaze into my eyes.

''There must be something very important to make you go against them,'' she says. ''It's a woman, isn't it?''

I shake my head. Another lie. And a transparent one.

She smiles unkindly. ''It's always a woman. You're going to be her savior, aren't you? How romantic. But it's impossible to fight them, Peter. Do you mind if I call you Peter? It's impossible to fight them, Peter, especially Mr. DeForest.''

''What is the secret they're trying to keep me away from?''

''And it's impossible for you to go anywhere. You know what they can do from a single office at headquarters or at Mead. They can trace you anyplace. They have access to every hotel and restaurant computer, every airline computer, every car rental. They'll know what you had for breakfast. Use a bank machine anywhere in the world, and they'll have you before you walk away. They'll make the world a box for you, Peter. Please don't mess with them. If you want to go somewhere, wait a year, wait two years. But don't go now. Get a job. Wait till they think you're just getting on with your life. Then do whatever the hell you have to do.''

''What is the secret?'' I ask again. ''Why all the trouble to keep me away?''

She shakes her head as if she's sorry. ''I don't know,'' she says, and sighs sympathetically. ''And I'm afraid for you. Why don't you call the office in the morning and ask for Mr. DeForest? I can put you through. I think he'll let you work something out.''

She continues to regard me with pleading eyes. If it's an act, it is quite convincing. But if she really is a secretary, then I feel sorry for her. The Organization is using her. She is their dupe, standing on the edge of a world that she thinks is exciting and exotic but that she doesn't understand at all.

Dupe or not, she looks so inviting. We are just inches apart, and I can see some youthful freckles beneath her makeup. Maybe it is just the shadowy light, or maybe it's the years of being alone pulling at me, but her lips seem plummish now, and her eyes are a bit watery. Her smell— not her perfume, but her natural smell—is very faint, but it is there. The tight jeans are suggestive, and the flannel shirt hangs a little loose and open. Something stirs as I contemplate her, something creeping through me, exciting and weakening me at the same time. She studies me, her face warm with feeling.

Trojan horses are always like that, inviting on the outside. They would be easy to spot if they were all horses or gifts from Greeks. The trouble is they never have the same disguise twice, though they always have the trustful eyes of a child. And of course they have a surprise waiting.

Her eyes hold mine. Her look is pained. She goes up on her toes and leans toward my ear. "They're going to take you out of circulation," she whispers, as if there might be a listening device in the room. "Out of circulation," she repeats. Her tone is confiding and concerned. "Those are their words, Peter. You know what that means."

In a world of masks it is rare to hear the soft sound of concern and sincerity, and now my instincts tell me she is for real. She really is a secretary. Or she is the best liar I have ever known. But my training tells me not to trust her; sincerity is a nonexistent commodity in the Work.

"I'm not afraid of you, Peter Gaines," she continues in a whisper so soft I can barely hear her. "I'm afraid *for* you. We know our bosses. Don't go back to Thailand."

We continue to face each other. She stands on her toes again and leans forward, and her kiss is just a soft peck on my chin. "I wanted to do that from the first time I saw you," she says.

A familiar excitement grows inside me, an exhilaration, a turbulence that is trying to take over. She seems so soft and desirous, not just feminine but magnetically female, the kind of willing and experienced woman I should be attracted to instead of Song. I reach out to slide my fingers through her hair, but she pushes my hand down. Then she tilts her head, and her mouth comes forward again, a wild and unrestrained kiss this time, a bite on my lip, and for an instant I feel the whip of her tongue. Then it is gone. We are facing each other again. She takes a deep breath as if regaining control.

"I'm sorry," she says in a gasp, her eyes wide in a kind

of horror and amazement at herself, her hand covering her mouth.

Without another word she turns on her heels and rushes away. Not the short, choppy steps that scuttled beside me after we got off the bus, but swift strides, her shoulders swinging back as she flees. Maybe it is the new Reeboks. Maybe it is the alluring walk of a Trojan horse. Either way, I feel a tinge of regret as she disappears down the hall.

12

ESCAPE

*A*ll this started just twenty-four hours ago. My dismissal and then a moment of courageous resolve as I stood outside headquarters building, a decision to change my life by undoing something terribly wrong. And already it has turned into something so complicated.

A single thought overwhelms me. It comes with no announcement. It just comes, and there it is. *Get away,* it says. *Get out of here now.* I know to trust it.

Not even a tote bag. Nothing that would indicate I am going somewhere. I can't chance a call to my mother or my sister, Beth. And I will leave the Prozac behind. My problem has not been chemical or biological. My problem is a place in me that a pill can never get to.

I check my wallet for the cash they gave me upon dismissal, a little more than eight thousand dollars, most of it in fifty-dollar bills. I pull on my jacket and glance around the room for other necessities; there is only one, the photo concealed in the paper towel roll. I slide it into my pocket and step into the hall.

Out on the sidewalk I go to the main street. There is a bank two blocks away. I enter and ask a teller to exchange my bills for twenties and hundreds, anything to switch currency, because the Organization sometimes laces currency with a microscopic filament that can be tracked up to two miles away. I leave the bank and time my arrival at a city bus stop. I step on the bus at the last moment. From inside I can conduct countersurveillance without detection.

It is not like in the movies, where a single vehicle follows right behind you or even at a safe and seemingly unobtrusive distance. If I am being watched, there will be a team of a half dozen cars, different models and years, each in cellular communication, some running on streets parallel to the bus, and alternately turning on and off the route so that no car follows the bus for more than a block or two at a time.

Or there could be no cars at all. It could all be in my mind. The line between controlled paranoia and real paranoia sometimes grows as thin as a spider's thread.

From the rear of the bus I study the flow of traffic and assess the ages and descriptions of the drivers. Station wagons and compacts are the Organization's favorites because they blend in more easily than the expected sedans. I look for male or female drivers, alone or together, and I dismiss cars with infants, children, or dogs. But I detect no pattern to the traffic, and I'm certain no car reappears after turning.

I change buses, careful not to backtrack or indicate any kind of evasive behavior. The bus meanders through Arlington toward the main terminal, which is in the dreariest part of town and accordingly only blocks from the state's unemployment office. Where I get off, the sidewalk is badly littered, and there are black youths grouped on corners and old white winos leaning against storefronts. As I walk past them all, I imagine eyes everywhere, eyes in the shadows and alleys and windows. Eyes watching. Minds wondering what I'll do.

I go directly to the unemployment office, enter the one-story building, and spend time surveying the job cards on the bulletin board. Cooks. Clerks. Laborers.

I leave, walk several blocks to a new mall, and alter-

nately window-shop and relax on benches that face the
direction I just came from. After all, I am retired, with no
agenda but to work my way back into American society.
And I am certain, almost certain, I am not being followed.

The next step is to locate the Greyhound station. Buses
are one of the few ways to travel between cities and states
without being logged into a computer or leaving a paper
trail of credit. Also, they make several stops, and it is
possible to purchase a ticket and get off anywhere in between without attracting attention.

As the late afternoon turns to early evening, I head to
the bus depot. What I experienced before as the wonder-
fully vibrant sounds and sights of American life are now
just a blur as my mind focuses elsewhere. I recall how
after Torpakai's death, her face and the smell of her body
stayed with me for so long. I continued to embrace her
for years. And then Anna too. Even after she had fled
from me, I could not forget her plain, straight hair and
the magnified eyes behind her thick glasses as she calmly
read to me from the *Phaedo*.

But now it is Songkha Chattkatavong who is in my
mind; I am with her, though I hardly know her. And it is
different from the absence of Torpakai and Anna. I feel
an emotion that I cannot name. Half haunted and half
mesmerized, accompanied by shame.

Shame. Sometimes I have felt that a part of me is an
unsolvable mystery; though I've wanted what is good,
there has often been a confusion of right and wrong. Life
is not as clear-cut as the sermons in church make it out
to be, where God has spoken, and good is good and bad
is bad, and all of it has been laid down since the beginning
of time.

Over the years there was never a clear pool in which I
could see what was right, just a muddy river of greater
evils and lesser evils, and so many times I have had to
choose the lesser evil. Like that man in Kyoto. Killing is
a despicable thing. But permitting him to live would have
been worse. More lives would have been lost. He had to

die. It was good that he died. So the evil thing was really a kind of good, and the good was not wholly good but stained with an evil. And there was no God to still the waters so that everything could be made more clear.

Sometimes too my own desires have made a game of good and evil, switching them in my head. Wrong suddenly is right. Only much later do I realize that I lied to myself and let my basest desires shape my thoughts and actions.

This is not something I speak about comfortably, and I've spoken of it only once before, six years ago, to Steven Vaal. It was the one time we had a chance to meet after leaving the Branscomb Institute. I was passing through the U.S. Embassy in Brussels, picking up new documentation as an associate at a Ford subsidiary in Europe, when I saw him ahead of me on the stairwell. There was supposed to be no contact between us. But it had been twelve years. I wanted to see him again.

I recalled a scenario we had devised way back in training, a typical conversation between two strangers in passing but with camouflaged meanings. We only had to plug in a few words to communicate the real message. Anyone overhearing us would think nothing of it, just a casual encounter and discussion.

"Excuse me just a moment," I said.

He turned toward me. "Yes? May I help?" His deep blue eyes gazed at me with no sign of recognition.

"I'm sorry. I don't know the city well, and I'm dying for a good American beer."

"Oh, then Briars Bar is the place for you," he answered nonchalantly. "It's a bit out of the way, though."

"Do you know the shortest way there?"

"The shortest way is not always the fastest. Take a taxi. And it's not too crowded there after ten."

I nodded my thanks. He turned and went his way.

It had taken ten seconds.

I got the address of Briars Bar and found it on a map. It was in the northern part of the city. I went there at six o'clock to check exits, lighting, and the clientele. One rear exit into an alley and a side exit onto a street. Dim. Middle class. Varieties of beer. Quiet music. Booths off to the side. Perfect.

I came back at ten-thirty. Vaal arrived at eleven. He went to the bar and surveyed the room in the mirror until he located me. Then, like in the old days, he headed to my booth with an expensive bottle of wine and some cheap pretzels.

He sat. There was no greeting between us because none was necessary. It had been more than a decade, but no time had passed since two Branscomb roommates would put down their books each night to find an out-of-the-way bar somewhere in Monterey or Carmel.

He poured two glasses, handed me one, and we silently toasted each other. I knew what Vaal would do next. He would pick up where we left off years before, continuing our boyish musings about whether the waitress was married and whether one of us could pick her up.

He nodded toward the blond waitress and spoke lowly to me in Chinese. *"Ni chieh de ta tze mo yang?"* Well, what do you think?

"Elle est certainement mariée," I said, switching languages the way we used to and holding up my end of the game.

"Kanojo wa kekkon shite inai," he answered, changing to Japanese. I say she's not married.

"Edinstvenniy sposob usnat eto," I replied in Russian. Only one way to find out. *"Davay, sproci eyo."* Go ahead and ask her.

Vaal smiled, and seemed to search his mind for another language. *"Dzisiaj jest twoja kolej, stary."* No, old friend, it's your turn. *"Ostatnim razem ja pytalem kelnerke."* I was the one who asked the waitress last time.

"You've learned Polish!" I said with surprise.

"Cam on anh," he replied in Vietnamese. Thanks.

We broke into laughter and toasted again. Then we sat back in a comfortable silence, and in that silence we munched pretzels and sipped the wine and just enjoyed being with each other again.

Only after we had finished the bottle did we talk—but not of operations, present or past, for that would breach the rule. And we did not ask if the other was married because the answer was clear. Instead over a second bottle of wine Steven Vaal and I spoke generally of the places we had been to and joked about places we would never go back to. And we agreed that fifteen months at Branscomb had not prepared us for the isolation and the difficulty of the Work. Such a changing world.

It was well after one o'clock when Steven motioned the waitress for the check. We both were tired, but I asked if we could talk just a moment longer.

He smiled sleepily and perhaps noted the troubled look on my face. "Sounds serious," he said. "Maybe we should order some more wine to clear our heads."

The wine came, and he poured two glasses to the brim. Then he rested his chin in his hands and feigned an expression of deep seriousness.

I did not speak at first, searching for the words. Then I asked Steven if over the years he had sometimes felt a struggle inside him, whether sometimes desires emerged suddenly—as if from night into day—coloring his perceptions, sometimes turning wrong into right in his mind, all of it in good conscience.

Steven seemed surprised. He put his glass down and looked away from me. I explained that I was not talking about a Jekyll and Hyde inside us, nothing so diabolical. Just desires that we sometimes feel crawling around under our skin, desires that are waiting. I told him I believed that no one ever *intends* to do anything wrong, but that somehow desires exert themselves in the name of good, creating fantasies that charm our reasonings. So we know that cheating on a test is wrong, except it is okay this one time. Sleeping with a neighbor's spouse is wrong, but maybe one time is okay. Lying under oath is wrong unless it saves our reputation. Chaos takes on the name of heroism. My Lai, Watergate, assassinations of great men, and every kind of terrorism are carried out not in the name of evil but always because someone saw them to be the good thing to do at the time.

Vaal was silent and still. Even his deep blue eyes didn't move. Then he sighed and nodded knowingly. He understood.

That was all I needed. I was happy, because there was someone who knew me, someone who understood that desires provoke fantasies and then fantasies stoke desires. I told Vaal one more thing: I confessed that I was never sure how far I would go in letting my desires persuade me but that I always sensed I was capable of absolutely anything—from the greatest heroism to the greatest destruction, all in the name of good.

Vaal nodded again, heavily, sadly. The whole time he had not spoken. Now he put up a hand to stop me. He drained his glass. It was time to go. I didn't mind. I was relieved that he understood. I was relieved that I had a real friend in the world. A mirror self.

As I head toward the Arlington Greyhound station I am surprised at how the past floods over me. I cannot block out the time I permitted my desires to stoke a fantasy that completely overwhelmed me. Sometimes things we do shock others, and sometimes things we do shock even ourselves.

It happened at the Fantasy Store. It was late, 1:15 in the morning, the day after I had been with Song in the mirrored room. I had everything planned. The attendants would be sleeping. I would find her, unlock the side door, and whisk her away. It would be her freedom, and it would be my own freedom as well.

I went to the fourth floor, the top floor of the building, where the women hired from around the world lived and slept. I had not been upstairs to the women's private quarters before, and when I reached the top of the stairs I was surprised at how lavish everything was: ornate molding, rich colors, the hallway closets full of attractive clothing, and twenty-five private rooms with fancy nameplates on the doors. I stepped down the corridor searching each of the closed doors for Song's name, but it was not there.

I became alarmed. Maybe they had really taken Song away this time. Or maybe her room was somewhere else because she had been rented from her family and not hired like the other women. The second and third floors had encounter rooms only, and the first floor had the reception area, the tech room, and a few more encounter rooms. There was only one other place she could be.

I returned to the first floor and found a stairway to the basement. I descended in the darkness and searched along the greasy wall to find the hall light switch. When the light came on, it revealed a row of rooms I had not known existed. No, they were not really rooms but more like cells, a corridor of damp cells, a dungeon. Leamer had avoided showing me the basement, saying we would get to it later.

At first there was only silence as I began to check the cells, and I felt a relief that they were empty. Then I detected a very faint humming or singing or something like a sad chanting, airy and clear. It was a breath of life, strange and sweet in the prison. I waited and listened. The faint sounds repeated. A woman's voice. There were three notes in all. Then the same three notes were sung again, this time a little differently. I stood listening as they were repeated twice more, and at first the sounds went low into a sadness and then higher, still aching with sadness but of a different tone.

Pulled by the soft sounds, I followed them down the narrow corridor. All the doors to the cells were open and dark and empty. I came to the cell with the faint singing. The door was closed and locked from the outside with a long bolt. I pulled the bolt back and entered noiselessly. A tiny bulb hung down from the ceiling, offering only a hint of light. But I could see her sitting on the corner of the bed, her feet on the cold cement floor, her eyes staring into a corner and her head swaying with the three melodic notes. The room was almost bare. I could make out only a chair and a small cot, like a child's bed.

Suddenly my legs felt weak, nearly buckling, and I put out my hand for the wall. I had not even thought about what conditions she might be living in. And I could only condemn myself. I was part of all this. Then I grew steady again because I was no longer going to be part of it. In minutes she would be free.

Song did not realize I was there until I had moved across the cell and stood over her. Then her soft sounds stopped. She did not seem afraid of me. Maybe she could see my eyes in the dimness, and knew that I was going to lead her out of there. I was going to save her.

But first I just stood silently, looking down at her. There was a kind of singing inside me now, a remarkable happiness. She was going to be free of this horrible place. Smiling, I leaned over and kissed her on the forehead as if she were an old love. I lifted her chin toward me so she could look into my face and see that I was on her side, see how much I cared for her. That I had come to rescue her.

"Everything is going to be different," I whispered in her language. "I am going to free you. You must come with me now."

She studied me a moment, then got to her feet. I put out my hand, and she reached for it. Then she reached with her other hand and took my whole arm, leaning against me with relief. She looked up at me, then suddenly threw her arms around me in a desperate embrace.

I held her tightly until her arms relaxed and she started to pull away. I looked into her face, and maybe it was my imagination, but I was sure I saw something promising in her eyes, and I thought she allowed herself to reach up toward me just a little with her mouth. She wanted me. It was so unexpected. I could not believe it. I leaned down hesitantly and kissed her on the lips. It was a soft, sweet kiss, her lips unmoving but slightly parted, and I had the distinct feeling that it was sweet for her also, because although she was stiff, she did not recoil in any way. Maybe it was the first kiss of her life, and she welcomed it. I whispered in English, "Song, you are what I want to be. You are perfect. You are perfection itself."

Then, slowly, other thoughts came to me, more powerful thoughts. My forehead began to perspire, and I heard myself whispering something different, inarticulate words about *desire* and *need* and *now*.

I could feel myself everywhere inside my skin, flushed with hot purposeful blood. Everything seemed blurred as a grayness seeped through me. But I knew she wanted me as much as I wanted her. Holding her hand, I sat down on the bed. She sat beside me, then turned her face and shifted away from me as if to say no. But it was only a momentary reaction, her natural shyness. I also felt a natural shyness. It was obvious she wanted me to kiss her again. I pushed back her flowing hair and stroked her neck with the flat of my fingers. Then I leaned into her and kissed her shoulder and turned her toward me so I could kiss her low on her throat.

Perhaps she felt me trembling as I eased her backward on the bed. I don't remember her resisting. We did not speak or undress. Her eyes were wide open, and I was pleased that somehow what was necessary for me was also necessary for her. She could see the goodness in me, and it had affected something in her. She knew I would free her and protect her. I was amazed that someone so pure as this could love me and have the same appetite that I had, that somewhere sealed up inside her was a disguised yearning for me. Silently she was even asking for me.

I had come to her room to lead her away, but now there would be something more. I would be the first one, and she would know what love was like. Much later, when she was safely home, she would remember these tender moments, the softness of my hand on her shoulder and across her stomach and on her leg, how gentle a man could be. In later years she would remember how I had aroused her, how I had held her and cared for her. She would remember me. This moment would be her friend.

After easing her backward, I leaned over her gently. Beside me on the wall was the thin shadow of my body over hers. This was our last chance, the last moments we had for each other. She remained motionless, holding her breath, waiting to be taken. We hung together on the brink. It was a special, timeless moment, each of us holding back so that the consummation would be even more pleasurable.

Then slowly, as if from a distance, I became aware that she was not looking into my eyes as I had thought, but that her head was turned far to the side and that she was twisting under my weight. I looked into her face and saw not her need for me but her silent rage. In the dimness I saw tears come from behind her eyes where they were hiding. They puddled and crept down her cheek.

I suddenly awakened as if from a fog or a great sickness, stunned with myself, shocked by what I had almost done. A tear started slowly from behind my own eye where it had been waiting. I reached out and brushed my hand across her hair again, then realized I did not have the right to do even that. The tear rolled from my eye, and it fell to her blouse, which was now open and exposing part of her breast. In the blur I could not remember how the blouse had gotten open. I shifted my weight, and she slid away from me, moving to a corner.

In the dim light I got up and found that my own shirt was pulled out and my pants partially undone, and I could not remember how. I quickly tucked my shirt in and straightened everything. Then, without looking back, I slipped away. So shaken, I can't recall what I did after leaving her cell. I only remember that the next day I stayed in my room, trying to piece together what happened, as waves of shame continued to break over me.

I know that self-forgiveness should be a part of life. But when things have turned so wrong, they continued to live inside us, and they must be made to turn again. It is not possible to set the clock back and change the past. But if I *could* set the clock back, I would. And this time nothing would stop me. No confusion. No lies to myself. No self-deception. Nothing. I would rescue her this time. I would take her away from there with the real affection I had felt for her the first time I saw her, a father's love for an innocent daughter. I would hurry her through the streets of Bangkok, return her to her village and leave money with her family so they could build their house and well. I would be as defiant and guiltless as she is. I would be a human being again.

But when it was possible I had not done any of that. In shame I left her there. That night. In her cell.

I did go back two nights later. But then her cell was empty. She had been taken north, this time for real. Two weeks later I was abruptly transferred from the Fantasy Plan.

Now I push through the door of the Greyhound bus depot. I make my way across the dirty checkerboard floor, past rows of old wooden seats, to the ticket window. The air echoes loudly with announcements of buses departing.

My immediate destination is unimportant, just to get away by Greyhound as quickly as possible to another city from which I can more easily leave the country, and then through a series of indirect routes make my way back to Song and maybe back to myself.

The boarding signs indicate a bus going north in minutes for Baltimore and then Philadelphia. I buy the ticket with cash and from a distance observe the ticket window to see if anyone approaches to inquire about my destination. Two minutes before the coach is to depart, I march to Section D. I wait until the driver starts the engine, then board, the last to get on. I sit in the rear.

My thoughts trace back over the last day and a half, which seem as long and perplexing as a lifetime. I think back over my actions since leaving the apartment and decide I have made no mistakes. I cannot evade them completely. They know exactly where I am going. But momentarily I have gained my freedom. From either Baltimore, Philadelphia, or points in between I can, without a reservation, pay cash at the last minute and board a flight to another city and then pay cash again to get out of the country. With only my real passport it isn't possible to travel without being tracked. But if my movements are swift and unpredictable enough, I might be able to zigzag my way to Thailand without being detained. Or maybe that is the point: that they will let me get back to Thailand because there I can be disposed of much more easily. No fuss. No mess.

But I can't worry about that now.

The bus proceeds north, and a kind of relief comes over me now that I have finally begun. I think of the fables where men set out to find the Golden Fleece or the Holy Grail after warnings from comrades and enemies alike and how sometimes there is a beautiful woman with a mysterious prediction or perhaps with a potion that will ward off evil happenings.

Then another feeling rises in me, a new sense of life and vibrancy. Today I made a turn at a crossroads that has been within me for so long; I have made the decision to be like Song. I will be blameless and pure and clear. No matter what the dangers or obstacles when I return to the Fantasy Store, even if there is death, there will be no more lies, not even to myself. There will be no more distortions, no more deceit, no more rewriting of my memory or shuffling of the truth.

But mixed with the sense of life and vibrancy is a kind of unease and even dread, because the wholly honest life is one I do not know and one I am not even sure I can find. I can see my past easily enough, with all the ugly twists and turns that led me to this crossroads, to the decision to be like Song. But now that I have made that turn, I feel that I am standing on a dangerously unstable precipice. And I am just now taking my first step forward.

PART II

So quick bright things come to confusion.

—William Shakespeare

13

*L*os Angeles sinks below me.

Korean Airlines Flight 24 rises and curls over the city, then speeds west with the sun. Around me conversations in many languages mingle with the air that whispers through little nozzles overhead.

After a few minutes we just seem to hang in the air, and through the window I can see everything: the green, choppy Pacific; a sleek black submarine maneuvering offshore; a string of rusty cargo boats that will stretch all the way to Japan. In my mind I can see even more: a nation of twenty million families clipping coupons, kissing children good night, making love to the same person, and burying their old people.

From up there the world looks spread out and safe. But I feel as if my life is happening inside a telescope. My movements over the past day can be tracked but not easily. I changed buses at a shack of a depot outside Baltimore and at the last second decided on a long detour to Pittsburgh, thinking that if I were unpredictable even to myself, it would be that much harder for others to track me. Still, each time the bus stopped I expected to see Catherine DeLaurentis struggling down the aisle with a suitcase and looking so surprised to find me there.

In Pittsburgh I discovered a discount store and bought clothes and a small travel bag, then went to the airport and paid cash for a short flight to Detroit, then on to Denver, then to Los Angeles.

LAX had dozens of foreign carriers, but I chose Korean Airlines because of the legroom. I booked myself to Tokyo by way of Seoul. But in Seoul I will change planes at the last minute and head for Thailand through a different route.

I stretch my legs and stare out the window as the plane races westward. For three hours the sky slowly darkens; then the sun finally leaps ahead of us, and it is black outside. I close my eyes and enter into a half-dreaming state, that collage world where images come and go freely with no introductions and no good-byes, a world of tall green fields, the embraces of Torpakai, Anna's wide eyes, and the slender, bare arm of Song.

Then my mind drifts backward to episodes of my youth. An ambush of memories. A birthday party when I was six or seven, when I wore my black Hopalong Cassidy suit and carried a pistol on each hip. Going to confession for the first time and seeing the dim silhouette of that man behind the screen who expected me to tell him every sin I had ever thought or done. And I remember the taste of the air in Scranton, a taste that announced to everyone that the coal dust had not yet settled even three decades after the mining had stopped.

When I was twelve, my father moved us to Cleveland, where he had gotten a job with a large pharmaceutical company called Webb & Webb. My father was a handsome man with a thin face and long, beautiful hands. The son of a German immigrant, he had learned to play the piano by ear from his grandmother. He never learned to read music, but he could play anything, waltzes, polkas, even big band music, and joked that the only key he couldn't master was the one to the front door. He taught us that America was a great and fair country, where anything was possible. His own life was a testimony to that. He returned from World War II with only a high school diploma and a flair for numbers, then worked his way from a shipping department through bookkeeping to accounting. My father loved the precision of numbers and solved accounting discrepancies with the same excitement that other people solve intricate puzzles.

You could say he was just a number cruncher. You could say he was just a man who sat in a cubicle with his calculator, counting dollars for people who made little pills. But he knew better. A product of the Great Depression, he counted himself fortunate to have a job and a three-bedroom house and a wife who never had to go to work. He also had a piano and at night he played Cole Porter and Gershwin by ear and some of his own moody jazz improvisations. My father would close his eyes and smile and tap his foot, and the world was okay with him.

He had his first heart attack when he was forty-three, younger than I am now. The doctors said it was probably genetic because his own father had died of a heart attack at a young age. After three months my father went back to his cubicle and lived for another twenty-seven years knowing that instant death lurked every moment inside his chest. He never referred to it.

If a psychiatrist knew of the conflicts I have felt, of how I have let myself be confused by life and at times dragged down by fantasies and desires, he would put me on the couch and ask me something ridiculous, like whether my father loved my mother. The answer is yes. The psychiatrist would ask what values I was taught. I would say Catholic and American. He would ask what neglects and terrible abuses my sister and I suffered at my father's hands. There were none. My father was a gentle man who tucked us in every single night and who believed that providing security for us was the most important thing he could do.

He lost his job when he was sixty-one, replaced by a younger man during a corporate takeover and suddenly thrown clear of the workaday life he had relied on so much. In his infrequent letters to me he said that now he was doing what he really loved, that he was at the piano all the time and finally learning to read music, even conquering some of the classical masterpieces. He joked that he would probably die at the piano, a quick coronary in the middle of the Beethoven *Appassionata,* and that he would just collapse over the keyboard with a final flourish.

But in my sister's letters, she wrote that he never went near the piano. He had no new strategy for happiness. He just sank into a depression, unready for that drawn-out period that precedes death, that period when you are not entirely of this world. He drank too much and complained of his bad luck and the failures of the national leaders to uphold the American dream. He reminded everyone that after he was gone, the world would go on just like before, the good and the bad, the bad and the good, and that we are all helpless to change it. He became more and more difficult for my mother to live with. His life never went onward, even one step.

Still, my father was a good man. Perhaps whatever good is in me came from him. But I will not repeat his mistakes.

The flight to Seoul is thirteen hours. I switch to Malaysian Airlines and head to Kuala Lumpur, a long seven-hour flight, and then take one last flight toward Thailand. No one arrests me at any of the changes. I am grateful but puzzled. Surely they have been able to follow my movements. Perhaps they are just a step behind. Or just a step ahead, waiting for me in Bangkok.

Bangkok. I take a breath as it comes back to me.

For most people the words ''Bangkok'' and ''Thailand'' conjure up images of ancient Siam: double-jointed dancers, *The Bridge on the River Kwai,* imposing mountains, and even a singing Yul Brynner. It is a nation that combines Chinese regalia with the splendor of the Indian Empire, for both civilizations have made their impact there. Yet it is the only country in the region that did not succumb to British, French, or Dutch colonial rule.

Casual tourists are always stunned by Thailand. They get drunk on ancient Siam's beauty and modern Thailand's potent beer. It is a colorful nation about the size of France, sandwiched between Cambodia and Laos on one side and Burma on the other. Travelers to the south discover gorgeous beaches along the Gulf of Siam.

But there are always two sides to a country, and the ugly side of Thailand is Bangkok. The Thai name for Bangkok is Krungthep—City of Angels. The name is ironic, for if there is a hell anywhere, it is Bangkok. Tour books portray it as a city of charm and magic, a halo of romance, with its palaces, golden domes and spires, hundreds of resplendent Buddhist temples, and mirrored highrise office buildings.

But look behind the lavish high-rises, and you'll find a thousand shacks. Examine the impressive estate homes, and you'll see the sprinkler-fed lawns stretching to fenced alleyways where the homeless wander all day and night. Four-lane highways intersect with dirt roads. Romantic Venice-like canals connect throughout the city with their greasy waters.

Krungthep. City of Angels. But Bangkok is really a crack where two worlds collide. It is a chaotic meeting of East and West, where immeasurably old thoughts live beside the very new. Every beauty that civilization has labored for can be found in Bangkok. But they are intertwined with every evil the human mind has imagined. Alongside executive towers are sweat factories where workers slave for a few cents a day from American and Japanese companies. Along with the ancient and ornate Buddhist temples are a thousand liquor dens, brothels, and every kind of human enterprise where people feed upon other people. The survivors exist in shantytowns, living the end of the world at each moment.

Krungthep. City of Angels. Collector of the young from the countryside. Five and a half million people. Hundreds of deaths a day and even more births, or rebirths. Look closely at the misery, and you think it is a world from the past. Look closely at the misery, and you think that Bangkok has not yet caught up to the West. Then pull back to see this misery alongside the sleek comfort of a modern world, and you know that Bangkok is not catching up.

And it is not the past. It is the frightening future. A supermodern city whose technology leaves its humanity far behind. It is the way the world is going to be.

We prepare to land at Don Muang Airport outside Bangkok. For the tenth time I retrieve the photograph from my pocket and gaze down at it. For the last year it has reminded me that Song is real. It reminds me that I abandoned her, not just at the Fantasy Store but a thousand times over the past eleven months, as I tried to ignore her in my mind. Each time she emerged in my thoughts I lied to myself, telling myself that my sudden reassignment to a desk job in Bulgaria made it impossible to help her or that it was all somehow for the best, that Leamer knew things I didn't, that the access Song could provide was vital for our country, and many others.

Eleven months. That is also how long they told me Song would be at the orphanage. Maybe a little less if she acquired the rudiments of English and Japanese quickly and if she learned her "special duties" well. Eleven months. That means Song should be back here in Bangkok right now.

The city is just awakening as I negotiate a taxi ride to its interior, sixteen miles away. The driver is Pakistani, and speaks only a little Thai, but he knows the way to the Old Farang Quarter southeast of Bangkok's Chinatown and not far from the busy and polluted Chao Phraya River, which snakes through the city.

I step out of the air-conditioned taxi at the corner of Silom and Rama IV Road. Across the street are the soccer fields of Lumphini Park. Although it is only seven-thirty, the streets are already suffocatingly hot and humid. This morning is like morning in so many Asian cities. Smoke and dust from motorbikes create a perpetual thickness in the air. Large flies move from shoulder to shoulder among the pedestrians, who ignore them. Store awnings roll out. Iron gates pull back. The street weaves and pulses with all sizes of vehicles, both motor-driven and hand-drawn.

The entire city is one mass of motion as workers arrive from the tenements, each with their hopes and plans and frustrations. A beggar ambles into an alley and squats to relieve himself. On the back of a scooter is an entire family: mother, father, child, and infant, with the infant's head flopped on the mother's shoulder, asleep amid the noise and dirt.

People. So many people. All fighting for a piece of the pavement. In the distance a Buddhist temple bell rings three times, and I think of the bell at my childhood church, and the hard pews, and my sister and I kneeling between my mother and father. The temple bell sounds again, a little more loudly this time, but the people around me don't seem to notice. I move down Silom Road against the flow of the crowd. The Thai world circles around me: the cadence of the language, the smells of spicy meat, businessmen with white shirts and briefcases, and the very poor shuffling nowhere.

I come to Thaniya Road, and now I am only a block from Song. It is a crooked street that extends just five blocks and is a mixture of "entertainment" parlors and family stores. A few steps down the block, and I see it, the older four-story building, painted in deep blue with a yellow door. Above the door is a neon sign that is bright even in the daylight, its hard orange light exploding on and off. In Thai letters it reads NARAI STEWARDESS TRAINING. The name is blatant enough that everyone knows what kind of business it is, but it is sufficiently vague that for a price the police will pass by on the other side.

Hanging just below the neon letters is a smaller sign, in Japanese katakana script, announcing a better-known name for the establishment, THE FANTASY STORE. Even as I look down the block at the storefront, three middle-aged Japanese men in business suits approach on unsteady legs. Disheveled after a night of drinking, they squint in the morning light. Two of them have cameras around their necks. They stop a short distance from the sign, swaying against each other. They seem to joke, then straighten their ties and nudge each other toward the yellow door. As one of them reaches for the handle, the door swings open, and a lovely young lady I have never seen before takes their hands and ushers them in.

The door closes.

I wait ten minutes, remembering the procedure: The Japanese men will pass through the lobby, where they can view the girls. Then they'll be led to their individual rooms where a Japanese-speaking hostess will show them a scrapbook—a kind of menu of fantasies—picturing erotic devices, positions, techniques, and groupings. If a client is bashful, he has only to point, and he will be escorted to an appropriate room equipped with the appropriate flesh and implements.

Suddenly I realize that Song could be one of the girls these Japanese men choose, and my stomach sinks as I imagine them undressing her and groping her. A rage swells within me. I try to control myself as I approach the Fantasy Store. Images of Song still play in my head, more vividly than ever now. I hear her words to me: "I will be a whore. And you will be my whorekeeper." I cringe in fear that I am too late, that she has already been humiliated and defeated, a different person altogether. The thought stuns me.

Yet just to be on the same block with her excites me again. The neon light seems to throb at the same rate as the pulse in my throat. I reach for the door, but it opens before I touch it. Young eyes flash against mine. A sleek, braceleted hand takes my wrist. There is a trapdoor feeling in my stomach because this is the point of no return. I hesitate. The woman grips my hand tighter and tugs, giving me a mischievous smile. I let her lead me in. The door closes behind me. I am back.

14

THE FANTASY STORE

It is a business like any other business. There is merchandise. There are customers who browse and others who know exactly what they want. And management's concern is always for the bottom line, which in this case is not money but access.

The Fantasy Store is a different reality from the crowded city outside. The waiting room is like a traditional Japanese home, spacious, Spartan, and bright, with pure white walls, plump floor cushions around low rectangular tables, tatami mats, and pairs of shoes in rows by the door. None of the outside noises filters in. The air flows with relaxing flute music. Somewhere is the gentle sound of a waterfall.

But unlike the traditional Japanese setting, a glass wall divides part of the room. On the other side, under bright lights, are about thirty-five human objects sitting on tiered benches. They are living toys for men and occasionally for women. From across the room I scan them all, looking for Song. Some are slouching or leaning to one side. Some are staring off. A few are reading or knitting. Some are just sitting with their knees together. None is talking. Each has a number pinned to their clothes, like contestants in a spelling bee, except here they are both contestant and prize.

I recognize only a few faces from a year ago. Either the turnover has been rapid, or others are with clients. I cannot find Song anywhere among them. Again I cringe to think that maybe she is off in a room with one of the Japanese men who just arrived. I pull my thoughts back. Every move must be strategic. I glance around the reception area for cameras that may have been installed since I left. I detect none, but I can't be sure.

My hostess wears a pastel green sarong that swirls around her shoulders and falls gracefully to her feet. If someone has shown her my picture and warned her that I was coming, her eyes betray nothing. Even if she had worked here during the weeks of my assignment, she still might not recognize me. Few of the women knew the true nature of the operations, and Leamer had kept me in the background as much as possible, overseeing the identification of customers and supervising the electronic support team in the tech room.

"I am Catha," the hostess says. Her words are slightly clipped, faintly British, but low and rich like caramel syrup. I feel as if her voice is stroking me. She laces her fingers in mine as if we are high school sweethearts standing in the hall waiting for the bell to ring. Her smile is friendly but with a cool distance that says she is not part of the merchandise. She gestures around the room and then to the girls behind the glass.

Of course they are not really girls. Though some are in their teens, most are in their early twenties, and a few considerably older. Women from across the world. Women from across my own country. Americans, Latins, Chinese. All types. Innocent-looking ones, blond Miss America types, movie star look-alikes, lesbian pairs, a fair-skinned redhead with large breasts. You never know what the next buyer will want. Even the straight buyers don't always crave a sleek young woman, so there are also heavier women, like rosy-cheeked mothers, paunchy with thick thighs. Some men, in the privacy of their rooms and away from friends, choose these matronly types to fulfill a fantasy. Freud would smile and say he knew it all along.

The women cannot see us because it is one-way glass. From their side they see only a mirror. I come closer and search again for Song, but she is not there. Maybe she is safe in her cell.

But I am aware of something different now. When I was here, except for Song there were only professionals behind the glass, handsomely rewarded specialists in a particular sexual act or deviation. But now there are others behind the glass—not professionals at all but scared little things. I am stunned. Of course I have known about the sex trade in Thailand, the tens of thousands of girls and boys sold into whoredom each year, used and abused until they are worn and ugly, or until they contract AIDS and are returned to their families in the countryside. But Leamer told me that the Fantasy Plan would use only professionals, what are known in the trade as Swans. Then, when I met Songkha, I assumed she was some sort of exception.

But now I see that she was the beginning of a new marketing trend. In front of me, in addition to the Swans, are what are called Fawns, frightened young girls and even two boys, who have been rented or sold by their families. They are the very, very poor. They are the fortuneless, for whom there is no straight line into the future.

I want to scream. I want to break the glass and free them. I want to tell them that I did not know about this part. That it is not my fault. That I am not responsible for their slavery. I think back to the Branscomb Institute and the idealism I shared with Vaal and how he would never have permitted his life to come to something so low. How is it possible that my intentions could have ended up like this?

But I hold myself back. Timing. Strategy. Every move must count. My hostess, Catha, gauges my expression. I force a smile and nod approvingly at the girls.

I know that Catha will treat me differently from her Japanese customers. Americans are not valuable to the

Fantasy Plan, so they aren't offered the luxury of retiring to a private suite to peruse photo albums and interview girls before making a selection. She will ask me to choose one here in the reception area. Then she will lead me to one of the side rooms reserved for less important customers, rooms that are less lavish and usually without cameras or microphones.

Catha points to the two Oriental boys on the right side of the front row, numbers 9 and 19, and then assesses my response to see if it is favorable. She gestures toward the back, where two middle-aged women, very bosomy with pretty faces, apparently Americans, sit quietly knitting.

"Number twenty-five," she says in crisp English, pointing to a woman in the upper-right-hand corner, a striking, wild-looking blue-eyed blonde in her early twenties who is holding a magazine. "You can notice the shape of her mouth. It is very appealing for many reasons. And of course her breasts have many purposes. We have had many compliments about her . . . special services." Catha smiles with no shyness at all.

Hearing voices, the contestants stop their reading and knitting and adjust their numbers. All eyes look up. But I know they can see nothing.

"It is one-way glass," she reassures me.

Most of the contestants sit up straight. The professionals—the Swans—smile as if on command and seem to be trying to pick up the sound of our voices so they can make some kind of contact through the one-way glass. Their smiles portray a combination of sweetness and evil, their eyes offering delicious promises to the invisible customer who has come to corrupt or be corrupted. There is no reluctance in their faces; they are on salary with incentive commissions. High client volume is their ticket, hoping to make what money they can before the inevitable deterioration of their beauty. Any one of them will take a customer with complete frankness and ease and even enjoy herself, not sexually perhaps but psychologically, as she strips away her clothes and uses her talents and nakedness to give her power over the man.

But the Fawns. Thai and Burmese girls with fake smiles that can't cover the tragedy in their eyes. They sit nervously, like shy schoolgirls in bleachers, arms wrapped around their legs, not wanting to sell anything. And these are only a few of the thousands upon thousands of minds trained to be submissive, trained to live out their unjust karmas, trained from birth to be victims. They can be brutalized and even killed, and no one will notice, let alone care. It is the perfect place for the Japanese deviate or any other deviate. That is what the Organization has created, a deviate's paradise.

I glance from one face to the other, avoiding their eyes. They are all dolls. They are not real. This could never be real.

"Where do they all come from?" I ask Catha in as pleasant a voice as I can muster. It is not a typical question, and I want to see how she will respond.

"Number eleven," she says, motioning to the large-breasted redhead on the third tier, "is from your country. From Minnesota. I am told it is cold there. Her specialty is leather. And everything that goes with it."

Unlike the other Swans, number 11 is now staring off numbly at a place only she can see. Maybe it is Minnesota. Maybe it is her parents. An old boyfriend. She toys absently with her red hair. Maybe she is staring at a sunset over one of Minnesota's ten thousand lakes.

I search them all again, hoping that somehow I have overlooked Song and that she is really there. It would be so simple then. I would rent her for an hour and leave quietly through the delivery entrance. But she is not here.

All the Swans and Fawns are wearing garments that reveal the slope of their naked shoulders, the curve of their calves. I recognize the oval face and lavender eye shadow in the second row. I even remember her name, Lisa, from New Mexico, part white, part Indian or Hispanic. She is wearing a pink vest that is buttoned tight to push up her breasts.

Catha squeezes my hand, then points to a heavyset woman in her late forties, apparently also an American.

"And number twenty-six there will surprise you. There is nothing she will not help you enjoy. She is available from every angle." Catha smiles cryptically. "And if you want the fullest massage, try number two. She is from Hong Kong. Or if you desire 'round-the-world' treatment, seventeen and eighteen are our best. They are from Bali. If you like feet, please turn your attention to number five."

She faces me and considers my expression. She has been trained to elicit lust, what men usually take as a sign of health and cling to as a feeling of their freedom and dominion, but that I have known mostly as an entrapment. In me it is that occasional greedy little monster that rattles its cage when it wants to, devouring my mind for the sake of my body.

Catha is growing slightly impatient. "If you have any special needs," she says, urging me, "I am sure we can accommodate. Nothing is unusual here. No taboos. Everything is okay. Okay?"

"Okay," I echo.

I search over the Fawns one more time, and again I want to smash the glass. They are attractive and young, like Song. And they are so frightened. But if Song were among them, she would not show any fear. She would appear composed and serene as she stared right into the glass challengingly, searching for the eyes of the invisible men, daring them to pick *her* so that she could denounce them for what they really are.

But Song is not here.

Several times already my eyes have gravitated to a young Thai girl, a teenager, sitting with her elbows on her knees, trying to hide her face in her hands. She is dressed in a sleeveless black leather outfit that hugs her body from the neck down. The leather pants are so tight in the crotch that I can see the seam of her anatomy. She moves her fingers away from her mouth, and I see that her lipstick liner is not precise, probably for lack of practice. The look on her face is heart-wrenchingly sad. Maybe she has been here only a short time. Maybe she went through training with Song.

"Number fifteen," I say, pointing to her.

"She is fine but still a student and not our best," Catha says.

"That's okay. I want her."

"Of course. She is trained in leather and all the pleasures that accompany. Is that what you desire today?"

She asks this the way a checkout clerk in a variety store asks, "Will that be all today?"

"Yes," I answer. "That is what I desire today."

"You have made a good choice. And because number fifteen is new, she comes with number eleven, from Minnesota. No extra charge." Catha smiles as if she's just put a free scoop of ice cream on my cone.

"No, I just want her. What is her name?"

"Please see the gentleman over there, and then I will take you to your room."

The price is $250, a small amount to most Japanese businessmen. I pay an old man at a desk in the hallway while Catha opens a door behind the glass and calls to number 15, then shouts harshly in words that are too rapid for me to follow.

Catha comes back to me.

"What is her name?" I ask again.

"She is number fifteen," she says, her smile still pinned in place.

Catha takes my hand again, and for a moment I'm afraid she'll lead me upstairs to one of the higher-numbered encounter rooms, richer and more comfortable, scented with secrets and servant girls, but rigged for closed-circuit filming that is monitored in the tech room. But we stay on the first floor. Catha walks slowly at my side, leading me down the plushly carpeted corridor. She stops at room 104, opens the door, and turns on the light, then dims it and faces me.

"Dominant or submissive?" she asks perfunctorily.

"What?"

"Which do you wish her to be?" Catha seems completely unaware of the absurdity of her question.

I flip a coin in my mind. "Dominant," I say.

"I will tell her to be dominant." Catha bows and leaves the door ajar.

I was in this encounter room once before, on my initial tour of the building shortly after my assignment. It is comfortable enough, and ornate, designed like an old-time New England boudoir, with a mahogany bed with four posts and a red-fringed canopy. On the far wall is a false bay window, with a landscape picture of estate grounds outside and in the distance men on horses on a fox hunt. There are two French-style chairs and an oak dresser. I catch a hint of perfume left over from the last occupant. And there is something else, something unmistakable, an air of sensuality and secrets and violence. I open the drawers and find what I expect: implements of bondage—assorted leather straps, iron shackles, three neatly curled whips, a mouth restraint, and variously shaped rubber probes and plastic pincers for every part of the anatomy.

I sit on the bed and scan the room. A wall mirror faces the bed, but I know that the hallway is on the other side of that wall. No cameras were there, as I recall. But I can't be sure now; while the room is for nonessential customers, occasionally there is a need to assess the performance of the employees. It is a business, after all, and quality control is the key to customer satisfaction. Anyway, I will soon know if there are cameras because someone will undoubtedly recognize me on a monitor back in the tech room.

The door opens, and there is a swish of leather as number 15 slips inside. The sleeveless bodysuit gives her the sleek look of a black cat. In the dim light she appears more exotic than when she was on display, the shadows hiding the soft fullness of her youth and giving her face a more angular look. In her hand is a riding crop. She gives me a stern look that is obviously practiced. She hits the riding crop against the palm of her hand. "Take off your shirt *now*," she commands, but her voice is halfhearted.

I grab the crop from her. "No. I don't want that," I say firmly.

She stares questioningly. "What you want? You want kinky? That okay. Please do." She goes to a drawer and takes out pincers and a whip and holds them out to me. "It okay to beat me." Her hands are trembling.

"What is your name?" I ask in Thai.

"You want me? We have fifty minutes. You take me however way you like. Then tell them I do you good."

"I asked you what your name is."

"Number fifteen. Very good girl. I the best."

Then with a single tug she unlaces her collar and the front of her leather bodysuit suddenly falls away. She stands uncovered to the waist. Her breasts are small but gracefully shaped. Her nipples are pointed disks with goose bumps, as she offers everything up to me with a fearful obedience.

I feel odd and nervous, as something ripples through me. I find myself stepping closer to number 15.

15

"**Y**ou want me?" she says again then closes her eyes, trying to shrink inside herself to escape my stare. There is heavy rouge high on her cheeks and a false dimple next to her mouth. The dark paint of her eyebrows slants upward in what is supposed to be a sinister look. But the corners of her mouth give her away, still trembling downward.

"I want to know your name," I say.

"Amkha," she replies in a small voice. She wraps her arms around herself, clumsily covering her breasts.

I pull up the front of her leather suit and retie it around her neck. "I want to talk," I say.

Uncertain, she looks at me. "They say some men look and talk but can't do."

I shake my head. "I asked for you because I'm trying to find someone."

Amkha edges around me carefully, as if I might leap at her, and sits fragilely on the edge of a chair about five feet away. She folds her hands nervously in her lap. "You won't say we just talk?" she asks.

"I'll say you were the best."

Her leather-covered bosom heaves with relief, and she

132

looks down at the floor, then shivers in the air-conditioned room. I pull the red blanket from the bed and swing it over her shoulders. She clutches it tightly, not thanking me, not looking up at me.

As I step back, I see that her heavy rouge covers some tiny pockmarks on her cheeks. And there are lines on her face, not from age but from wear. She is a girl who has already experienced too much. Her eyes are neither youthful nor hard. They are eyes that have forgotten youth or perhaps have never known it. She clutches the blanket with one hand and with the other hand attempts to hide her face as she did in the reception room.

"Amkha," I say, "is anyone downstairs now in the little sleeping rooms?"

She looks at me curiously and shakes her head.

"They said you are new here. Is that true?"

She nods.

"Where were you before? Where did they have you for training? Was it in the north near Chiang Mai?"

She nods once to all my questions.

"What is the name of the place?"

"Kon kampra," she says tonelessly.

I piece the words together literally: *Kon kampra*—people with no family. Apparently the Thai word for "orphanage."

"What is the name of the *kon kampra*?" I ask.

"Tee Natiew," she answers. The words mean "wonderful place," probably named by someone in the Organization with a penchant for the sardonic.

"I'm looking for someone," I continue in English. "Do you know Songkha Chattkatavong?"

For the first time her eyes fasten on to me, and she does not blink.

"You know her," I say. "Is she okay?"

She just stares at me.

"Is she here?" I ask. "You must tell me."

Amkha shakes her head and looks down. "Songkha be here already, to Krungthep, this place here. She make baby here. She at *kon kampra* again."

I look away, stunned. "She has a baby? Are you sure it was Songkha?"

"*Kamlang,*" she says.

Kamlang. Forced.

"Bad man hurt her. At night he come in her room. He *kamlang* her."

"Leamer," I say to myself. Who else knew about her cell? My stomach turns at the thought of his body on top of Song. But why would he let her get pregnant? And then stay pregnant? There must be some reason.

"Songkha say to me she think they make movie," Amkha says. "They show he *kamlang* her."

"Maybe," I answer, not sure whether her cell was really monitored. If it was, Leamer never told me. Maybe even my own night visit there was filmed. And now I understand why he had me transferred so suddenly and finally had me dismissed.

"Is she all right now?" I ask. "Is she safe?"

"She has baby now. So she lucky, she not work for long time."

"Can you tell me how to find the orphanage?"

She shrugs. "*Tahng nua.*" North.

"Where?"

"*Kon kampra tank yu dan lang pra puttaroop sirung.*"

Something about the orphanage's being behind a Buddha with many colors. Literally a "rainbow Buddha." But that doesn't make sense. I ask again, but she only repeats the same words, *pra puttaroop sirung*—rainbow Buddha.

"Can you read a map?" I ask.

She shakes her head.

"Can you read at all?"

"My family not teach me."

I wonder about Songkha's own family. Am I the only one in the world who cares for Song? And why do I care? Is she just a warped passion in my mind, a fantasy that grows stronger each day? Why don't I care as much for Amkha, who is right in front of me now, so real, and suffering?

I take a breath and switch to her language. "Is Songkha still at the orphanage? Is the baby okay?"

"Still there. The children like her baby."

"The children? What children?"

"From all countries."

"Then it's a real orphanage," I say. "A real *kon kampra.*"

"*Mai!*" she shouts. No! "But children there. Many kinds."

She sees that I don't understand.

"Many colors and looks. Little children. Grow the children. Someday for here, for Krungthep. They from every country, all country in world." She pulls the blanket tighter as if she is freezing. "American childs there too, and Mexico childs."

She sees the look on my face and frowns contemptuously. Her fear of me wanes, and her words come out like invisible claws. "You Americans go and steal from houses," she says sharply. "Steal children. From schools. From beds at night."

I recoil as her claws find their mark. But what she is saying goes far beyond what the Fantasy Plan entailed. There must be some other explanation.

"How many children?" I ask.

"*Hok jet.*" Six or seven. "*Puak khao mee phom si thong lae ta si namngen lae suay ngam mark.*"

I translate in my head: The children have blond hair and blue eyes, and they are very desirable-looking. Very expensive.

My stomach turns, and one thought possesses my mind now: to find out what is happening, why there are children involved. The answers will have to come from the workers in the tech room.

"Thank you, Amkha," I say. "Thank you for your help." I get up.

Amkha grabs my shirt and points at the bell that rings after fifty minutes, a short hour of therapy at twice the psychiatrist's rate. "Too early!" she says. "They think I no good, that I not do you good."

"I will tell them you were the best."

I open the door and look down the empty hallway. I wonder why no one has recognized me, why there has been no opposition up to now. Maybe because the hostess, Catha, is new and because there was no camera in the room. Or maybe they're not looking for me at all. Not expecting me. Or is it some kind of trap?

I start down the hall and glance back. Amkha stands at the door with a dumbfounded expression, not even knowing enough to cry. "I am sorry," I say, and smile to show her that I mean it. Then I feel a sudden falling inside myself as she covers the small pockmarks on her face again, pathetically afraid, still clutching the blanket and shivering in the doorway. I want to take her with me, to free her. But how many others are here who need to be freed? And not just here but in hundreds of places throughout Bangkok. And even if I freed Amkha, would she understand? Or does she think this is her lot, her karma? Does she believe she has been destined to be this pathetic creature?

I will come back for her.

But even as I say these words in my head, I know I am lying again. There seems to be no one I haven't lied to and no way to stop the lies. I have a way of slipping and sliding around: half-truths, easy promises that I can list off to myself, and conveniently revised memories, altering in my mind what I have done and then making noble promises to fulfill the unfinished things sometime later. I will be a truer person in the future.

I turn away, willfully ignoring her. I have done nothing to Amkha, and I am not responsible for her. I did not bring her into this world. I did not sell her to this place. I did nothing to hurt her, nothing that I must take back and make better. Someone else is responsible for what has happened to her. There are too many innocent ones, and I cannot save the whole world.

I am not responsible for them all.

I am not responsible for them all.

16

LISA FROM NEW MEXICO

What is impossible in this world? Nothing. Everything that can be fantasized, everything terrible and cruel, can be made real somewhere.

That's what fills my mind as I make my way down the corridor toward the tech room at the other end of the building. Three quarters of the encounter rooms I pass are empty at this time of day, but every few feet there are different smells from the open doors: oils, perfumes, sweat, urine, marijuana. And from the closed doors come noises of pleasure: a gasp with a cry, whispers and whimpers, two women giggling, a man shouting a single word, a woman's high-pitched groan, obviously fake. Behind a few of the closed doors there are no sounds at all, causing the mind to wonder even more.

The tech room is on the first floor, just beyond the last of these rooms. It is strange how the two realms can border on each other, how close together they are yet how vastly separate: one, a series of chambers with something for everyone's imagination; the other, a sterile and calculating world of technology, with reels and fluorescent lights and clicking machines that care nothing for flesh and fear and pain.

The door to the tech room is unmarked and has a button type of combination lock. Four-seven-eight-two-two. So much for the efficiency of the Organization. I push it open.

The room has not changed either. American furniture, walnut veneer, high-backed leather chairs, thick carpeting. At first glance it seems like any business communications room, with fax machines, computer terminals, and photo-copiers. But looking closer, you see recording equipment and television monitors recessed into the walls, each la-beled with a different room number. Despite the sophisti-cation, the devices are just high-tech eyes and ears. Mechanical Peeping Toms.

When I was here, I supervised two tech workers, a hus-band-and-wife team whom I knew as Mr. and Mrs. Pearce and who had been here since the start of the operation. As I enter, the two of them are huddled in front of a single monitor, oblivious of my presence.

Mr. Pearce is about fifty, with a scraggly beard and an intensity that makes him look like a coffeehouse beatnik absorbed in analyzing life's meaning. But unless he has changed in the last eleven months, it is not life's meaning but computers that occupies his mind. He lives in a world of bits and bytes, where electrical currents and speed fac-tors are more real than people and their problems. Mrs. Pearce is tall and halfway attractive, even in her baggy blouse and with her dark hair pulled back tight and curled in a bun. Together they are technicians of the first order, repairing equipment, cataloging tapes, making color and tracking adjustments, going about their work efficiently and with a minimum of excessive motion. They are a stiff, uncommunicative couple who find satisfaction in the precision and organization of things. I look around the room at the dozen or so video recorders, their digital clocks each showing exactly the same minute.

When I knew them before, I was always amazed that Mr. and Mrs. Pearce seemed to take no interest in the performances on the screens. They had seen it all before. I wondered what happens if fantasies are played out every day in front of your very eyes. Do you become stone cold, erotically dead? Or are you forced to become even more inventive than the rest, with a hidden life that would be the envy of us all?

Screens flicker with close-up images of bodies that I can't see clearly from this angle. But Mr. and Mrs. Pearce continue to stand transfixed before just one monitor. Mrs. Pearce is trembling terribly at what she sees. Her husband looks sickly green as he stares at the screen, then places his head in his hands.

He looks up and notices me. He seems surprised but relieved. "Can you stop it, Mr. Harmon?" he says in a meek voice, using the name I had when I worked here a year ago. He points to the screen. "It gets worse each week. This is the second time for that man there."

Mrs. Pearce doesn't speak to me, but her furious eyes demand: *Do something!* And I realize what special "service" the man on the screen has paid for. It did not happen in the few weeks I was here, though I had been warned that it might.

But we all know the rule: *Never interfere.* Whatever is happening on the monitor is happening to only one person, and it may ultimately provide A-C-C-E-S-S that will benefit thousands or even millions. One person in exchange for a million. It is a reasonable trade.

I quickly come closer. The monitor shows the back of a Japanese man, his rolls of fat lapping over a towel wrapped around his waist. He kneels at the end of a bed. At the other end, naked and cringing, is Lisa from New Mexico, the part Hispanic or Indian girl with the lavender eye shadow. When she was behind the one-way glass, she was wearing a pink vest that pushed her breasts up, but now she is naked and shivering with fear, holding herself in her crisscrossed arms, her whole face trembling. And though the building is air-conditioned, the man in the towel is sweating like he has just stepped from a sauna. There is an excitement burning inside him, some hatred or fiery necessity.

I can't see his left hand, but I know what is in it. He is not speaking to Lisa, just staring at her. Then he moves closer and with his right hand pins her neck to the headboard. She slaps at him, then punches and grabs at his wrist, trying to get free, but he overpowers her. He opens her legs, parts his towel, and seemingly rips his way into her. He howls as he immediately begins to come, then shudders and falls on her.

This is only the beginning. Mr. and Mrs. Pearce also know what is going to happen, and they turn to me pleadingly as if I can somehow stop the most taboo act in Japan, the one act that the Organization longs to capture on film because it places the diplomat or the executive in its hands forever. The words ''hideous'' and ''pornographic'' are too tame to describe it. Even within the Organization the act is never named outright in reports, only alluded to.

What is impossible to this world? Everything that can be fantasized is made real somewhere. On the monitor I see the crazed animal imagination that is about to be acted out. And now a glimmer of what was hidden from the camera's view by his wide body: an unsheathed blade in his left hand, just one inch long, curved. He moves forward again on his knees, and through the microphone I can hear him panting. Lisa from New Mexico presses back against the headboard, terrified. He pulls the towel free from his waist, exposing himself, then turns and looks around the room as if to make sure he is alone, his round bald head and his ecstatic, crazed expression caught forever by the camera. Then he turns back to Lisa.

Mrs. Pearce looks to me imploringly for my answer. Above the monitor are the numbers 227—second floor, room 227. I know exactly where the room is and how to get there. But it will take thirty seconds.

17

THE ULTIMATE TABOO

*W*e are double-sided beings.

One side of us is sunny, with a luminous warmth and sympathy for others in the world. But the other side of us grabbing, lustful, demanding everything for ourselves.

The Japanese have a word for that other side: *ura*. It means the hidden and angry side of us that we don't show the world, the part of us that needs to possess and dominate and sometimes even violate to the extreme. The Japanese say it is natural, just part of being human and that its origin is deep inside all of us, a tangle of cerebral and chemical elements that simply cannot be sorted out.

Ura thoughts appear like mirages, in those twilight moments as we drift off to sleep or when we awaken in the morning and lie silently with our little fantasies. Sometimes we can't shake free of them. Forbidden images appear again and again, uninvited.

The back side of every society has places to accommodate these fantasies: "dance" clubs, X-rated movies and magazines, and now computer games, CD ROM, and Internet private rooms, places where we surrender to our imaginations, letting our *ura* side be stoked. What is it we want at such places? Mostly we want the regular, and then a little extra, something deviating as much as possible toward the extreme, something we can't begin to get at home.

Yet even in those places we ride our appetites with some lingering degree of conscience. A thin thread of deliberation always remains. But at the Fantasy Store it is different. Deliberation and conscience can be tossed aside. This is a special business, the business of access, and everything is designed to unbridle whatever *ura* need the customer arrives with and then to stoke the fire to any degree of heat imaginable. Given license and opportunity, the *ura* side becomes the ultimate access.

But some Japanese have a special *ura* fantasy I've never seen anywhere else. It is sexual power taken to the extreme. Unbridled. Unconscious. But very deliberate. It is the ultimate domination.

Cutting.

I once stopped at a newsstand on a street corner in Tokyo and peered into a comic book showing realistic drawings of women bring brutalized by men, their cheeks and bodies carefully sliced open, their faces in a tortured agony that no civilized society should ever depict. But the comic books were there on public corners for any man to pick up and peruse and take home if he cared to. Hundreds of artists work full-time sketching these acts. Story editors edit them. Publication houses print them. In color. Mutilation for entertainment's sake. Mutilation for one's own personal adult enjoyment.

I watched men on the sidewalk, not just Japanese men but tourists too, as they stopped for a momentary diversion, a quick thrill, unabashedly flipping through the most horrific pictures of what humans might do to humans.

But oddly these depictions of men mutilating women are not acted out in Japanese society. It is not like in the States, where a clever bank robbery is broadcast on Sunday night TV and the next morning imitated in a dozen cities across the nation. No, Japan has something going for it. Japan is a social corset, a nation of obedience to the group. Even *dis*obedience is expressed in prescribed ways. Each person sees himself or herself as part of a vast web of obligations to the family, the corporation, and the nation. Maintain those obligations, and society is safe. Break just one strand of that web, and you threaten the strength of the whole, the fabric of society's sanity. And more. You've lost face as well as your affiliation with the group.

But what happens when Japanese men leave their homeland? Does the social corset come off? One lace at a time? Or all buttons and hooks at once?

I learned the answer to that the first week I was assigned to Bangkok. A psychiatrist with the Organization arrived to brief me on the Fantasy Plan's psychological components. I even remember her name, Dr. Elaine McDonald. Chopped brown hair, no makeup, dressed in a plain suit with a man's tie. Her hand was cold and stiff when I shook it, and her lips were white and bloodless as she sat stiffly and explained the Fantasy Plan in clinical terms.

"When the target group leaves their homeland," she said, "they also leave behind the pressures to conform. They'll do anything here. And your little sex shop provides the perfect place."

She saw me flinch at the word "your." We sat facing each other, Dr. McDonald speaking patiently, as if I might be too dense to understand her psychological profundity.

"Take the Rape of Nanking in 1937," she continued. "Even their worst enemies couldn't understand how those mannerly Japanese could act in such a way. And the correct answer is that yes, they are mannerly and obedient when feeling the pressure of their own society. But abroad they're like college kids on campus: no parents, no curfews. Obedience and discipline snap."

Then she stopped and halfway smiled as she read my thoughts. "You think I'm a racist," she said. "But I'm not. I'm only reporting what many Japanese psychologists agree is the case. We are scientists. Scientists uncover the facts and then report them. The facts are simple. It is the Japanese who are racist. They despise other nations as mulattoes and mixed tribes. *Konketsujis* is the word they have for them, mongrels. They feel they are justified in being brutal to them. Here at your brothel you'll find out just how brutal they can be."

For the first time she smiled naturally. "Are you following me?" she asked.

I understood enough to take her by the elbow and usher her to the lobby and the front door. She stopped to study the girls behind the glass. "You have a good product selection," she commented matter-of-factly. Then she looked at me. "You know, the Organization didn't invent the human psychology. We only use it."

There was almost a chill in the air after she left. It wasn't just her words that echoed in my thought. I also heard the phrase that Japanese men often repeated as they studied the women waiting on the tiers. "They are women of no importance," they would say. And in my mind I thought of Song. *A woman of no importance.* And the many others. Two hundred thousand others in Thailand. *All of them women of no importance.*

And I wondered if some Japanese men might come here to live out the ultimate erotic taboo. The Organization would undoubtedly condone it, even encourage it. Every woman was expendable, a chrysanthemum whose erotic beauty could be snipped, pruned, and slashed. And after the mess had been cleaned up, the Organization would own the obsessed man, have complete access to his corporate or political secrets, complete power over his every move. After all, cutting was not the sickness of *our* psychology. It was that of the Japanese.

"Never interfere" are the words that go through my mind as I race through the lab door to get to the second floor and to Lisa with the lavender eye shadow from New Mexico in room 227. *Never interfere because it is happening to only one person and the access we receive benefits so many. It is a trade-off that must be made.*

As I run down the hall, a petite Asian girl ushers a young Japanese man to a room. I push past them, nearly knocking them both down. Then I see a tall American woman standing farther down the hall near the stairway. It is Penny O'Hara. It is Catherine DeLaurentis. She is not looking around bewilderedly like a newcomer to this place. She seems right at home, coming toward me with authority as I go for the stairs. She puts out her arms to stop me, grabbing at my shirt.

I shove her aside and race up the stairs, knowing I am already too late.

18

A WOMAN OF NO IMPORTANCE

The lock gives from the force of my shoulder, and the door flies open.

Across the room the sheets are already stained red, and there are red zebra stripes running down Lisa's arms. Blood pulses out at her wrists. She is paralyzed in terror as the fat Japanese man pins her neck against the headboard and completes yet another stripe, a lengthwise cut that starts at the smooth flesh of her wrist and goes up over her shoulder to the base of her neck. A line of droplets squeeze through the parted skin and then pour out where an artery has been cut. He turns his head toward me slowly, his brow lowered with indignation as if to complain that he has paid his money and should not be interrupted.

He says something in Japanese, a cursing tone, something I don't understand, but in my mind I hear, *She's a woman of no importance.*

He releases her throat and spins toward me on all fours. He smiles and adjusts his rectangular glasses like a doctor trying to get a better look at his patient. A flicker of wry amusement crosses his face. He has already forgotten his victim, as oblivious of her as a man who has just turned away from a urinal. He slides from the bed with surprising nimbleness, short and naked and middle-aged. His body is fat and sagging like a miniature sumo wrestler's, except that it is smeared with her blood. Even his half-sized member, erect but barely protruding from the swell of his stomach, has red drops on its tip.

Behind him Lisa collapses back, gulping air and staring in shock at the red bath where her blood pulses out and spreads across the sheets.

He remains focused on me, coming toward me quickly, not concerned that I am much larger than he. The knife is hidden in his hand, and now he reveals it, shouting furiously, and pointing to the door. The scene is unreal. It is a movie.

I put out my hands, trying to fend him off as I sidestep around him to get to Lisa from New Mexico, who is now coughing a stream of blood from her nostrils. I don't want to fight him. I only want to run to her before the last bit of red life has pulsed away. I want to embrace her, or give her last rites or cradle her so that her last fading knowledge will be of being held.

He swipes at me with the knife, then on the backswing swipes again. As he follows through, his leg swings high hitting me hard next to my right ear. My head echoes, my vision blurs, and I realize I am lying on the floor. He leaps through the blur, stabbing at me, and I roll to the side, keep rolling, scrambling, but he is moving faster and kicking out at me viciously.

I spin to my feet, and we face each other again. That same mocking smile on his face. He lashes out with the blade again, and it all happens so suddenly. He is knocked to the floor, and I see my foot on his throat. His eyes show terror as I cut off his breathing completely, not even a gasp. He stabs at my leg, tearing through the pants and puncturing my calf. The weight of my foot on his neck increases, and his eyes bulge. He continues to swipe at my calf, my pant leg in shreds, blood pouring down my shoe and onto his cheeks and lips. He won't stop struggling, and my foot presses down harder, as if it is acting of its own accord. There is a slight crack, not like a twig or a pencil, but softer, like knuckles popping gently.

Then the heap is motionless; the smeared and spotted flesh sags even more, and urine squirts up from between his legs. My foot remains on his neck, and more of my blood pours down my leg onto his chin and to the floor.

I turn to Lisa on the bed. But the American woman is with her now. O'Hara. DeLaurentis. Trying to straighten the striped figure and brush back the dark hair that covers Lisa's face. Her body is still slumped, her head falling to the side like a doll's. The air seems sucked out of the room.

"He's killed her," Catherine DeLaurentis gasps.

The blood drains from the long openings on Lisa's arms, but there are still spurts from the open arteries. "Her heart is beating!" I shout.

Catherine DeLaurentis shakes the naked woman's shoulders, then tears off her own blouse and with great strength rips a strip of cloth for a tourniquet. She quickly ties it above one of Lisa's elbows, and it immediately slows the pulsing blood. Then she rips another strip and ties it tightly around the other arm. After a moment Lisa's eyes flutter to consciousness.

DeLaurentis looks down at her own hands, then blots them on the sheets. Embarrassed in just her white bra, she covers herself with her arms, then turns to the man's body on the floor.

"Oh, my God," she says softly in a stunned voice. "You killed him. Shit! Do you know who he is?"

"What about her?" I say, pointing to Lisa.

She erupts. "You don't know what you've done! He's a scientist, a physicist! On a special council in Japan."

She looks directly over my head to a spot above the door. She knows exactly where the camera is. She shouts to the people watching in the tech room. "Get security up here now! Now! And get this girl to a hospital." She turns back to me, no longer self-consciously covering her bra. "Maybe he was a pig," she says, trying to calm herself.

"But shit, this shouldn't have happened. You don't understand. There are things you don't know."

I want to laugh at the absurdity of her words. "And what about her?" I say again.

"I ran to her first, didn't I? Not to him. I slowed the bleeding, didn't I? But you have no idea what you've done!"

DeLaurentis goes back to the bed and gazes down at Lisa from New Mexico, whose eyes stare fixedly in shock. Her torso is smeared with red, and her legs are twisted open, rudely exposing her, but the redness no longer spills out as before. I go to the other side of the bed, and together we take Lisa by the shoulders and ease her down flat. Then we bend her knees, and place a pillow under her head. DeLaurentis covers Lisa to the neck with a sheet that immediately soaks in the bright red streaks.

"The ambulance will be here," DeLaurentis says soothingly to her, stroking her hair. Then she stands and wipes her own hands clean again.

DeLaurentis tears another strip from her blouse and without speaking kneels in front of me and wraps my leg tightly above the knee, making a tourniquet with a final and painful twist. With another strip she carefully dabs at my leg, then scrubs at the blood on my shoe.

"Your cuts are deep," she says, trying to keep a calm voice, "but there aren't too many. We'll take you to a hospital."

"Sure you will," I say.

"You'll be safe."

I laugh. "Who the hell are you?" I step back from her. A stab of pain goes through my leg where the muscle is punctured. And I see that her eyes aren't brown at all, but green. I should have noticed the contacts before. Or is she wearing contacts now? My mind reaches for some reason why she is here, why she knows the rooms and locations of the cameras. "You were my replacement, weren't you?" I say. "They got a woman to do the job, didn't they?"

She shakes her head. "I have as little to do with this place as possible."

"You know your way around."

She doesn't answer at first, then admits, "It's hideous here. But it's necessary."

She doesn't have to say the word. *Access.* I look to the bed and wonder what kind of access justifies Lisa from New Mexico streaked in blood. "Yes, we're going to keep the Japanese out of the digital phone trade," I say contemptuously. "Or maybe take back the VCR market." I point to Lisa on the bed. "She's certainly worth that."

"I said he was a scientist!"

"I don't give a fuck!" I shout back. Then it begins to dawn. The Fantasy Plan has reeled in an unexpected prize, a bigger secret than corporate executives or government bureaucrats could provide. This man was an astrophysicist or maybe a biochemist. Or maybe it is just more lies.

"Another creative story, Penny?"

"It's true he's a scientist," she snaps angrily, "more important to us—*and* the world—than you could ever realize. But you screwed up, as usual."

"Who are you?" I let the question hang a moment. "Who are you?" I demand again. "You're not O'Hara or DeLaurentis. Who the hell are you?"

She looks for a place to sit down. There is nowhere except the bed, and she avoids it.

"My real name is Rennard," she finally says, still standing and wiping her eyes with the back of her hands. Realizing she has smeared her mascara, she tries to blot it with what is left of her blouse.

"Rennard," I say. "Great. And do you have a first name, or are you thinking one up now?"

"Catherine," she says. "My first name really is Catherine. I'm the deputy assistant to Charles DeForest."

"And of course that's the truth."

"Fuck you, Gaines."

"Fuck you. You planned it all back there on the bus. You never lived in that apartment at all."

"Of course not. We had to know if you were coming back."

"And while you're at it, catch me on film in your bed?"

"How would I know they were going to put a camera in that bedroom?"

"That's right, the team set it up without you knowing."

She eyes me with anger. "Fuck you. I'm not some whore, Gaines. You stepped into it yourself, just like you bumbled into this one. Don't blame me."

I looked around the room. The scene is like a horror movie. Red-streaked sheets. Lisa's eyes darting in confusion. The naked man on his back, his penis still dribbling, and the smell of urine almost overwhelming.

He is the second man I have killed in my lifetime. As a boy I always imagined a face-to-face encounter having more honor. A shoot-out of some sort across a littered street or a dusty corral, one-on-one, with fingers twitching until we slap leather, the fastest man walking away. But here there is only his motionless flesh and the urine. And on the bed, a sticky redness. It is strange that blood should be such a color. What else in nature is so bright, except a few flowers and some tropical fish?

The Thai doctor from the dispensary comes quickly through the door. He glances at the Japanese scientist, then rushes to Lisa on the bed, checking her pulse and gently slapping her face to keep her awake. He speaks to her soothingly in English, telling her a vehicle is coming now.

My leg is cramping, but it has nearly stopped bleeding. I test it as I go to the door, then look back at Lisa from New Mexico. She is still in shock, but more alert now, delicately touching the sides of her face, as if trying to make sure she is still alive.

Catherine Rennard or whoever she is follows me as I hobble into the hall. "What has the Fantasy Plan uncovered?" I demand.

She gives me a snort of disgust. "You are really stupid."

"Of course you can't tell me; it's bigger than I could possibly realize. Synthetic fuel or fiber optics. Well, fuck you, O'Hara, or DeLaurentis, or Rennard, or whoever the fuck you are today. I don't care how important anything is.''

"It affects everyone, Gaines. Me, you, even that family of yours in Ohio.''

"Right,'' I say, and take the stairs, leaning heavily on the rail. I can hear her following me, but no security comes. When I push open the door to the tech room, monitor 227 is still on. The scene looks exactly the way we left it, but greenish and slightly distorted, as if it is being broadcast from some faraway planet.

Mr. and Mrs. Pearce look relieved that it is over. "The ambulance just arrived,'' Mrs. Pearce says to me, her words coming out like a gasp. "Everything's gone too far. Thank you for stopping it, Mr. Harmon.''

Rennard points at Mrs. Pearce. "Security was supposed to be called as soon as he got here! Why weren't they called?''

"We were a little occupied with room two-two-seven,'' Mrs. Pearce answers angrily.

"Get them now!'' Rennard shouts. Mrs. Pearce doesn't move. Rennard turns to Mr. Pearce. "You! Get security now!''

"Yes, I've got their extension here somewhere.'' He begins looking slowly through some drawers.

"We used to have a young woman here,'' I announce loudly. "Songkha Chattkatavong.'' Mrs. Pearce nods to me. "I interviewed her about a year ago. I want all the tapes and papers on her interviews and any other tapes of what went on in her cell.''

Mr. Pearce starts to move, then looks at Catherine Rennard.

"He's inactive,'' Rennard says. "Off the payroll. Inactive!''

Mrs. Pearce ignores her and types something at a nearby computer. "There's only one tape on her,'' she says to me. "S–four– one-one-four.'' She goes quickly to the storage files and comes back with a single videocassette. "This is all there is, maybe three hours at the most.''

"Is there a copy?"

"Not as far as I know. You take it."

"Where is she now?"

Mrs. Pearce shakes her head, glancing for a moment at Rennard. "Probably that other place. Ask her. She knows where it is."

I look to Rennard, who is silent. "How could a woman tolerate all this?" I say.

"Oh, I should be some hysterical creature who can't do the rational and patriotic thing. What do you expect me to be, Gaines, menstrual?"

"That would be an improvement."

"They didn't want you coming back," she snaps. "Mr. DeForest warned us about you. He said you were weak and you'd screw things up, and he was right. That's why he got rid of you."

"I thought it was Leamer who fired me."

"Shit. Leamer is nobody."

"What about this girl?" I say, pointing to the videocassette. "Is it true she's pregnant?"

"Is it true?" Catherine Rennard says with a sneer. "No one should know better than you, Gaines. Or did you forget we have cameras around this place? Take the video, and enjoy it, Mr. Morality. You're a father."

Something jams inside my mind. She's telling me I had sex with Song. She's telling me I raped her. I try to think. I try to remember.

No, she's a liar. I am not capable of doing what she claims. I remember going to Song's cell that night to rescue her. I remember the confusion in my mind, and misunderstanding Song's gestures. But no, I did not take Song. I did not use her. I could not have. I don't think so. But so much of it was a blur. And the rest of that night was a blur. No, not a blur, a black hole.

Maybe I can't trust myself anymore. Maybe I have rewritten my own history in my head, blocked it all out and hidden my thoughts from myself for eleven months while stuck behind a desk in Bulgaria. No, I have not rewritten my history. I did not do anything to Song. I am certain.

I admired her and tried to care for her. Rennard is trying to trick me.

Rennard's words break through my thoughts. "They won't let you interfere again, Gaines. There are no more chances."

I shake my head clear of doubts. "And what about the orphanage and the children there, little children?"

"Drop it, Gaines," she says.

"Access," I say with disgust, and feel a surge of the same disgust toward myself.

I have to get out immediately. I look down, and my shoes are bloody again. My pants leg is sticking to my skin, and the tourniquet is too tight. I reach down and loosen it.

Mrs. Pearce is still standing. Her eyes move from my shredded pants leg up to my face. "Thank you, Mr. Harmon," she says again.

I move as quickly as I can through the hallway, then stop, overcome with the sense that in all the chaos I am forgetting something. I check for my wallet. Miraculously it's still in my pocket. I have my glasses. I have the videocassette. I am still alive. And though I don't know what the operation has uncovered, I know my direction: north, to find the orphanage and Song in the hill country of Thailand. But of course the Organization knows my destination too.

I limp into the lobby, trailing spots of blood along the floor. I look through the one-way glass again. The girls are sitting as they were before. Nothing has changed. But I still have the nagging feeling I am forgetting something.

I turn back and hobble down the hall to room 104. Amkha, number 15, is still there in her leather bodysuit, sitting cross-legged on the floor, weeping into her arms. She looks up as I enter, her hands automatically covering her cheeks. I kneel by her side. I must tell her not to worry. I must tell her that I will come back for her. And this time I really will. Not like before, when I left Song.

But the instant I think it, I know it is not true. It is another lie to myself.

I pull the blanket around Amkha and study her for a moment. Suddenly everything is simple and clear.

I help her to her feet. I take her hand. Together we walk down the hall as she weeps silently. A soft fluid drains from her nose. Her eyes are red and swollen, and her face is frozen straight ahead as we march quickly through the lobby. She does not glance even once at the one-way glass.

Then we are out the front door.

19

GOLDEN

*E*verything is golden.

The walls, the carpet, the blanket, the door, they are all golden. The videocassette on the floor is golden. Even the window and the dust particles floating in the air above me are golden. My hands are golden too. Amkha lies next to me on her side, wrapped in a blanket as golden as a Buddhist monk's robe.

The golden face of my watch says seven o'clock. The sun is low on the horizon, its radiant yellow and orange hues slanting in through the window and washing over everything. I can't remember if it's morning or evening.

I am on the floor of a shack, on a mattress so thin I can feel the cracks between the boards beneath me. There are cracks in the slatted walls, and golden beams of light stream in there also, like rays through a cathedral window. It is soft, warm light that says not to worry, each day is new.

Amkha faces away from me, clutching the golden blanket tightly. I look around the room for her leather clothes and don't see them. She must still be wearing them.

It is morning. I remember now. In Bangkok, outside the Fantasy Store, we ran down Silom Road to the river. I

156

smile to think what a curious sight we were—Amkha wrapped in her blanket, her black leather bodysuit beneath it, and I in my shredded pants—as we hobbled at a half run past fifty amazed tourists, pushed our way to the head of a line, and hopped into a *hong yao*—one of those long-tail motor-driven boats—which took us across the Chao Phraya to the west side of the river. And then into Bangkok's maze of canals with a million shacks and sinewy waterways in which to hide, a world so different from the palaces and temples and high rises of the east side. It is a world where Thai life is as it used to be, a damp and dirty existence on rickety boat homes, with women bathing waist high in their sarongs and washing their teeth in the brown water.

We paid the boatman and managed to flag down a taxi, then persuaded the driver to zigzag through side streets and to backtrack several times. Finally he pulled over and demanded money. I paid him in American cash, and soon we headed straight north in a different taxi. The whole time Amkha remained completely wrapped beneath the blanket, her head on her knees as she wept in fear, or maybe in relief, I'm not sure which.

North of Bangkok the sky was so much cleaner. The lush grasses and trees fed the air with fresh oxygen, replenishing the whole world around us. By two in the afternoon we came to the town of Bang Pa In, south of the old capital of Ayutthaya. The driver would take us no farther, so we got out. We hurried away from the commercial section, with its touristy jewelry shops, massage parlors, and cheap restaurants. We crossed some railroad tracks and took a gravel street into the poorer part of town. My arm was around Amkha as she held the blanket tightly with both hands. I noticed for the first time that she was barefoot, but the stones didn't seem to hurt her.

All the houses looked the same to me: unpainted, slatted buildings with straw roofs. One house had a round Coca-Cola sign on its door, and Amkha pointed toward it. I knocked and pushed the door open. In the cool dimness was an assortment of fruits, soft drinks, and candy. An old woman in a chair did not get up.

Through Amkha I asked if there was a place we could rest. The old woman ignored me and spoke to Amkha, seeming to scold her as Amkha stood with her eyes fixed on the floor. The woman said something else, and Amkha slowly parted the blanket to reveal her leather costume, her head bowed and chin trembling. The woman's words became even harsher, so defeating that I thought Amkha might collapse. She began to cry again, and I took her hand to lead her outside. But the woman shook her head, got up, and led us out back and up a steep climb of stairs to this shack raised ten feet off the ground.

I wonder now if it has been possible to follow us, somehow to trace our movements. There is not even a lock on the door of the shack, and I have no gun. As a fist fighter I am only average, certainly no match for what they will send.

There are soft footsteps on the gravel outside. I scramble to my feet, a stabbing pain shooting up my leg. I hobble to the side of the door as someone climbs the steps. The door opens a crack, and a wrinkled brown hand reaches in and sets two apples and two Cokes on the floor. The door closes again.

I limp back to the mattress and lie down, drained. There is a throbbing in my leg, and I examine the wound. I don't remember how, but one of my pants legs has been removed, perhaps cut off, and the slashes on my leg have been washed and bandaged.

Amkha stirs and looks toward me with vacant eyes. She waits to see if I will reach for her, but I don't. Then she throws back the blanket and stands, her black leather bodysuit a stark contrast with the golden light. Standing sideways so I see her profile, she undoes the strap of her neck and seductively lowers the leather top. Her breasts are bathed in the golden light. Then she reaches up and undoes her hair, and it falls to her shoulders. Slowly, routinely she slides her bodysuit down over her hips. She is wearing no panties. She faces me naked, a golden statue. Then she kneels down next to me and inches closer, offering herself up to me as some kind of repayment, as if this is what I would expect. Her body is all she has to give in return for my kindness.

I pull back, but she presses closer to me. Her breasts flatten against my chest. I wrap my arms around her, and her body tenses as she waits. But she is a wounded bird, a ball of pain and confusion, with a forced and fearful smile. She is not a fantasy. She is the face of honest humanity. I hold her until there is nothing sexual in our embrace, and she finally relaxes, then weeps again.

There is a creak as the door opens. I sit up quickly and spin to the side. A pair of black drawstring pants and a white peasant shirt, both neatly folded, are placed inside.

Amkha goes to the door and slips the clothes on. Now she is any peasant girl on the road, walking along and carrying a bundle of wood or leading a cow.

She comes back and stands above me, studying my face. "You want to have Songkha?" she asks, and there is a hint of jealousy in her voice, as if Song might take away her new friend.

Do I want to *have* Song? If I am honest, I will tell her yes. Layers of dreams and fantasies still emerge, and I dare not even trust myself with the secret that I am exhilarated just to think that I once touched Song's hair and neck. But I am living a terrible contradiction: that I want to *have* Song, and at the same instant I want to redeem myself by *not* having her, and instead *being* like her, and actually finding and helping her. Two conflicting selfishnesses drive me. Two unfinished threads of my life seem so completely woven into one fabric: my need to seize her and my need to mend myself.

Here in the soft golden light with Amkha I am overwhelmed by the fact that it is not just my life that is confused and knotted, but that the whole world seems bruised and requires so much healing. With or without me it will all go on—the good and the bad, the bad and the good—and I wonder if in this universe of distress and pain whether finding and helping one small creature like Song can make any difference at all.

"You like Songkha as a pleasure girl?" she says.

"She is just a friend," I answer, and realize I have lied again.

The golden light grows dimmer. I was wrong: It is evening, not morning. There are no candles, and the dusk invades the room. I go to the door and come back with the apples and Cokes. We sit facing each other, munching and drinking and trying to smile as the light fades until we are shadows to each other. A weariness overtakes me, and I lie back as Amkha disappears completely within the growing wall of darkness. Then I hear a soft rustling as she slides under my sheet with me. She is still in her peasant clothes, but she nestles close, her warm breath against my shoulder. It seems like only seconds, and her breathing becomes regular and deep. Maybe it is just a movement of her head as she sleeps, but it seems as if she kisses my shoulder lightly.

I lie awake, struggling with Rennard's words and the possibility that I have blotted out some deed from my mind, a depraved secret that would make me an outcast everywhere. No, I didn't hurt Song. It is not possible. But now I wonder if I can trust myself. Maybe they videotaped me in Song's cell that night, and then the proof that I did not hurt her will be on the videocassette.

Amkha stirs gently, and I can smell her beside me. Her hair does not have the sweet fragrance of papaya shampoo or coconut conditioner. And there is no piped-in music or rich fragrances of perfumes or gentle sounds of a waterfall. There is no fantasy here. The only thing artificial is the faintest scent of her makeup. The rest of her is musty with dried perspiration. I put my arm around her and pull her close. Her smell is human. So human. Not a fantasy, but real.

20

SMILES

There is a tiny old man kneeling at my feet. He smiles up at me as he feels his way up my inseam to my crotch. He stretches the measuring tape and makes a white X on the fabric. He smiles at me again.

I have been a hundred places in the world, but the Thais are the only people who have a smile for every emotion—including contempt, and hate. Maybe his smile isn't contempt or hate. Maybe I just look comical to him. Six feet two, unshaven, unwashed, with a torn calf, standing perfectly still as he fits me for new pants and a shirt. I'd rather buy from the rack. But no tourist buys from the rack in Thailand. And that's what I am now: a tourist.

There are other tourists around me in this air-conditioned clothing store. Three British women finger a roll of exotic silk, while an American couple browses in the corner. And there is a collegiate-looking young man with a Nike cap and a backpack bargaining with a Thai saleswoman. She smiles at him, but her smile is somehow expressionless.

Through the window I keep my eyes on Amkha. She is speaking to a Thai man, who turns and walks away. She disappears from view, then returns and stands in front of the store, looking around innocently. I am not spying on her. And I am not paranoid. She enters the store and comes over to where I stand. She smiles at the tailor, then smiles up at me. There are smiles everywhere.

I am desperate to get to the city of Chiang Mai, but I force myself to stay clearheaded. I have only a strategy, not a full plan. The details will have to unfold as I go. We are still three hundred miles from Chiang Mai. They know where I am going and will try to stop me. Flying is out of the question, and the railroad is too easy to check. We will have to go by bus—not the express line but local buses, which will take us only forty to sixty miles at a time. We will board in a small town and change routes several times before reaching Chiang Mai.

About seven bus rides. That's what I figure it will take to get there. It's the best way for a tourist to travel if he wants to see the real Thailand, and especially if he wants to avoid other foreigners. I give Amkha enough money to purchase our first tickets north. She leaves, and I wonder if she will stay with me or just take the money and flee.

After the fitting and stitching, I emerge from the store trying to disguise my limp as I take my first steps in the new gray pants and white silk shirt. The morning air is compressed, heated, and dirty, and my face immediately beads with sweat. I have no bag, nothing in my hands except the videocassette of Song.

Amkha reappears. She has not deserted me. Her eyes are wide open and shining. She is a peasant girl again, and I am amazed at how she blends in with the colors of the street. Her face is washed and clean. She is much prettier without all the makeup. There is something renewed and bright about her, a certain light in her eyes that wasn't there before.

She takes my hand and leads me to a nearby alley. My leg aches, and next to her I feel old, very old. In the alley she reaches around me with both arms and hugs my waist the way a child sometimes does. Yet her embrace is a little too long for just a polite thank-you. She smiles up at me again. I can't decode the smile. Maybe it says that I am the single most important thing in her world. Or maybe it is a nervous smile. Then I see that her eyes are watering. But I cannot read her tears any better than her smile.

"Songkha," she says to me in a broken voice. "I am afraid. But I help you find."

"Thank you," I say. "You are very brave."

"You and I good friends." She smiles tearfully, then adds, "Best friends."

"Yes," I say. "Best friends."

She leads me down the alley to a street corner away from the tourist area. Within minutes an ancient bus arrives, looking much like a battered school bus from my boyhood days except that it is blue with two yellow stripes and an underinflated back tire. It is already crowded when we board. We sit three across: a young boy next to the window with a chicken in his arms, then Amkha, then me sitting sideways with both legs in the aisle. It is stifling hot, and the air smells of motor oil and bodies. Already my new shirt is soaked. The peasant families around us keep looking over and smiling, probably in amused wonder. Their country is crawling with middle-class Americans, Japanese, and Europeans, but it is rare for a Thai family to be elbow to elbow, third class, with one of these walking wallets.

The bus lurches forward, and in minutes we are rolling across wide and fertile plains, Thailand's rice bowl. The roar of the transmission drowns out the insects and the birds, leaving me only the visual realm of the countryside arrayed in many greens. We pass isolated hamlets, cottages with sagging grass roofs, and farm families slogging through muddy fields on both sides of the road. Despite the mud, it all looks so clean, so simple, so uncomplicated.

The drone of the engine is hypnotic and tiring. I have to force myself to stay alert. I must figure out what the Fantasy Plan has uncovered. Why would the Organization permit that fat Japanese scientist to live out his horrific fantasy? What access could justify it? Maybe the answers revolve around some remarkable advance in satellite or undersea technology that the Japanese won't share with us.

And why would the Organization have children at the orphanage? It must be more than a school for seduction. And why was I transferred and later dismissed, only to be pursued by Rennard to learn if I was coming back? Somehow it all has to do with Song. But maybe there is no great secret. Maybe people like Catherine Rennard are just addicted to the access game, and the game must go on.

The old bus strains as we begin a slow climb. It will be even steeper when we reach the lower extremities of the Himalayan foothills, which will rise like huge mountains themselves, covering the northern provinces.

We get off the bus in another small town. Amkha says there will be an hour wait for the next bus. She takes my hand and walks me down a lane. We come to an old stone temple and a tall plaster statue of the Buddha. Amkha approaches slowly and bows, then kneels and seems to pray.

I stand face-to-face with this image of the Buddha. It is nearly ten feet high and was probably manufactured on some assembly line somewhere. It is not the fat, grinning Buddha you see in Chinese restaurants but the lean, mysterious Buddha of South Asia, with a faint, enigmatic smile, standing poised and serene, knowing all. It is just cheap plaster, but something in me responds. It is not a face like any I know. It is a boy's face and a girl's face both, youthful and ageless. Its eyes are lowered; its palm is open as if holding out an invisible secret, its calmness beckoning me and seeming to ask a question. I understand then why Amkha bows. Its calm grace is an image of something in her, perhaps in everyone, something deeper than our desires and loneliness and fears.

Maybe that is why every village has a Buddha, a reminder everywhere that we can pick ourselves up from the muck of the world, master our demons, and raise ourselves to find tranquillity.

We hurry back to the corner when the next bus arrives, this one a shocking green. Our journey north continues, wobbling along with random jerks. We pass more villages and hamlets, each with its statue of the Buddha. Buddhas everywhere, helping people transcend the everyday world.

But I could never be a Buddhist. I don't want to transcend the world, and I can't hope to save it. I have come here only to gain a certain freedom from my own past. And my actions are not karmic. They aren't conditioned by a long chain of previous lives. I have always had a choice, even when I have made the wrong one. And the Buddhists are mistaken about something else: There is no reincarnation, no revolving door from this life to the next. That is just wishful thinking. Each life is a straight line from the womb to the grave. The end is final.

I wonder about Song. Did she consider her life some sort of karmic retribution, a necessary cleansing? Would she acquiesce to it all, permitting herself to be polluted by men, and then stoically say it was meant to be? I cannot imagine it. She knew she had choices, and she defiantly fought for them.

The bus lurches around a curve and thumps across a foot-deep pothole. I brace myself by holding to the seat in front of me. I glance over at Amkha, who is looking up at me, smiling a different smile now, a happy smile. It seems odd that she is not frightened to be heading back to the orphanage, and I wonder why.

I feel the elevation in my ears as we begin a twisting climb into the hill country. At a hilltop the road winds downward, like a gray ribbon across the green land. I realize that even if I make it to the orphanage, it will be an even more difficult journey out. These are the back roads, in a back province, in the back part of a half-backward nation. I will find Song and escape, or I will disappear here. Fall right off the earth. Last-known whereabouts, they will say, was a brothel in Bangkok where I went to release a casual desire and ended up murdering an important Japanese scientist.

Two hours later we pass Sirikit Dam and a nameless hamlet to the right. Amkha sleeps against my shoulder, a soft weight. I like the feel of her hair as it blows across my neck. The air is moist from a recent downpour, and there are heavy smells from the mountain forests. We climb still farther, entering a world even more foreign, a place of tribal cultures—the Karen, the Hmong, and the Lahu—and also a home to bandits. We stop briefly in the town of Phrae and then at Lampang, where I wake Amkha gently to change buses again.

We begin the last leg of our journey to Chiang Mai. The sun sets below the mountains, and it seems as if the dusk and then the darkness rise out of the earth. We wind over another hill and then see the lights of a modern city below us. Chiang Mai. It is a smaller version of Bangkok, with its own train station and airport. A quarter of a million people in this commercial island in the hill country, a destination for thousands of tourists. As we begin the slow descent, civilization closes in around me again, and I feel claustrophobic and trapped.

The bus fights the grade in the darkness, a brake-burning mile down. Chiang Mai's lights ripple in the thin air: street lights, modern neon signs, and streams of car lights moving slowly through the city. Amkha awakens and looks at me with yet another enigmatic smile.

As we get closer to Chiang Mai, I feel a queasy tension growing. Perhaps it is only another fantasy, but it seems as if this modern city, this oasis in the mountains, is another kind of personal crossroads. Maybe my trek here is karmic after all, for I feel as if something is waiting for me here. And I am afraid that a wrong turn will lead me somewhere else, someplace even more remote, someplace from which there will be no way out at all.

21

THE VIDEO

I slip the videotape in, and the machine starts automatically. But the screen shows only white spots. I look around the room, wanting to ask what is wrong with the monitor. The elderly Chinese man and his wife sit at a small table, gulping rice from little bowls. Amkha sits with them, their conversation low, as if sharing secrets.

We found this herb shop after I decided it wasn't safe to stay at any of the hotels. We wandered Chiang Mai for half an hour. Then finally Amkha pointed to the shop, told me her father was Chinese, and we just knocked on the door and offered some cash in exchange for food and a corner in which to sleep. They would accept no money but ushered us in.

The front room of the herb shop could be a thousand years old: a long counter with an ancient scale, and behind the counter a wall lined with tall jars and glasses labeled in Chinese. Medicine, not food. The ingredients are probably the usual: ginseng, leaves and weeds from various hills, fungi from a tree in such and such a province, lion's teeth ground to a powder. I saw what could be a bull's penis in a clear liquid, and there was a dark jar that might be coagulated pig's blood.

But here in the back room it is a mixture of modern and traditional worlds—more tall jars, but also a microwave, a small air conditioner, and this video player and TV.

The fuzzy picture suddenly clears, but there is still no sound. The scene is a dirt street in a poor town. The hand-held camera jiggles as it focuses on a wobbly bicycle coming down the street, then zooms in closer on the face of Songkha Chattkatavong, perspiring as she approaches a wooden hut on the bicycle. Over her shoulder is a sack with what must be rice from a store. The camera swings to the left, toward another girl, most likely a sister, who is a year or two older than Songkha, coming through the door of the hut. She helps Song lower the sack to the ground. As in a silent film I see their lips move without sound. Song and her sister appear to laugh at something. Song rests the bike against the corner of the hut. Then, each taking a grip on the bag of rice, they carry it inside together.

I realize the film is a kind of product review, a commercial taken by someone in the Organization who was trolling the villages for special girls, not the typical girls sent south by the families.

There is a moment of snow on the monitor, and then another scene comes into focus, this one inside a hut. The camera pans left to right. The room is dim, but I can make out a chair where a man sits, probably Song's father, and a large mat in front of him, where his three girls are huddled. In the middle is Song. The girls face the camera, expressionless. Then each stands, and one by one turns slowly in a circle as if someone off camera is inspecting her. Song is the most attractive. The other two girls are directed away. Song stands alone in the middle of the room, looking into the camera.

Another moment of snow and then static. The picture comes into focus, showing Songkha sitting across a table with the man who is probably her father. He has a stubble of beard but is trying to look his best, sitting erect with his collar buttoned and a brown tie poorly knotted and off center. The room is dingy and unfamiliar—another hut somewhere—perhaps near Song's village. She is wearing a plain white blouse, and her hands are pulled behind her. She keeps looking at the Thai man as if expecting him to change his mind. She says something, but he turns to avoid her eyes, then looks back to the interviewer again.

The interviewer is Caucasian and has his back to the camera. Only his shoulder and part of his head are visible. His hair is yellowish blond and thinning. He speaks to someone else in the room, his voice resonant and authoritative. "Don't untie her," he says. "She'll be okay. Let's get this over with."

It is strange how voices change so little, much less than a face and often less than a person himself. Even after years we sometimes recognize a single "hello" at the other end of a phone.

The blond-haired man switches to Thai, speaking fluently to Song's father. I try to follow the words but can catch only phrases, courtesies that initiate a conversation. Then his tone changes, and Song's father nods solemnly. The blond-haired interviewer places three bundles of money in front of him—Thai notes wrapped in rubber bands. The father does not count the money or even touch it but just nods again. Song is still looking at him.

The interviewer then pushes a piece of paper forward and sets a pen in front of the man, who scribbles a mark. It is standard procedure, signing for the money and getting the contract on film in order to establish the family's complicity in the bargain and give the Organization leverage if they later try to back out.

Her father gets up and stuffs the money into his pockets. He looks toward Song with a sad expression, maybe saying that he is sorry that this is necessary. Then he turns away. Her eyes follow him until the door closes. The interviewer shuffles some papers, then makes some perfunctory motion with his hand, a kind of dismissal. She rises unsteadily, her hands still behind her back. The blond-haired man says something about two years not being such a long time. Song stiffens, then spits on him. Someone pushes her out of the camera's frame.

As the interviewer wipes his cheeks with his sleeve, he glances back at the camera. I freeze the frame and catch a three-quarter profile. His thinning hair gives him an even higher forehead than he had before. His handsome, angular face looks narrower now, and gaunt. He is wearing round-rimmed glasses, as he did years ago, and the glasses reflect the glare from the camera's light.

I advance the tape in increments. His face continues its slow turn toward the camera, toward me. His cheeks are more hollowed, but he is smiling an easy and friendly smile, a smile I remember well. I even want to smile back, so fond are my memories of him.

The glare from the glasses disappears, and now I see his eyes as they stare right at me, eyes that are tired but eyes that I would recognize anywhere in the world. Deep blue. The bluest eyes I have ever seen.

I stare at the face frozen on the television monitor, and I recall sauntering through the Branscomb campus with Steven Vaal eighteen years before. How clear and self-assured he was. His certainty that if there was any significance to living, it was not in chloroform jobs and the depressing ''good life.'' He would mold some permanent good in the world, make or shape something really important. And his muscular frame—that strong wrestler's grip when he took my hand and looked me in the eye and said that the Branscomb Institute was our beginning, that we both were embarking on exciting and rewarding careers. I've always imagined him rising through the ranks, undertaking some noble service more significant than my own, something truly meaningful.

I recall six years ago in Brussels, when we sat down over wine and pretzels, and I talked to him about desires, how they sometimes created fantasies that charmed our thoughts and turned wrong into right. I remember how carefully he had listened when I told him about the power of desires and fantasies, how each stoked the other, confusing the mind so that it might choose anything. I remember Vaal nodded his understanding, without speaking.

Then we went our separate ways again.

Now he is here on the screen, freeze-framed in a peasant village where he has come to recruit a seventeen-year-old into prostitution. Maybe he took my words about fantasies and constructed them into a scheme for access. Maybe I am the originator of the Fantasy Plan.

I press the play button, and the tape begins again. Steven Vaal continues to look right at me for several seconds, his irresistible smile still in place. Then he turns away, and the tape continues.

22

SONGKHA

A loud rush of static on the machine. I glance toward Amkha and the elderly Chinese couple, but they are so absorbed in their conversation and rice that they don't notice the noise.

A different picture comes into focus. The same picture I saw through the tech room monitor last year, when Leamer first brought Songkha Chattkatavong to the Fantasy Store. The date on the screen is "March 27," the time "14:41." Again I am struck by Song's composure and her uncorrupted beauty and modesty. I recall my impulse, even then, to protect her from what they wanted her to be.

I fast-forward and stop at the next scene. This one includes me. It is the next day, "March 28," when I interviewed Song after they had dressed her in a shoulderless wraparound with fake gold loop earrings. I remember how I was unable to pull my eyes away from her, caught in a contradictory excitement that longed both to rescue her and to possess her. Now, intent on observing myself and not just her this time, I watch the scene from beginning to end.

Another patch of static and another scene.

Plush red carpet and four people. No, six people. No, only two. Song and I are reflected in the mirrors on the walls. The camera was running the whole time we were in that room. Songkha drops a cassette and a moment later pulls the whole rack over. The sound quality is not good, but I hear myself shouting for her to stop it. Then she takes the wig out from the drawer, and the mask and handcuffs, and everything is in a pile on the floor. I can't hear what she is saying to me, but she starts to unbutton her wraparound. "Don't!" I cry out in her language. "I will help you!" But then I am brushing my lips over her. The microphone does not pick up my whisper about coming to her room in the early morning to help her escape, but the camera records her pulling her dress to the floor and me turning away, not looking.

I glance over to the table, where Amkha and the Chinese couple are eating. The couple continue to fill their mouths with rice, but Amkha is staring at the screen, her eyes showing a mixture of pain and alarm. I turn back to the monitor in time to see reflections of me fleeing the mirrored room.

Another rush of static.

The tape is no longer in full color, just shades of lighter and darker green from a special "starlight" camera used in low-light circumstances. It takes a moment for me to realize it is Song's cell, lit by that single dim bulb. Among the shadows I can make out her form on the edge of the bed. The camera cannot pick up all the details, nor was it intended to. It was for surveillance rather than entrapment. I see a darker shape come toward her, and I know who it is. The audio is hollow, recording my breathing as if I am in a cave. I hear myself tell her that I will take her out of there. I will free her. She gets to her feet and takes my hand, then throws her arms around me. For a moment our faces are one shadow as I bend and kiss her. Then I sit down on the bed and pull her toward me. I ease her backward. We are one shapeless shadow as I lean over her.

In my memory we were together only for seconds, but on the video it is clear that it was minutes. In the faint light the camera cannot distinguish depth, whether I am next to her, or leaning over her, or completely on top of her. There is some movement, but maybe I am just trying to get comfortable. I don't know. I don't know. This is not how I remembered it. Now I am confused. Have I done something awful and blocked it from my own mind? No, it isn't possible.

Then I see Song slide away from me, pulling her blouse closed and moving off the screen. I rise slowly, adjust my clothes, and I too move away.

Suddenly another swish of static. I turn from the TV monitor toward the table again, but Amkha has fled. I am tempted to go after her, but I look back to the monitor as another scene begins. The date on the screen reads "May 7," the time "09:41." I can tell by the background that it is at the Fantasy Store in Bangkok. That means her training at the orphanage ended after less than two months, and for some reason they brought her back early. I recognize the setting as encounter room 223, the one with a fake fireplace and red-canopied bed. The camera is hidden in the wall by the door, and it films Song entering, wearing a traditional Japanese kimono, her back to the camera, her hair tucked tightly in a bun. She turns and faces the person who follows her in. From the position of the camera I can see only that he is slender and well tailored, probably a Japanese, with short hair combed to the side. He stops opposite her and stands with his legs apart, waiting for something.

There are no words and no sounds except the man's gruff breathing picked up by an overhead microphone. He stands there, as if waiting for her to proceed. Then Song steps directly in front of the man, takes his face in her hands, and kisses him long and full on the mouth. But it is playacting. There is a stiffness to it. He snaps his fingers. She steps back and bows. She undoes her kimono. It falls away in layers at her feet, and she steps out of it in a strapless peach-colored bra and black panties. For a moment she freezes. Her face drains into a moment of horror, and she shrinks back. Then she approaches him again with a wooden smile and releases her hair, which tumbles down over one cup of her bra. I am sickened, but I cannot take my eyes away.

The man claps his hand four times, loudly. Immediately she helps him slip off his coat, maneuvering him around so he faces the camera. He is a narrow-faced Japanese, with a thin mustache and a serious look, almost a sad look. He is breathing heavily with excitement. Under his gray coat he wears a tailored vest with a burgundy-striped necktie. She places the coat neatly across a chair. He claps his hands again, three times now, and she immediately loosens his tie. Then two claps, and she begins pulling his shirttails out. Something twists inside me. The man just stands as she undoes his belt. His pants collapse to the floor around his ankles. Then a single clap. Slowly Song-kha goes to one knee before him. Then the other knee. And I am falling off the edge of the world.

23

DISSOLVING

I haven't told you that I cry. Nothing unmanly, I assure you. It began about a year ago, standing in the shower, with my face raised into the spray. I hadn't planned it, and at first I didn't even realize I was crying, the shower hiding it from the world and nearly from myself.

Now sometimes, when I awaken in the early-morning darkness, I find myself sitting with my legs limp over the side of the bed, my body anchored with the weight of depression. My eyes begin to water. Quiet tears. Tears, as if washing away the effect of my life or melting some immense meaninglessness. Or perhaps it is because I hear age whispering around me in the dark. Maybe it is all those things together. I don't know. But the tears pass as the sun rises and I get busy with my day.

Now I sit cross-legged on the mat in the back of this store. The night sky is black and liquidy through the side window. Surrounding me are the odors of various powders, dried skins, and who knows what else. Amkha has not come back, or else she is that dark shape curled on the bare floor across the room. I have no pillow, only a blanket that is not thick enough to keep me warm at this altitude. But it is better than risking the comfort of a Chiang Mai hotel, where they could easily track me.

The tears are not yet coming, but I know they will come, such an uncontrollable sadness over the world and over what I may have done to Song. I close my eyes, and the video replays in my head: two shadows merging on Song's bed. Regardless of what it looked like, I could not have done the unspeakable. Song was forced, Amkha said. *Kamlang.* And then pregnant. And Catherine Rennard said I was the one. But I did not force her. I did not do anything but hold her. I am sure.

Then comes the clapping of hands and the image of Song going to her knees in front of that man. That man. That man. Maybe another Japanese scientist. The image of her on her knees goes no further in my mind because I was unable to watch. I looked away and then reached back and shut off the recorder, telling myself that what I was seeing happened months ago and that it was long over. Perhaps there are hours of additional footage, I don't know. I couldn't turn the machine back on. And I don't understand why she was brought back to Bangkok so quickly. Why was she being used? Is she part of the secret they are trying to conceal?

Now the tears begin to come. I am dissolving. I am coming apart. I am always alone when the tears come, so I do not have to catch or hide them or try to blot them. I lie down on my back on the mat, and the tears roll over the corners of my eyes, and I try to recall what kind of person I was as a young man. So far away, it is difficult to remember now. The years are a sleepy blur. I feel as if I came into the world and then joined the Organization and then was suddenly out again, and now I am here: My only reality is the present—me on this mat, on this floor, tearful—a train traveler through life who has somehow napped through his stop and awakened in a strange land.

There is movement on the other side of the room. A turning and then a sleepy moan. I hear Amkha struggle to her feet and move quietly toward me. I can even hear her shivering and breathing. She comes to the mat.

"Amkha," I say, "I did not force Song. No *kamlang.* It is not my child."

Amkha lies down, careful not to touch me, not even taking the blanket. I move an inch closer and toss an end over her. She pulls it tight and, still shivering, moves an inch away.

I get up and light a candle, then stand by the window, my mind plagued by dead-end questions. What crucial access has the Fantasy Plan gained? What momentous secret are they so anxious to protect? An entirely new generation of computers or lasers with nearly unimaginable functions and applications? The development of a synthetic drug that would replace cocaine and capture the world's market? Maybe a vaccine for AIDS, which is now being withheld for some unfathomable reason.

My mind cannot reach any further. The only thing I know for sure is that Steven Vaal is connected to the Fantasy Plan. When I find the orphanage, I may find him as well as Song. He will know the secret the Organization could not share with me.

I blow out the candle. The glow from the night sky enters the room, its soft hush creating patches and shadows on the walls, spreading out over the blanket on the shivering Amkha.

I lie down behind her again, pulling her close to me in order to warm her. Her waist is so small. She does not resist. Then I feel her tears on my arm and realize that she was not shivering but sobbing silently.

"Tomorrow will be different," I whisper to her. "Tomorrow will be different." And that is all I can say.

24

THE KILLING

She awakens me early, with her hands moving lightly over my body. I think it is her way of telling me to get up and also that she believes me that I am not the one who forced Song. I hug her like a brother, to show her that I do care, then stand and help her to her feet.

We wash quickly from a large basin, each of us privately, back to back. Then I send her for a tourist map of the northern country, which will be easy to find since tourism is Chiang Mai's primary source of revenue.

Amkha leaves, and a deep depression sweeps over me. I have fooled myself again, pretending that I have come here to shield Song from all the men who will use her. But my motives are more selfish than that. I know that despite my youthful plans, I never really defied that middle-ground complacency I abhorred. The Organization was like any other organization, with rules, and orders, and a conspiracy of mediocrity and conformity. I never strove beyond myself. I never leaned out over that rim of existence, putting everything on the line for some principle, or a person, or justice, or some piece of truth that was larger than I was. Like my father, I lived in a cubicle, though mine was geographically larger.

Amkha returns with a map that spells out the locations and descriptions of each major temple, statue, and monastery in the area. I spread it out on the floor for her to see. But she cannot read a map. She cannot see any landscape or roads on the flat paper; she sees only wiggly lines and strange marks. I trace the roads and streams with my finger, reading the narrations out loud. "Wat Pongsanuk, with its tiered roof and four Buddha statues around a bo tree." "Wat Chang Kham, the 'Elephant-Supported Temple.' " "Wat Phra Kaew, which was split by lightning to reveal a dazzling emerald Buddha." "Wat Ton." I stop there. The brief description reads: "The temple Wat Ton sits up on a hill in a remote area 41 miles north of Chiang Mai. The closest town is tiny Ban Ton, but it is a difficult trek even from there. Wat Ton has a 30-meter-high statue of the Buddha. The huge and unusual statue is carved from a glistening white marble that appears to change colors—blue, red, and green—as it reflects the many moods of the sky at sunset and dawn."

I point to a dot on the map. "Wat Ton," I say. "A temple near Ban Ton. *Kon kampra*," I add, remembering the Thai words for "orphanage," and then recall the Organization's name for it. *"Tee Natiew,"* I say. Wonderful Place.

For the first time since we fled Bangkok Amkha looks afraid. "Wat Ton," she repeats, and nods. "*Kon kampra* at Wat Ton."

She looks strangely at the dot, her hands trembling. *"Tee Natiew,"* she whispers to me, her eyes now starting to tear. Amkha backs away from the map as if it is a snake ready to strike. "Very much terrible," she says. Then she goes to a cabinet in the corner of the room. I see her take out a gun. She brings it to me. It is an old pistol that she has found here, a revolver with an oddly curved handle and an ugly steel barrel that glimmers in the low light. It is an old Japanese weapon, apparently left over from the brief occupation in the forties.

It rests in my hands, heavy and awkward and slightly oily, and I recall the first person I killed, the man in Kyoto.

It was not like the spontaneous killing of the man at the Fantasy Store. No, the killing of the man in Kyoto was deliberate, calculated. I still wonder why I was called upon to do it. I had always thought there were special people for assignments like that, what we vaguely referred to as the Skills Team. I knew nothing about his personal life, not even his name. But I was told that he was a senior leader of the Yakuza, the brutal Japanese Mafia. Killing him would send a message that would protect Americans in Japan from being kidnapped and ransomed. It wasn't a pleasant assignment, they said. It was necessary, that's all.

But to me he was just a small man on the street, who took the same route home each night. He was not my enemy, and I was not a soldier. They told me that killing him would be simple because I didn't know him and had never even met him. There would be no emotional attachment, nothing to recover from. The hard part, they said, was the background: finding the hour he returned home, tracing the route, locating a deserted place before he reached his house. I just had to do it and then walk away.

But setting it up turned out to be the only easy part. His routine was regular: same train, same hour, same dark side street every night. It was late and drizzling, and he was carrying an umbrella and wearing a brown derby hat. For someone so important, he did not seem to be taking any precautions. I timed it so we walked toward each other on the sidewalk not far from his house. As he came closer, I was surprised to see that he was much older than I had thought and a little frail. But I focused on the thought that the Yakuza leaders were merciless and that American lives were at stake.

Everything happened so fast. I try now to recall what I was thinking at that precise moment, but I can remember no thoughts, only acute sensations: his dark shape, the weight of the weapon in my hand, adjusting my breathing. There was no idea of revenge or hate, and I could feel no necessity in what I was to do.

They had told me to fire several times at his head, execution style, but to do it in slow succession or else the weapon would ride up as I fired, making it impossible to hold on the target. Yes, they called him the target, as if he were a cardboard silhouette.

He was suddenly so close. I raised the weapon. It was an eternal second from the time my mind willed to pull the trigger and my body followed its guidance. I fired only once. The noise seemed so close to my ear, so violent that it was like the explosion of the universe or of my own heart.

He jerked, and his derby flew backward as if yanked by a string. The lower part of his face exploded downward, shredding his jaw and part of his throat. He fell, and in the dim light I could see he was still moving, twitching, then grabbing at his throat as if trying to choke himself or maybe trying to tear open his throat so he could breathe. His blood glistened like oil through his fingers. He struggled to sit up, his round face looking at me in surprise. I couldn't bring myself to shoot again. I wanted to take it all back. I wished he would just die. Or live. Or something. I wanted to kneel and call for help and somehow rescue him. Then he fell backward and didn't move, his hands still on his throat, the face of his wristwatch reflecting in the dim streetlight: twelve minutes after nine. The second hand sweeping on without him, the whole world continuing on.

They said I might feel an exhilaration, a kind of savage high, a surge of the kill. But I just looked in disbelief at the weapon that had carried out the deed and then at the hands that had caused the sin. I threw the gun down. It clanged on the walkway. I did not run. I walked stiffly away. Already I could feel myself trying to deny it, coiling it back in my mind, never to face it again.

Now I look down at the old pistol in my hand. I turn it over slowly and check the cylinder. It is empty. Amkha opens her hands and presses five bullets into my palm.

"Are there more?" I hear myself saying, still remembering the man lying on the sidewalk in Kyoto.

She shakes her head. Her chin is quivering. I know the

violence that the gun will cause, and I don't want her to see it.

"I can find the orphanage now," I say. "You don't have to come."

But Amkha reaches for the gun and shows me how it tucks inside her loose blouse, almost without showing. She wants to help me. I nod and smile, thanking her.

We get ready to go. The man lying on the sidewalk recedes to the back of my mind. I am only a few miles from Song now. So close.

Amkha has the pistol under her blouse as we go through the door into the front room of the herb store. She stands casually at the counter, speaking pleasantly to the Chinese wife, joking with her about something.

Then it occurs to me how easily Amkha is coping with this situation. Effortlessly. Willingly. And I begin to wonder if it is all too willingly.

25

TOO EASY

It was easy. Too easy, I think. Making my way out of the States and to Thailand, then escaping from Bangkok, and now getting out of Chiang Mai.

The Mercedes diesel minibus takes us through the center of town. I count ten passengers, including Amkha and me. In front of us is a European couple, a barrel-chested man with his wife, speaking German with a Bavarian accent. I eavesdrop. He is a dentist who can't leave his work behind, commenting every few minutes on the marvelous condition of the Thai people's teeth. Behind me is a middle-aged couple from Texas, relieved to be out of the humidity and riding in air-conditioned comfort again. Behind them is an older American couple with two young boys, probably grandsons they are taking around the world.

The lady at the C. K. Travel Service signed Amkha and me up for this famous "Two-Day Tour," which is supposed to take us north to the caves of Chiang Dao, then to a hill tribe village, and then to the Golden Triangle area of opium-growing fame. But we will not be completing the two-day tour. Or even one day. We will be getting off after just forty miles.

The minibus heads north on Ratchawaong Road, toward

a main shopping area. On the sidewalks people are buying, selling, haggling, probably stealing. There are billboards in English, advertising car rentals and ATMs. There is even a McDonald's, its twin arches rising above the buildings around it. Progress everywhere. A Thai boy carries a boom box on his shoulder and bounces to the music. More progress. And I know there are other intrusions of progress here: AIDS ravaging the north country, overflowing the hospitals as each year thousands of women return from their "family service" in Bangkok.

The driver stops at the Tantrapan shopping area, explaining that this is the last pickup. Through the crowd I see a collegiate-looking young man making his way toward us. I recognize him. Amkha sees him too and looks over at me concerned. It is the same young man who was bargaining with the woman at the tailor shop, only now he is without his Nike cap and backpack. He boards and nods pleasantly to all the passengers, including Amkha and me, then takes a seat in the rear.

The minibus pulls away.

All along it has been too easy. They have known where I was every step of the way.

I keep my head turned partway to the side, looking out the window and keeping an eye on the man. We cross the Ping River, passing a hillside of cliff-hanging condos like the ones in Marin County, complete with pools, solar heat, and satellite dishes. This place is an anomaly. It is an oasis. The wealthiest part of California seems to be transported here, surrounded by primitive tribes, mosquitoes, and malaria.

Behind us one of the boys speaks to the young man. He answers politely that he has been sent here by the Peace Corps. I listen carefully to his American accent. Nondistinguishable, with colorless vowels. Probably from California. Probably from Branscomb.

We head directly north on Road 11. Towns roll past, and dirt roads lead off to higher climbs. There are no power lines. No road signs. Just hills folding into more hills.

Amkha moves forward and sits by the driver, surveying the terrain. I keep shifting my attention between her and the young man in the rear. The town of Ban Ton is about fifteen miles ahead now. I look out the window, hoping for a glimpse of the rainbow Buddha of Wat Ton. But our map shows that the road does not pass directly by it. Now the young man leans his head against the window and seems to be dozing. I look forward. Amkha grows agitated, turning nervously and looking through the windows on either side as if recognizing landmarks. But it all looks the same to me, a blur of jungle woods. Raw nature. We are in the middle of nowhere.

Minutes later she turns around. Her face tells me.

I check the young man again. His eyes are closed, his head nodding forward. But I must be ready for the unexpected. Surprise is deadly because in that first instant of surprise the mind doubts what it sees and gives away the edge. I stand and glance toward him one last time, waiting for him to spring forward with a gun and stop me. He still dozes. I make my move quickly. But the aisle is now blocked by the barrel-chested dentist.

"This isn't a tourist spot," he says in perfect English. "You can't get off here."

I push him backward, but he grabs my shirt by the collar, trying to force me into my seat. I swing my elbow, a chop to his mouth. A quick shove, and he lands in his wife's lap. I shout for the driver to stop. I look around. The young man in back is now awake but as surprised as the other passengers. The dentist struggles to get up, but Amkha is there, reaching past me and pressing the Japanese gun hard against the man's face. She even knows enough to cock it. His eyes are huge and focused on the gun as he stays motionless in his wife's lap. The minibus pulls to the side of the road.

In a second Amkha and I are outside in the unforgiving heat. I wave the driver on. He closes the door. The dentist starts to the front, then sits back down and glares at us as the vehicle pulls away.

Amkha and I are alone, with only a hot breeze and the rustle of green nature around us. In a way it is a perfect spot. Not even a crossroads. No immediate reference point that we can be traced back to. My leg aches as I turn in a circle, taking in the remote and savage land. It is a harsh dose of reality, and for a moment I struggle to remember why I am here: that I am reversing the course of my life, and I hope I will save Song in the doing. Regardless, I have come too far to stop now.

Amkha still holds the gun, trembling.

"Put it away," I say, but she stands there frozen, the gun still cocked. I reach for it, and she backs away. If all along this has been a ploy and she is part of it, then this is the perfect place to kill me. I focus only on the trigger and ready myself to leap at her with the slightest movement of her finger.

"I keep," she says, studying me. Then she carefully uncocks the gun and tucks it into her waist again. She pulls her blouse over it.

With Amkha at the side of my vision, I take out the map. She points northeast, the general direction of the Wat Ton and the rainbow Buddha. Is she using her peasant's sense of the world, or is this also part of the plan? The map shows there is only jungle between us and there, about ten miles cross-country, and then steep hills. The map also indicates a dirt road a few miles north, heading to Ban Ton. But we cannot chance it.

Amkha points to some trampled-down grass leading away from the road and into the jungle woods in the general direction we want. It is just a faint path, maybe traversed by a lone woodcutter or by animals.

Something within me begins. I step off the road toward the threadlike trail. There are thorns at first, and the grass is alive with insects that swarm up into our faces. We wave them away and continue waving until we reach the edge of the jungle woods. Large ferns form a luxuriant green curtain. We brush through the ferns, to enter a dim and strangely cavernous jungle.

26

THE WAY IN

I expected a maze of branches and vines and monstrous plants that I would have to fight through. But it is like stepping into a cathedral or a forgotten temple. Dark tree trunks stretch upward a hundred feet like tall pillars. The canopy permits in only fingers of sunlight, reaching downward to where we stand. The light appears cruel and foreboding as it alternates with shadows and mixes on the ground with shades of green and black, like smudges on a painting.

The hot breeze is gone now, replaced by a hotter dampness. The jungle is silent, as if all the noisy creatures saw us coming. The branches are motionless. Here the earth is not yet shackled. It is monstrous and free, as if time has collapsed and we have traveled back to the beginning of the earth when humans still blundered about. I can hear my own breath and even feel the pounding and rush of my blood.

I search for the trail, while keeping an eye on the bulge in Amkha's blouse. The trail is just faint marks, clumps churned up on the ground. Warm water seeps into my shoes. I keep walking, limping. I push away some dead branches between trees, then hold them for Amkha to pass.

She clings to my shirt now, as if for reassurance, as she focuses on the trail and on stepping over roots without tripping.

I have no instinct for the outdoors. There is no geometry here, no straight lines, no ready-made formulas. Just curves and forks and winding tangents, everything voluptuous and reckless and unrestrained. I long for the familiarity of a rectangular door or the precision of a straight street with perfect intersections.

Then something familiar grabs my eye: a small geometric design, a perfect octagon, five inches wide, brown and flat and raised on a stick a foot above the brown ground. It is a sensor. Twenty-meter range in all directions. I look around but can see no others. How many have we passed? How many are ahead? Electronic eyes everywhere. I have come all this distance, and still someone sits in a tech room studying me: I am an iridescent green blip moving across someone's tracking screen. I am overwhelmed by the futility of it all.

There are parrot voices above, laughing at me, or maybe they are encouraging me on. I point out the sensor to Amkha, but she doesn't understand. I search for more sensors and see only strange-looking mushrooms that sprout from rotting trunks.

I am determined to continue. I go forward, and Amkha follows. We hit a patch of bleached sunlight where the canopy opens overhead. At our feet are tiny flowers, brilliant violet and orange. Gnats play in the light. As we pass through the light, I can taste the sun's warmth.

Then Amkha clutches my wrist and points to a brown and yellow crack in the earth. I freeze. The crack moves, winding away from us. It stops, and again it is just a crack in the earth. We wait, and the crack slithers away.

I mop my face with my sleeve, which has been torn by some low branches. Amkha raises the front of her shirt to wipe the perspiration from her forehead. Fragments from leaves stick to her hair, and I brush them away. She smiles and coughs. There is an odd kind of dust in the air, tiny particles of mold or shredded leaves floating.

We walk through mud and over more roots. The jungle is lush with oxygen and rich with damp smells. Even with the map and keeping an eye on the flirting sun, I am no longer certain our direction is correct. I am exhausted, and my body craves food.

Then Amkha starts to cry. I take her wrist and encourage her forward for some distance. Suddenly there is another thick curtain of ferns. That means we have reached an outer edge of the jungle, with sunlight on the other side. We push through the ferns, and we are out, standing on a hill, looking at other hills, and down into a grassy valley.

Below are a stream and a single thatched-roof hut. We are back among some kind of humanity. The sun is lower, its yellow rays slanting from our right.

I lead Amkha down the hill on the slippery grass. Far below, the brook looks so innocent, the thatched-roof hut looks miniature and delicate. Seeing it makes me think of food and the orphanage. I wonder how far off course we are. How many more hills to go.

Amkha slips, and I catch her against me, a kind of embrace. Her head is against my mouth, and I taste the perspiration in her hair. It is sweet. For a moment there seems to be no urgency. We are just two human beings embracing. There may be no one else on the planet, and suddenly she seems so precious to me.

Then another flat octagon at my feet. This one green, hiding in the deep grass. I kick it, and it shatters.

We descend farther, side by side. A quarter of the way down I look up and can see two fingers of a huge white hand extending from behind the slope of a hill to our left. We descend a little farther, and the full arm comes into view. We reach the valley floor, and the huge Buddha faces us: bright white marble against an emerald hill.

Amkha stops.

"I never see this side of him before," she says, and bows to the marble icon, which is still a mile off. The statue is huge, one of the Buddha's hands reaching out gracefully, its palm upward to the sky as if receiving bless-

ings; the other palm raised in our direction as if waving
to us or maybe warning us to halt and go back. Around
us there is complete silence. A voice inside me emerges,
as if distantly—perhaps the statue's voice—a wordless
warning not to continue.

The sun sets lower, and I have the distinct impression
that I have lived these moments before. Or died them. Or
dreamed them. The sky changes color above me, and the
distant hills begin to change with it. Amkha bows every
few steps as the white marble statue alternately reflects
the yellow, blue, and then the red of the sky. The ground
levels as we get closer to the statue, and to the orphanage,
and to what else, I don't know.

There is another octagon in the grass. A few steps later
I see another. I imagine a thousand of them spread
throughout the valley. And that warning voice. I sense the
edge of my life creeping closer. I do not want to die. I
am afraid, and I hate myself for being afraid. But it is not
a sin to want to live. And it is not too late to go back
through the jungle and to the road, and to Bangkok, and
to my mother and sister in Ohio, and to a new job that
concerns only myself and not the world or people distant
to me, and let the world go on, the good and the bad, the
bad and the good.

I see another little octagon. I crush it beneath my feet.

My decision is made. But they know I am coming. They
even know when and from which direction. I think they
have known everything from the very beginning.

PART
III

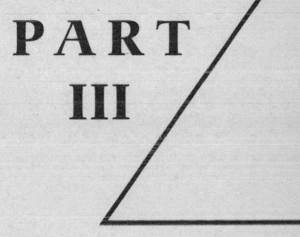

They came out of unholy dark-nesses and attacked the heavens.

—FROM DIALOGUES OF CHIOS

27

OLD FRIEND

Vaal's smile is welcoming, as if remembering our history. He looks older, of course, but not as old as I feel. He stands at the statue's feet, dwarfed by the huge Buddha which seems aflame as the white marble reflects the red sunset.

Vaal's blond hair is mixed with gray now and combed straight back in fine strands. The round-rimmed glasses give him a kind of professorial look. I come closer and see those blue eyes. He chuckles amiably as he points to my torn shirt and mud-caked shoes. *"Ni de yang tze chen nan ken,"* he says in Chinese. You're a sight.

"Tu m'as fait prendre un petit voyage," I reply. You've sent me on a bit of a trip.

"Da," he answers, then shakes his head at me. There is a smile on his face, but it is a pained smile. *"Mojet bit tebe ne nado bilo prihodit suda, Petr,"* he says, and there is a hint of anger or frustration in the words. Maybe you shouldn't have come here, Peter.

"Maybe not," I reply in English, ending the language game. "But I'm here."

He grips my shoulders with two hands, ignoring the sweat and dirt. I can feel the strength in his arms. Despite

195

the professorial look, he has stayed fit all these years and still has a powerful and athletic body. Vaal steps back and extends his hand. I take it, cautiously, unsure whether we are meeting now as friends or foes.

He smiles again, a troubled smile. His eyes are tired, with dark circles under them, and his face seems drained. Vaal is dressed like an executive on his day off: golfing shirt, casual slacks, and Reebok walking shoes. His shirt could be worn more loosely, but he has it tucked in, perhaps to show that he is not concealing a gun.

The burly German dentist has undoubtedly reached the orphanage by now and reported that Amkha is carrying a revolver. But Vaal says nothing about it. He puts a hand on my shoulder again. "Mosquitoes will be up in a few minutes, Peter. Best we be getting in."

I look up at the tall statue of the Buddha. The sun has dropped below the hills, and the marble is now the same faint purple color as the air. I see that enigmatic smile and the half-closed eyes that seem to gaze down on Vaal and Amkha and me. I hear the sound of water and see a trickle running over the Buddha's feet at the base of the statue. Vaal notices my interest. "Sixteenth century," he says with admiration in his voice. "Really something, isn't it?"

He points back through the valley. "About two miles off there's a monastery in some caves. When the Japanese came through in the forties, the monks went underground so they could escape the world and live undisturbed." Then Vaal adds pointedly, "Of course, we can't escape the world, can we, Peter? We can only try to make it better."

I nod.

"Come on," he says.

He leads us around the side of the Buddha. I have an eerie feeling that the statue is turning its head, following us with its eyes. I actually glance up, but it remains facing forward, motionless and detached.

Jungle growth rises up behind the statue. Vaal steps into a nearly invisible trail. We walk for about twenty yards with wide leaves brushing the length of our bodies. Then we are out and standing on a ridge.

The ground descends steeply before us, then flattens into a valley. There is a clearing in it, and in the clearing are a half dozen stucco buildings—the so-called orphanage—surrounded by a stone wall. The orphanage looks serene from this distance, like a villa seeming to float in the valley with a kind of surreal strangeness.

Darkness comes fast, and the trees, the valley, and the villa itself glide into a velvety black. Vaal puts up a hand, telling us to wait. An amber light begins to glow around the stone wall until it circles the orphanage like a halo. The halo grows brighter, and I realize it is from special sodium bulbs, timed to go on at nightfall. Now I see that the bulbs are lighting a bare dirt perimeter that runs just outside the wall.

"Watch your step," Vaal says softly. He leads the way.

The amber light helps illuminate our path downward. We descend surprisingly easily, as if on a walkway. In minutes we reach the valley floor and push through more layers of jungle growth to arrive at the edge of the dirt perimeter in front of the wall. The dirt is raked. It is a kind of dry moat with no path through it. Vaal sidesteps at the edge of the dirt, and keeps sidestepping until he comes to a narrow stone path and a simple black-and-white sign staked to the ground. In Thai script it identifies the place as *kon kampra,* an orphanage.

"It's safe to cross here," he says, pointing to the path. "But don't step off it." He turns to Amkha and repeats the instruction in Thai, to make sure she understands.

We go forward in single file. At the wall there is a heavy iron gate with a mossy archway. I hear muted voices, young women's voices. With two hands Vaal forces the iron gate open. It creaks noisily, and the women's voices change to a whisper. He steps aside and motions for me to enter first, then Amkha, who clings to me quivering.

Vaal enters last, pushing hard on the gate. It closes behind us with a loud clang. Then he slides a bolt into place, and I hear the click of a heavy lock. I have arrived at *Tee Natiew.* Wonderful Place.

*　　*　　*

I am so close. I can even picture a happy ending.

Steven Vaal and I sit at a table in one of the stucco buildings. The room is lit only by a candle in the middle of the table. Somewhere in the background is the drone of the generator supplying energy to the perimeter lights. Occasionally there are voices from other rooms and perhaps other buildings.

I still feel danger, but there is also opportunity. Songkha Chattkatavong is somewhere inside this compound. Maybe I can buy her freedom. Or Vaal will just let me take her away. Maybe she is nothing to the Plan. One more body. One more set of legs.

Our meal is Thai noodles with a few shrimp. Mexican food is hot; Thai food is incendiary. So along with an expensive bottle of Chardonnay, there is a large pitcher of cool water. All of it is served by a young Indonesian girl, about fifteen, who has made several trips in and out, her head bowed all the while, not daring to look us in the face.

At my insistence, Amkha is here too. But she keeps her distance from Vaal, squatting alone peasant style in a dim corner. A bowl rests on her knee as she eats hungrily. She does not take her eyes off me.

"Tell me what's happening in the States," Vaal says, breaking the silence. His attitude is too casual and too pleasant. He pours more wine, as if we are dining at a Parisian café.

"I was only there four or five days," I reply, my mind trying to anticipate what is coming. "Not long enough to catch the mood."

"I'm only in and out of there myself. God, I really miss it." The corners of his eyes crinkle. "We're a long way from Branscomb, aren't we?"

I nod. "You were going to avoid the chloroform life," I say. "And change the world. Did you do it?"

"To an extent, maybe," he answers. "And you were going to find happiness living on the edge. Did you find it, Peter?" he asks in a half-mocking tone.

I don't have to answer because he knows I didn't.

He puts his glass down. Despite the friendly conversation, I sense a hardness about him, or maybe it's a kind of settledness that comes with a certainty about one's life and the actions one has chosen. So different from the way I feel.

"We both thought life was some kind of game," he continues. "But games have rules, and life doesn't." There's a bite in his voice. "The world's a damn street fight, Peter. What's fair one day might not be fair the next."

"What did the Fantasy Plan uncover?" I ask.

His tone is softer. "I'm happy to see you. I really am. But I'm sad you made it this far. I never should have assigned you to the Fantasy Plan in the first place."

"It's your operation, isn't it? Leamer works for you?"

He nods. "And it's only right that you know I'm the one who had you dismissed."

"Yes," I say. "You are DeForest."

"And right now I wish I weren't. I wish I were one of those people back home in a car pool on their way to an eight to five, and worried about the dandelions in the lawn."

"But then you couldn't change the world."

Vaal laughs heartily. "Still the same humor," he says.

"Why don't you just say what you're getting at, Steven?"

"It's simple, Peter. There are things more important than you. More important than me. There's a world to be maintained, and things aren't always fair. The Work comes first."

"I think I understand that."

"No, you don't," he snaps. "Every operation you were on, you put yourself first. You let yourself get absorbed. Everyplace you went you gave away a piece of yourself. There's no room for that. You've got to stay detached and steady—no matter what—or you can't keep the perspective."

Vaal looks up at the ceiling and takes a breath. "Initially I assigned you to the Plan because I saw the chance for us to work together. I guess it was my own stupid sentimentality that wanted to bring you on. I should have known you couldn't take it. If there's one thing I learned from this, it's that there's no room for personal feelings, Peter. The stakes are too high.''

He sips his wine. "So when I saw the video of you and that girl, I had you transferred out of Bangkok." Vaal eyes me strangely. "What is it with you and her anyway?"

"She doesn't deserve what you've done to her."

"How much of yourself did you give away this time?"

I feel stupid and ashamed and cannot bring myself to look at him. "Is she here?" I ask.

He shakes his head noncommittally. "Actually, in this case your sentimentality ended up working to everyone's favor. We dismissed you back at headquarters, expecting you to try to find her. After they went through your apartment and found the photo in the paper towel roll, I knew you would. You're pretty easy to figure out. I even guaranteed them at headquarters that you'd be back."

"Is that why nobody stopped me?"

"Practically escorted you the whole way, just to make sure you didn't change your mind."

"Not for old times' sake, I suppose."

"I wish, Peter. Shit, I really wish. But I wanted you back because you're important to the Plan."

"Then why didn't you just assign me here?"

"We'll get to that. First there's the little matter of the gentleman you killed at the Fantasy Store."

That seems like a century ago, a different life. But my body tenses as I recall it. "He wasn't a gentleman," I say. "He was a murderer."

"For now let us say he was both. You did a lot of damage to the Plan. We didn't expect that. He was a physicist, and we needed him."

"What has the Fantasy Plan uncovered?" I demand.

The flickering candlelight accents the hollows of Vaal's face, making him look like an alien. "There are ingredients out there for an international collision of proportions you can't imagine," he says.

"Those ingredients are always out there. That's your job security," I add, not hiding the sarcasm.

"The Fantasy Plan is our security. And I don't mean just for us personally but for all Americans and the Japanese too. And Chinese, British, and Russian as well. Maybe a million lives are at stake. We have to stop it all before it happens."

"And for some reason you need sentimental me."

Vaal chuckles. "Yes, sentimental you. But I have to admit you surprised me when you killed that physicist at the Fantasy Store. I didn't think you were capable of that again."

"Again?"

He is silent a moment and checks Amkha, who has finished eating and is trying to listen. "After the elimination," he answers quietly, gauging my expression.

It is seconds before I realize what he is talking about: the old man in Kyoto two years ago. Things become clearer.

"I had hopes for you then, Peter. But I had to see if you could put aside your sympathies. Actually you performed better than I expected. You followed through all the way, though it was messy. But afterward you couldn't handle it emotionally. You disappeared for weeks. You probably still worry about him."

"Who was he?"

"You see, you do worry about him." Vaal shakes his head, as if I am stupid and completely missing the point. "God, I never should have assigned you to the Plan. It was my fault."

Anger mounts in me. "He wasn't some leader in the Yakuza, was he? He was just an old man on his way home to his family at night. Just a little test for me. A victim of no importance, is that it?"

Vaal leans forward, his own voice rising. "How can you be so smart and so stupid at the same time, Peter? That old man's life is a small thing compared to what's about to happen out there."

"What did the Plan uncover?" I say again.

Steven Vaal nods as if it is time for me to know. He drains the glass of wine, then pushes back his plate and stands. For a moment he stretches. "Come," he says. "Let me show you the grounds."

28

TRINITY TWO

*T*here is only one reason Vaal would give me this night tour: to impress upon my mind that Wonderful Place is escape-proof, that even the contemplation of escape is a waste of time.

"It's a fortress," he assures me as we walk through the compound, "a fortress designed to keep people in."

But I see no guard towers, no patrols, no dogs, not even any sensors. Ironically that creates a psychological deterrence more effective than any physical one. The mind suspects there is much more here than an unguarded stone wall with rotting mortar.

Amkha stays close to my side, gripping my hand tightly and keeping her distance from Vaal as we come closer to the wall. He must know Amkha has the revolver. But he does not even glance at her.

Over our heads there is only the black night. But around us is the glow of the amber lights aimed over the walls, with splinters of yellow reflecting back on the villa buildings and trees. I can see that Wonderful Place may actually have been an orphanage once or perhaps a poor monastery; now it is just a kind of prison.

"I met your assistant," I say.

"My assistant?" He raises his eyebrows. "Oh, you mean Catherine. Well, she stretches things a bit. But she does work for me. She happened to be in the States when you were dismissed, so we decided to use her. She's on short-term contracts, just like you were, but I think she'll make career level. She's totally committed. I guess you found that out."

"Where is she now?"

"Around here somewhere."

As we walk, Vaal points out that the mossy walls are only eight and a half feet high at most, and in places the stones have crumbled even lower. "Quite an easy jump," he says. "One leap and you're over."

"And into a minefield," I say, picturing the raked dirt perimeter we came through. "If it really *is* a minefield."

"You think it's a hoax?"

"The guards at Alcatraz invented the story of San Francisco Bay's being shark-infested. It made escape seem even more hopeless."

He doesn't reply.

"Why not use safer technology?" I ask. "Like infrared scanners."

"It wouldn't be a deterrent. The people don't understand technology. So we have to use old methods. Primitive but effective. We've had a few sad incidents, but after that word got around."

I scrutinize each quadrant as we walk, counting eight stucco buildings in all. There is candlelight through some windows and shadow movements inside. Two of the buildings have reflecting windows. "How many people work here?" I ask.

"Enough to get the job done. Over there is our tech room, where we monitor the sensors. The whole area is scanned for miles."

Amkha is looking around nervously, seeming to shiver in the hot air. I have no way of knowing exactly what happened to her in these buildings or the horror of the memories coming back to her now. I loosen her grip from my wrist and take her hand firmly in mine.

At the far end of the grounds we come to a low point in the wall, where it has crumbled to chest level. Vaal rests his arms on top of the stones and gazes out at the flat dirt perimeter. We stand there together, taking in the night, listening to chattering and scratching from the small jungle animals on the other side. The amber lights make the perimeter soil look sandy, like the surface of the moon. The lights shine across it, onto tall grasses and giant palms that disappear upward into the night. Neither of us speaks for several minutes, each of us waiting for the other's move.

"Little Boy and Fat Man," he finally says.

"What?"

"The names of the two bombs we dropped on Japan. At the surrender their leaders agreed they'd renounce war forever. Of course they didn't have a choice. We took charge of their military and wrote their constitution, including the part about them never having any offensive forces again—land, air, or sea."

"So they got smart," I say. "Now their offense is computers and cars and fiber optics, and the Fantasy Plan is probably going to rewrite those rules too. Is that what this is all about?"

"Hardly. After the war, nobody thought Japan would ever recover. They didn't get billions in aid like Europe did. Hell, they didn't get any aid at all. Through brains and hard work, in a relatively short time they went from having no economy to having the world's most productive economy. Now other nations are demanding sanctions against them, claiming the Japanese are monopolizing technologies and outmaneuvering the competition, then buying them up. And the more Japan gets bashed, the more some of its leaders realize how difficult it will be to secure their nation's stability over the long run. Western nations look down the road about thirty years, but an ancient nation like Japan looks down the road three hundred years."

"So you devised the Fantasy Plan to destabilize them," I say.

"Actually you're the one who gave me the idea. Control a man's fantasies, and you control the man. Get him by the balls and he's all yours."

My mind races back to our conversation in Brussels. A pleasant evening over wine and pretzels, a private conversation, a personal revelation, now twisted and used for access. Access. Or is Vaal playing with me?

"Hold his balls," Vaal continues, "and you can control a corporation or a government."

"You don't need my help for that, Steven. Why am I here?"

"Remember the letter the Japanese delivered to Roosevelt? It said every nation had to find its proper station in the world. The next day they attacked Pearl Harbor."

"So? That was half a century ago."

"But their nationalism hasn't changed. They're a society based on race, aren't they? And as Japan gets bashed from around the world the new prime minister and one of his senior cabinet ministers are thinking that other nations ought to be taught respect again. They're reconsidering the old way, a ladder of nations with the superior nation on top."

"Except Japan's already on top," I counter with a laugh.

"But economics runs in cycles. You know they've always viewed themselves as islanders, alone in the world and under siege. Circle the wagons and all that, like in the Tokugawa era, and again in the 1930s."

"The Organization has the siege mentality, Steven," I say. "What does the Organization think the Japanese are going to do, build another war machine?"

For the first time Vaal checks Amkha's expression to see if she is following the conversation. She is not even looking at us but huddling close to me, her head turned back toward the buildings.

"Yes," he says quietly. "Another war machine. Bigger and better than last time."

I shake my head incredulously. "Has the Organization

gone paranoid, Vaal? You can always conjure up a new villain. Who's next, Polynesia?''

"I'm sharing facts, Peter, not speculation.''

"Your facts are wrong. The Japanese are against any kind of military buildup.''

"The Japanese *people* are against any kind of military buildup,'' he replies sharply. "But there's an office buried in their defense bureaucracy that's developing offensive weapons again, with the consent of the new prime minister. Its code name is *dai ni san mi ittai*—Trinity Two. It's happening. It's a reality. I'm telling you because I need you to understand.''

"I don't believe it. We've got treaties. Japan's already protected under our nuclear umbrella.''

"Treaties? Are you stupid? They saw us abandon Vietnam. They saw us drop Taiwan like a hot potato and recognize the People's Republic. And we haven't done a damn thing about North Korea's nuclear buildup. As we stand here the Chinese have three hundred nuclear warheads mounted on intermediate- and long-range missiles, bombers, and subs. Japan's prime minister understands the West, Peter. He knows if push comes to shove we're not going to rush out to save yellow skin again. We'd rally all right—around America. You'd see bumper stickers across the U.S. saying Remember Pearl Harbor. It would be payback time.''

Vaal checks Amkha again. She seems hypnotized by one of the buildings behind us. "Japan has the fourth largest defense budget in the world, behind France and Germany,'' he continues. "Last year thirty-eight percent of their defensive money went for offensive research at Trinity Two. First-strike capabilities. They're famous for first strikes, or don't you remember?''

"It would take them decades to match our military or even the Chinese military.''

Vaal's face is set and hard. "Except Trinity Two is like a sequel to a bad movie. The original Trinity was the code name of that site near Alamogordo, New Mexico, where Oppenheimer developed Little Boy and Fat Man. Now the

Trinity Two team has their own versions of Little Boy and Fat Man.''

I shake my head in disbelief. ''Not after what their people experienced in World War Two, and their government's efforts to disarm the nuclear nations.''

''Unsuccessful efforts. And now they're importing plutonium waste. Tons of it.''

''For their reactors, for chrissakes!''

''They don't need plutonium for their reactors. Uranium is cheaper, and there's enough uranium out there to run every fucking reactor in the world for a hundred years. So why are they importing plutonium? And why are they continuing to build breeder reactors that produce even more plutonium, when other countries have stopped building them? Go ahead and tell me why, Peter. There's only one reason.''

''You're trying too hard to convince me, Vaal. What's the real story? What are you covering up?''

He gives me a strange look, as if he has just noticed me for the first time and doesn't like what he sees.

''I'm telling you a secret office in the Japanese government is preparing the nuclear option. First strike. And Trinity Two has already detonated a nuclear device on an island in the Pacific. Just one explosion, Peter, about a quarter of the size of what hit Hiroshima.'' Vaal smiles knowingly. ''But they were clever and timed it with a Chinese detonation so the tremors might be confused as coming from China. They're conducting the rest of their research through computer simulations. Input the data, add the variables, and see what happens. You've got virtual A-bombs. It's like test-crashing a holocaust on a computer. Doesn't pollute the air and the world community doesn't have to know. And Japan's space research already gives them the technology they need for missile systems to deliver a bomb just about anywhere.''

''Then leak it to the press. The Japanese people would be so outraged they'd shut 'em down in an hour.''

''Even if we turned over all our evidence, the Trinity Two team would just claim it was defense research. It would look like more Japan bashing on our part." Vaal faces me squarely. "Six months away, maybe nine, and secretly they'll have everything in place."

"That still doesn't mean they're a danger to us," I counter.

"What it means is they won't need our protection anymore. What it means is we lose control of the region and Japan becomes the dominant power. What it means is that a nation with a militaristic and expansionist history can make its own decisions against China or Russia or North Korea and against any other country, including us, that it sees as a threat. And if Japan's leaders can eventually convince the people that in the long run military power and not economics offers them the greatest security, what do you think the people will do? I'll tell you. They'll follow like worker ants."

He pauses to let it sink in. "But we can stop it or at least stall it for some time because the Fantasy Plan got us the access—a couple of Trinity Two scientists on film, in rather compromising positions you might say. A Dr. Inoki and a Dr. Kenji Yanaga."

"Then use them to stop it. You still don't need me."

"Dr. Inoki is dead. You killed him."

"So use the other one."

"Yes, Dr. Yanaga is the key now. If things go right, we'll have access within a few weeks. Hardly anyone in the world will know, Peter, but we will have maintained the balance of power on the planet again."

There is no bragging in Vaal's voice, no conceit on his face, no grandiose gesture or heroic undertone to anything about him; just a matter-of-fact firmness. Another day at the office.

"And what's the cost?" I say.

"Minimum."

"Just the women here," I correct him. "And the others in Bangkok."

"Wake the hell up, Gaines. What do you think sacrifice is anyway? Ask any American or Japanese or Chinese if having those girls lie on their backs is worth the access we'll get. They have it a hell of a lot easier than a lot of soldiers."

"And the children here. Are they soldiers too?"

"God, you're missing the point. There's only a handful, and personally I was against using them. But we don't have to agonize over right and wrong here. The costs are small, and the gains are enormous, absolutely enormous—not only for us but for everyone in Asia, including the Japanese people. What'll happen if Trinity·Two completes its program, and then the prime minister sees a need to threaten China or North Korea, and one of them decides to strike Japan first? How many will die then? Go calculate."

"Calculate," I repeat. "It's all fucking statistics to you. But it's the girls and the children who pay the price, not you."

"I don't pay a price?" The anger grows on his face. "You think I want all this? Shit. I don't want any of it. But life's a trade-off, and it's going to cost a few more lives. Three to be exact. For the sake of thousands, maybe millions."

"A trade-off," I whisper to myself. I think of Lisa from New Mexico, with red stripes down her body. Disgust rises in me. My eyes go to Amkha's waist. Vaal knows about the revolver but he let us keep it, maybe hoping to win me over. He wants me on his side. But why? I can reach for the gun right now and end this. I imagine Vaal's expression as I pull out the revolver and take control. I could just shoot him. One more man killed. My heart beats rapidly, more from excitement than fear.

But the numbers. They are so reasonable in my mind, so sane. A few for the sake of thousands. Logic speaks loudly. I can't afford to think of just myself, or even Song, if so many lives are at stake.

Vaal stares across the eerily lighted perimeter to the thick jungle wall. I face him, the revolver no longer in my thoughts. "You said three lives to get this access."

"Come," he says without looking at me. "The mosquitoes are biting, and we should be getting inside."

"Who are they?" I demand.

29

DARWIN'S UNIVERSE

Vaal does not answer. And he will not tell me why he needs me here.

He turns and heads back toward the buildings. Amkha watches him, then squeezes my hand. She is uncomfortable in the night and with Vaal, and the mosquitoes are eating her. I had hardly noticed them but now realize that the ones circling the amber lights are finding their way to where we stand.

We follow Vaal past one of the stucco buildings to another small building. He opens the door and steps in, disappearing for a moment. Then a match is struck, and a candle lit. A soft glow blossoms over the room. It is not a hut but an attractive cottage, its familiarity so inviting, creating a kind of universal coziness. Overhead a fan moves slowly, and there are two single beds, a dresser, and even a bookcase offering a number of volumes. Attractive ruffled curtains around the windows complete the quaint look of a vacation home.

Vaal gestures around the room, telling us it is ours. "There are no locks here," he says casually. "No need for them. Good night, Peter." He goes to the door, then turns back. "Oh, by the way, the revolver won't do you any good. Why don't you just give it to me?"

Amkha understands. She looks at me and shakes her head.

"Why didn't you take it when we got here?" I say.

"Because you would have thought we were on different sides. You wouldn't have listened or understood that we both want the same thing, a peaceful world for as many people as possible." He steps toward Amkha and holds out his hand. "Give me the gun, please," he says.

Amkha reaches under her blouse and removes the weapon. It is heavy, and she raises it in both hands, pointing it directly at Vaal.

His expression hardens. "Give me the gun," he repeats. *"Churn khrup!"* Now!

She takes a step back, moving her thumbs onto the hammer. But this is not the time to fight. Five bullets are not enough against Vaal and Rennard and who knows how many others guarding this place. And the old pistol could even explode in Amkha's face.

"It's okay," I say, already searching my mind for another plan. "Give it to him."

Vaal moves closer to her. "I'm afraid you're going to hurt yourself," he says casually, then springs at her and snatches the gun away. He turns it around and levels it at Amkha. "You bitch!" he shouts, and pulls the hammer all the way back. "You want to see how it works?"

I move quickly in front of Amkha. "Don't, Vaal! You have no right!"

"I have every right!" he shouts, keeping the gun on us. His hands are shaking with fury. "You're the one who had no right to bring her here. Another sentimental mistake, Gaines. God damn you!"

He uncocks the revolver and lowers it. "There's no escape," he repeats. "I promise. So don't try." Still shaking with anger, he turns and leaves.

Amkha is trembling with fear. "You are very brave," I say.

"Why you not fight him?" she shouts angrily. "He very bad man. Use girls." She begins to cry. "He take me for pleasure two times. Hurt me."

I reach for her and hold her, stroking her hair as she hugs me around the waist, still crying. "He won't hurt you any more," I promise her. I wait until she relaxes in my embrace. Then I sit down on the bed, and my mind swims in all of Vaal's words: Giving away pieces of myself. The Japanese—siege mentality. A ladder of nations. Economic collapse. Trinity Two. Only Dr. Yanaga is left. Japanese worker ants. We can halt it. And the cost. Women soldiers on their backs. Three lives. We both want the same thing, a peaceful world for as many people as possible.

Yes, I can see the possibilities. Nationalism again leading to imperialism. It is every nation's dream, but not every nation has the military might.

I look around the room. No bars on the windows. No lock on the door. A pitcher of cool water on the dresser, and two glasses, as if he'd known exactly how many were coming. Clean clothes in the drawers: folded shirts and pants. Dozens of books on the bookshelf: the works of Thomas Hardy, poems by Shakespeare and Shelley. And the Bible, resting beside a pocket version of the Buddha's sermons.

Everything so civilized in this charming cottage. It masks a world of Darwinism; no, it masks an entire universe of Darwinism swirling our planet and solar system. The primal earth cools; we crawl out of the dark sink and after aeons climb up into a human swamp. There are only a handful of absolutes. The rest we make up as we go along. We learn to wear clothes, put on civil faces, take up manners of a culture, and then begin eating one another. The strong eat the weak and then battle others who are strong. And there are so few who want to stop it.

I am angry at Vaal for using Amkha and who knows how many others. But now exhaustion is overtaking me. My body clock is still halfway around the world, and I shake my head furiously, trying to fling off the sleep. I have not forgotten Song. I have not forgotten why I came here. I will just set the candle down and lie back on the bed and pull a sheet over my clothes. I won't sleep, only rest a few minutes, then get up and search the other buildings for Song. But it is such an exertion just to think of it. The sheets feel cool and fresh. My head quickly sinks into a heaviness, and I long to lighten my mind with restful dreams.

The bed shifts as there is a weight next to me. Amkha slides in, the single bed requiring that she nestle close. She is still trembling, and I pull her against me.

The mountain air has cooled, and the warmth of her is so comforting that for a moment the cruel Darwinian universe flees from my mind. I breathe more evenly and caress Amkha's shoulder, running my hand down her arm. I am so tired. I don't have to find Song tonight. In the morning. For now it would be so soothing just to lay my hand on Amkha's stomach and feel it rise and fall. I let my hand sweep down her shoulder to the small of her back. Her skin is so smooth. I pull her more tightly against me. My mind wanders, and I think of rolling over and embracing her. Is it my imagination, or are her hips thrust out to me in invitation?

Then that Darwinian universe comes back to me. It is chaos. Chaos. Despite the coziness of this cottage, Wonderful Place is a sex school; its purpose to elicit the animal in us. In me.

I loosen my embrace of Amkha. Her breathing is soft and regular. Already she is asleep.

30

CHAMELEON

The door jolts open. Catherine Rennard steps inside and looks down at me in bed, then at Amkha, who sits up quickly, clutching the sheet against her bare breasts.

"Thank you for knocking," I say.

"Everything is wide open here," she remarks in a matter-of-fact tone.

"That's what I hear," I say.

Rennard is wearing no makeup, but the light freckles under her eyes make her look even younger than before. Now this chameleon could be a good-looking mother in the bleachers of a Little League game or at a ballet studio watching her young daughter practice.

She points to Amkha. "You never should have taken her out of Bangkok, Gaines. You're even softer than we thought. And you've only made things worse for her."

"Why did Vaal want me here?" I say.

"Vaal?"

"Charles DeForest," I say, correcting myself.

"He doesn't tell me everything. From the beginning he only said he didn't want you hurt."

I throw back the covers and stand, still in my clothes from yesterday. "He says you're not his assistant," I announce.

"Not officially maybe. But I fill in. Sort of a Jane-of-all-trades."

"Sort of good at being whoever you need to be."

"Catherine Rennard *is* my real name," she says sharply.

"Of course. And your middle name really is Penny," I add, "but your family made jokes—"

"Stop it!" She nods toward Amkha. "That one has to go back. She's trouble."

"And what will happen to her?"

"Nothing."

Rennard is lying, of course. They will kill Amkha. She is one life that Vaal has indicated is expendable. Song's life is probably another.

"It's almost time for the first meal," Rennard announces. "Everything is run strictly by the clock here."

"Amkha stays with me," I say.

"Someone is coming for her."

"She stays with me," I repeat.

"All right, get ready then," she declares sternly, trying to stay in command. She turns and leaves.

It takes Amkha and me only a few minutes to wash, sponging ourselves with cold water from a basin. I put on a fresh shirt and pants from the dresser. I hold out a clean jumpsuit that was left for Amkha, powder blue, with a zipper down the front. She won't touch it, and without comment she slips back into yesterday's clothes.

We step outside, and Rennard is waiting. I see the grounds in the daylight for the first time. There is a grassy quadrangle in the middle of the buildings. In the distance is the wall. Beyond it is the emerald jungle, and rising behind the jungle is the top of the Buddha, its back to the orphanage. In the morning light the rear of its head sparkles a beautiful pinkish yellow.

"DeForest says you're in charge here," I say to Rennard.

"Exercise time," she announces, and stands waiting.

A moment later a man emerges from one of the buildings: the burly dentist, wearing a side holster, with what looks like a .45 automatic. He is followed by his wife. The dentist eyes Amkha and me, suppressing a grin.

He pulls a whistle from his pocket and blows it shrilly. Almost instantly twenty-five to thirty young women—all of them Fawns—spring from two other buildings and group into a militarylike formation, three ranks deep. It is like a Japanese corporation where the day begins by massing together for calisthenics and a pep talk. As in a Japanese corporation, each of them wears an identical work uniform, a one-piece jumper like the one left for Amkha. These are the soldiers for the cause, except there are no names on their uniforms, just numbers stenciled above the pockets.

I search the ranks for the one face I am looking for. From where I stand it seems the majority of them are Thai or Burmese, but there are also a few Caucasians, maybe Americans. There are no children, but there is one Fawn who is either African or African American. Black slavery again. Then I notice two boys in the ranks, one an Asian and the other apparently Caucasian, both in their early teens, thin with attractive, angular faces. All of them stand perfectly still and attentive.

The whistle sounds again, two short bursts this time, followed by one long. The Fawns begin a series of stretches, followed by side bends, jumping jacks, and other exercises, a memorized regimen that requires no additional commands. They all look so much alike in their uniforms. Or has Song changed so much? Or is it possible that I have forgotten what she looks like or have altered her appearance in my mind?

Amkha clings to me, her forehead against my sleeve like a shy child. She once was in such a formation.

"Physical exercise in the morning and then again in the late afternoon," Rennard announces.

"For body tone obviously," I remark, and watch her face.

"Bodies are important," she answers unapologetically. "But for the Plan they have to learn basic language studies too. Over there," she says, pointing to a stucco building off to our right, with reflecting windows. "Japanese and English conversation."

I point to the building next to it, also with mirrored windows. "And let me guess. Over there you have courses in 'human relations,' where they are forced to watch certain types of films. And you hope they'll get used to it all and will no longer be embarrassed and humiliated. Then you'll make them perform those same acts till a shell forms over their minds and every perversion will be as ordinary as eating rice."

The dentist shouts at one of the Fawns who is lagging behind. A few others seem to weaken as the exercises take their toll. The dentist's wife shouts and prods them.

"Seems you've got it all figured out," she says. "But you're forgetting the pictures of Nagasaki: skin melting off bodies, limbs fused together, swollen heads from radiation. If we lose this access, next time it'll be Beijing or Pyongyang or San Francisco. In the real world, Gaines, we have to choose which wrongs are acceptable."

"That seems to be the party line."

"And it's the right one. Look, I used to be squeamish about this before I understood the importance of it."

I know too well what she means and how it happens. The more horrific your job in the Work, the more desensitized you have to become, not denying the horror of it, just affirming its necessity. Results count. Disassociation with the means becomes a necessity. After a while the emotional well dries up.

"What about the woman in Bangkok," I say, "the one with slices all over her body? What are your justifications for that?"

She points a finger at me. "It's you men, Gaines." Her eyes are hard and accusing. "Don't blame me because every one of you has some sex fantasy that drives you crazy. All we're doing is tapping those fantasies to trap the ones who can stop the Trinity Two project."

"You think that you're holding the world together, that men raping these girls can stop violence in the world. Whatever happened to the gentler sex?"

"Gentler sex," she repeats scornfully. "Look, I didn't start out with you big boys at Branscomb. I came up the hard way, from a nothing family. Back when you were studying Chinese and Latin, I was trying to survive in New York as a waitress and a model. I got lucky and became friends with some dignitaries at the UN."

"Friends, like up close and personal, I bet."

"Yeah, I fucked them, Gaines. I fucked UN dignitaries, from dozens of countries. Is that what you want me to admit? Yeah, I was a prostitute."

"And then the Organization offered you a chance to fuck the dignitaries on film."

She doesn't flinch. "I gave them access. And I showed headquarters there was more to me than bedroom talents. They saw how capable I was, and after a while they put me on contract, small assignments at first, but then they gave me this training center."

"So you worked your way up to the bottom," I say, pointing to the exercising group.

"There isn't a more important assignment," she snaps back.

"You and DeForest make a fine team. But you're still a prostitute."

"And what are you, Gaines?" She smiles at me now, a knowing smile.

Her words are more than a slap. They are a club across my face. I've followed orders, more accommodating than any prostitute, even killing the old man in Kyoto without challenging the reason.

Rennard's lips bend to a thin, superior smile, as if she knows some dirty secret from my past. "And what is your fantasy, Peter?" She points to Amkha. "Is she your fantasy? Should I tell you something about your little whore here?"

I squeeze Amkha tighter. "Leave her alone," I say.

"Oh, no, this is show-and-tell time. She's a novice, Gaines, but she's done it all, absolutely everything, and she knows how to assess the needs of every man's fantasy, including yours. She knows how to put you at ease and perform any act you can think of, even some you've never imagined. I'm sure you've already had the pleasure.''

"I have not!" I look down at Amkha. She is struggling to follow what Rennard is saying.

Rennard smiles cruelly. "Or maybe your fantasy is rescuing young Asian girls. You're so decent, Gaines. Nothing slick or shady in your background. Let me tell you something else about this one. She can down shots of whiskey and freebase cocaine. Oh, I bet she cuddles so sweet alongside you. But all the while she's completely detached while tickling your pleasure points with her mouth or any other part of her. She's been using you, Gaines. It's nothing but a survival game for her since you took her out of Bangkok.''

Amkha understands enough. Her anger is now greater than her fear, and she goes for Rennard. I grab her and hold her back.

Rennard points at Amkha. "If she quits, she's a traitor, to us and to her family.''

"You'll kill her.''

"She'll go back to Bangkok, and we'll remind her that if she doesn't improve, her family will lose the money, and everyone in her village will know she's been making her living with her ass in the air.''

In a fury Amkha tries to step past me again. I hold her tight.

At that moment a whistle blows. The exercises change, concluding with body twists and leg splits. Suddenly the group is assembled again, standing erect as before and breathing heavily, except for two bodies that remain bent over, gasping desperately.

"So Amkha goes back to Bangkok," I say. "What about Songkha? Where is she?''

"That's another story.''

"A person! Not a story! Who was that man with Song on the video?''

"A partner of the one you killed in Bangkok. A Dr. Yanaga, and we need him.''

Anger races through me. ''The same thing has happened

to Song, hasn't it? You let some fucking physicist slice her, and now you're blackmailing him!''

"Lay off, Gaines. No one's cut her.''

"She's alive?''

"Of course she's alive. But that's not the point. The point is that through her we have the perfect access to stop Trinity Two.''

"How could she be that important?''

"Men's sex fantasies, Gaines. Yanaga wanted to command the purest virgin, and we got her for him. He wanted to ritualize it. A personal toy to relieve the many mental pressures of his nuclear research work. And now Yanaga is in our hands. The best access we could ask for.''

"And what's the cost, Rennard?''

"You know the cost. He wants her.''

"To come to Japan?''

"She had his baby, Gaines,'' she says, and laughs as if I am stupid.

I stare, dumbfounded. "You said it was my baby.''

She laughs again. "A little joke, get it?''

I feel an immense relief to be certain that I did not erase something terrible from my memory, that it was just another of Rennard's lies. Then immediately something else crowds my thought. "But you let her get pregnant,'' I say. "You can't use her anymore.''

"We *helped* her get pregnant. It's the best access. With DNA we can prove it's his, and we've already started building a case of street rape against him. Yanaga and his whole family can be shamed and shunned, and we can even have him put away if we want to. But he's holding a few cards of his own. He won't help us unless we help him.''

Then the implications begin to dawn. "No genetic link,'' I say. "Yanaga wants no genetic link to himself. No mongrels. No pollution of his gene pool. He'll cut her, Rennard. And the baby.''

"No, I think he's more reasonable than the other one.''

"But he'll kill them.''

"Yes.''

"How fucking reasonable is that?"

"Think big for once, Gaines. There are a lot of lives at stake, not just a few."

I search my mind for some counterargument. "You don't know that you can trust him! You're going to trade Song and her baby, but you don't even know that he'll stop the rearming."

"Shame is a very effective weapon in Japan."

I turn back toward the group. Many of them are still bent over, catching their breaths. Maybe Song is there somewhere. Maybe Song is that one in the second row, third from the right. No, she is shorter than Song. But I can't be sure because of the distance and the sweaty hair stuck to her face. I search them all again, comparing shapes and sizes. Fawns. Even the boys and women look so much alike in the powder blue uniforms.

Rennard starts to say something else, but I can't hear her through my fury. I want to grab her and choke her and then run to the ranks and search for Song and, if she's not there, take control somehow and go from building to building until I find her, and then we'll escape together.

Someone is shouting at me, and it is Amkha. And I realize I have left her behind and am stumbling like a drunken man toward the group. The burly dentist is ready this time. He pulls out his sidearm and steps toward me. I move quickly away from him, left to right along the first row, searching the faces, each person so different despite the uniforms. They breathe heavily, looking straight ahead with tired and empty expressions, as if I am not there at all.

The dentist grabs my shirt from behind and twists it at the neck, a stranglehold. I put up my hands as if giving up—a schoolyard ploy when you are outmatched. I slowly turn around, hands raised, then swiftly bring my fist down on the bridge of his nose. I feel it crack, and he bends over, clutching his face and catching the blood. The gun falls, and he immediately goes for it, groping on all fours. He grabs it. I kick his wrist, and the .45 spins away. I kick him again, catching him under his chin. I turn toward his wife, but she is already racing toward one of the mirrored buildings. I have only a few minutes to find Song.

I move quickly down the second rank, searching for Song, staring into more blank faces. Then the third rank. I beat back an urge to cry, and I don't know if it is for all of them together or for each of them individually. Or maybe it is for Song because she is not here. Or only for myself because I cannot find her.

Rennard shouts something at the Fawns. The three rows of uniforms abruptly face left. They begin to march around me. I quickly go to my knees to find the gun as marching feet step around me on both sides. Rennard gives another command, and they keep marching, but in place, and I can't find the gun through their legs. Rennard breaks through the lines and stoops down next to me: the chameleon, able to change speech and appearance and mood at will. Now she changes again. "You like a fight, don't you, Peter?" she says, laughing. "You never quit."

I see the gun and reach for it. Rennard pulls hard at my arm. "I like fighters, Peter," she says, now kneeling close and sliding two fingers between the buttons of my shirt, feeling my chest. Her lips are slightly parted, and her eyes are no longer hard and accusing but soft and inviting, and I remember her wild kiss at the apartment, her suddenly demanding mouth, and the brief flutter of her tongue. And now I can hear her mind—or maybe it is my mind—saying: *Dump this girl you brought with you, and dump the one you're looking for, and join us again, Peter. And we can do whatever you want, any fantasy you have. I am the teacher, and I can give you anything, fulfill every desire.*

At some perverse level something in me switches. An ancient instinct arises. There is a tingling and a momentary tensing of my muscles, and then I feel relaxed. I feel dangerous. No anger or fear. Just strength and cunning and calculation, as if half of my humanness has turned off and a confident animal part is asserting itself. Or maybe it is the reverse: My humanness has finally been switched on. I want to stop this insanity. All of it. I will begin by killing this woman called Catherine Rennard.

I push her away, searching for the gun. But Amkha already has it and is standing there, pointing the .45 at Rennard. She steps toward Rennard evenly, carefully, a glare in her eyes. The marching Fawns see her. They scream and scatter. Still aiming at Rennard, Amkha tries to pull the trigger. It doesn't budge. She struggles with two fingers to pull it. Nothing.

I move quickly toward her, and she lets the weapon slide into my hand, heavy and cold. I release the safety and spin around toward Rennard. My mind flashes to the two people I have already killed: the man in Kyoto, his splintered facial bones, and how he sat up grabbing desperately at his jaw and throat; the scientist in Bangkok, his sagging body, and the urine squirting between his legs. Catherine Rennard will be number three. And I don't care.

There is an explosion from somewhere and more screams from the Fawns and then from Amkha. I duck low and brace myself, every muscle ready, every nerve tensed and prepared for battle. Then I realize that the explosion is from the weapon in my own hand.

31

I spin downward into a blackness without end, a tunnel with no place to grasp, no place to stop my fall. I feel the reality around me becoming frighteningly small, receding each instant . . . falling.

I discover Torpakai in the snow, her torso cut in half but still wiggling like a severed worm, her arm beckoning to me. She struggles to sit up so she can look at me. A sad but loving smile.

I continue falling . . . and I see Anna's eyes, magnified behind her thick glasses, a book of Plato in her hands, and a look of horror as she steps back from me and races away. . . .

Spiraling even farther downward . . .

I see the old man in Kyoto as our paths come closer, and I wonder why he keeps such a regular schedule if he has so much to hide. His face is before me, and I raise the gun. He smiles kindly and puts out his hand to shake mine. I am the one who is afraid, and I must rise above myself and do what is necessary. . . .

I continue falling . . . and there is Lisa from New Mexico, looking in amazement at red stripes covering her body, oozing red, spurting red, and she is laughing at the stripes, saying she is only one person. . . .

225

Spiraling . . . to discover my father in his cubicle behind his desk, a pencil between his teeth as he works his calculator. I call to him, and he begins to stand, a grin on his face. His mouth moves soundlessly, and I know the words: how the world will go on without him, the good and the bad, the bad and the good. Suddenly the desk collapses, and the cubicle walls, and everything breaks into tiny pieces of glass, and then my father collapses, his ribs and then his heart shattering into tiny pieces, and my mother and my sister and I scurry to pick up the shards of his heart one by one, clutching them to our chests, our fingers bleeding. . . .

. . . spiraling . . .

. . . What is your fantasy, Gaines?

. . . What is your fantasy, Gaines?

It is Catherine Rennard's voice singing and ringing inside my head, swirling in the pool within the dark tunnel around me, everything real and unreal. . . .

Your fantasy is that Fawn Songkha Chattkatavong.

This time it is a different voice; it is my voice. . . . Your fantasy is Song, the voice continues. Not just to be with her, to look at her, to admire her . . . but to have her.

Then Song enters the dark swirl, enters my soul in a yellow flower dress as she steps onto the dirt perimeter surrounding Wonderful Place, smiling across at me, where I stand safely outside the perimeter. I know what is going to happen. I see it even before it happens: the explosion and the jumble of meat and bones. I feel her foot approaching the hidden place, and I wave her away. But she steps toward it as if God had put that place there and is now directing her foot. She stops on the spot and beckons me to step closer, her arms outstretched for me, begging me to come to her. But then I will be caught in the explosion too. And I feel as if the universe had mapped this moment out a million years ago, the exact spot where she will step, the explosion I see in my mind. The universe getting even with me; or maybe the universe is saving Song from something even much worse. . . .

*   *   *

A comforting warmth on my eyes as my mind emerges from the cloud. My eyelids flutter open to see the sunlight slanting in through a window next to me. A ceiling fan turns, offering a breath of air. Someone is standing over the bed, looking down on me.

"You're a real surprise, Peter."

The words hurt my ears and my head.

"A real surprise," he says again.

Vaal isn't smiling, but his eyes seem no less friendly than before.

"May I?" he asks, and sits down gently on the edge of the bed. "Next time you should pick on someone your own size." He chuckles lightly.

"What happened?"

"What happened is you underestimated her. A woman got the better of you."

"I guess I'm out of the club," I say weakly.

He smiles, his eyes crinkling. "You always did have a comeback."

"So now what?" I say.

"Peter, you've got to understand. The world is not as easy and wide open as we once thought."

"Killing Songkha and her child is wrong," I say.

He shakes his head solemnly. "Poor Peter. You've been in the field too long, not in Command and Control. We don't choose right and wrong. When we have an objective, we do what we need to do, that's all. Our choices funnel down, and we go where the funnel goes. We do what's necessary. Even having those two killed."

There is no animosity in Steven Vaal's voice and no anger coming from him now. There is no darkness in his eyes, no brooding over all this. He has accepted the terrible necessity of it all and settled it within himself. The funnel justifies it.

But for some reason he is still trying to persuade me, trying to win me over.

He continues to gauge me. "If you had used that gun, Peter. If you had killed her or me or someone else and then managed to escape from here—which is impossible—

you would have been sorry. Maybe not right away. Maybe not for a few years. But then you'd see the terrible damage. Your nights would be filled with houses on fire and melting children. And every day you'd have to live with it.''

His words hit hard. I can think of no response. ''Back at headquarters,'' I finally say, ''do they know what you're doing?''

''At certain levels.''

''What about the government?''

''The government?'' He breaks into a laugh. ''They want peace, and we want peace. They set the objective: security. And expect us to make it happen. So our options funnel down, Peter.''

''In our favor, of course.''

''Keeping the planet stable is in everyone's favor,'' he replies. ''It's a win-win situation, for all of us, including Japan. But we can't let anyone put us in a win-lose position because then our options funnel down a different way, and we'd have to use our military muscle. That's what we want to avoid.''

''There are other Fantasy Plans and other orphanages, aren't there?'' I say.

''Egypt and South Africa and a few other places, including Washington, D.C. Fantasies everywhere, Peter. And some of the best access we'll ever get.''

I sit up slowly in the bed, shaking my head. It throbs terribly.

Vaal continues. ''Hiroshima and Nagasaki taught the world that the unthinkable can be thought. And the fact is, Peter, that some of the Japanese in power are now considering the option themselves. The victims of that weapon are taking up the same weapon. And why shouldn't they want it when Iran and even India and Pakistan have it? There's nothing sinister about our intentions. We just need to keep the control, that's all. To keep the peace. And that's our duty.''

''Sounds like the Organization should get the Nobel Peace Prize.''

"Look, I don't run the world. Nobody does. It's a runaway train, and all we can do is force it onto a side rail where it'll do the least damage. That's all we're trying to do, side-rail the train."

There is no smugness in Vaal's voice. His earnestness amazes me. But why is he bothering to tell me all this? I have a trapdoor feeling in my stomach.

"Is Songkha here?" I ask.

"No. But the point you need to understand is that girl has become the key, Peter, to stopping it all. The best access on the planet. Access that will stall a fucking war."

My mind races backward to the first time I saw Song, and to Leamer's words: "*First-class access. A special order for someone we've targeted.*"

"I'm sorry," Vaal adds, and he sounds legitimately sorry.

I struggle to get up. "Oh, don't worry, Steven. Choices funnel down, you know. Hey, no hard feelings."

He pushes me back down on the bed. "She's only one person, Peter."

"And the infant is another person. That's only two. Who's the third life, Steven?"

But I don't have to ask because I already know the answer. "Why me?" I say.

He shakes his head helplessly. "I'm sorry," he says.

"I want to know why, Vaal. You owe me that much."

"The girl and the child are only part of the bargain. Unfortunately there's another issue. Yanaga wants you. And he found out your name and where your family lives."

"Why? What does he want with me and my family?"

"It's your own fault, Peter. You were supposed to walk away after the elimination. But you threw the gun down on the street."

It all comes together in my mind. "The man in Kyoto," I say softly. "Who was he?"

"Our first attempt to force Yanaga to work with us. We threatened him with the extermination of his family—one by one. He put his wife and kids in hiding, so all we had left was his father.''

"The old man.''

"Actually it was two birds with one stone. Our test of you and a way to get at Yanaga. Unfortunately for you Yanaga is connected, and had Japanese intelligence run an international search on the gun and prints. He wants your head.''

"You set me up.''

"It's your blunder, Peter, not mine. Don't blame me.''

"But you got me to come back, Steven.''

"I knew you would. But I didn't force you. Sometimes we are even inside the minds of others, remember? You put yourself here, not me. But that doesn't mean I like the situation, Peter.''

"Why didn't you just assign me here?''

"Would you have come here if you'd been ordered? Especially after you'd been transferred away? You're sentimental, Peter, but not dumb.''

"But you could kill Yanaga. That would stop him.''

"We thought about it. But that wouldn't end Trinity Two. Then we got lucky, and Yanaga and some friends bought tickets to Bangkok for a little holiday, and we made sure they ended up at the Fantasy Store. He loved that place. Came back half a dozen times by himself, then made a special request: a true virgin. No fake stuff, he said. So we brought that girl down from the orphanage, and he liked the menu.'' Vaal shakes his head. "But God, her temper! She scared him at first, so we had to encourage him. She finally broke down and became his little whore. I think he actually came to like her.''

I try to get up but fall back on the bed, weak from a sudden surge of depression as Song's face grips my mind. That first day: her haunting eyes, unafraid. Her pride. Her strength. How I longed that someone so pure would want me. Then the video of Song kneeling before Yanaga. Her wooden smile as she looked up at him. The same man who will now kill her. And her child. And kill me as well, with perfect satisfaction. And with all the misery in the world, what do three more deaths matter to anyone? The cold mathematics of it all.

I hear my father's melancholy words, and I can see that we all are merely struggling for a piece of life. Our portions aren't equal or fair, and they're not meant to be. And we cannot change anything. The globe just continues to spin.

I shake my head vigorously to reject the thoughts. The instinct for self-preservation surfaces. *I will not die. I refuse to die.*

Vaal has no chance to react as my hands shoot out and clutch his throat. I spring up and push him backward against the wall. I will snap his neck. I must make it quick because he is stronger than I am.

At first he instinctively fights against me, but then he lets his arms fall to his sides uncontestingly. We are eye to eye. And I see what he is telling me: that he will give me a chance to change my mind because it doesn't matter if I kill him. *He* doesn't matter, just as *I* don't matter. And *Song* doesn't matter. The *baby* doesn't matter. We all are people of no importance.

My hands continue to tighten the grip, and his face contorts. He waits for me to back off, waits for me to realize that there is a greater good for a greater number, that the world must be spared a push-button holocaust, spared all the mushroom clouds—even if we are the price.

But I will not stop. I will live. I will live. In a second he will be the third person I have killed. Three men. Three different men. Everything races through my mind. Is one death different from three? Are three different from ten thousand or a million? Song and her child. Even if they live, what would their lives be like? Even if I live, what would my life be like?

Now Vaal finally struggles, pulling desperately at my hands. He is so much stronger, and I will not be able to hold him for long. But a rage builds inside my skin, giving me more power, and with the rage comes a clarity, like a door swinging open into a great field. And in this clarity I can see that the future war is not the worst thing of all—

no, not even the terrible moments of heat and light and naked energy ripping upward and outward. People will die then, but I cannot feel them. I cannot save them. They will need their own hero to save them in their own moment.

Because the worst thing of all is not some far-off, possible evil but *this* evil happening now to Song, and to Lisa from New Mexico, and to the children, all of them no more than access, no more than sacrifices to quell the wrath of the Atomic God. Yes, evil will always go on, with new faces and new justifications, and we can do so little. But this one thing I *can* do. No, it is not personal. It is not just to save myself. I can stop *this* evil. I can stop *this* evil here.

Vaal struggles in a fury to breathe. The fear in his eyes grows. There is a burbling in his nose, and mucus ejects. He wrestles and pulls at my wrists, nearly yanking them free. I catch him by surprise, throw his balance off, and push him to the floor, on top of him and at his throat again. I feel an unfamiliar lust sweep over me, a lust for this man's death, the adrenaline mixed with a cold clinical desire to kill him. I will make it quick. With all my weight I shove back on his throat as he tries to push against my hands. His mouth opens and contorts terribly. My third kill, and maybe later I will be responsible for more, maybe a million more. But the Atomic God is not worth Song or her child or Lisa or Amkha or any one of them. If they have to die, the world will be too dirty to go on.

Vaal's eyes bulge, and suddenly his powerful forearms swing upwardly against my hands, which are locked hard around his neck. There is a distinct crunching sound as something breaks in my right wrist. But there is no pain yet, just a radiating numbness. I try to squeeze harder, using the adrenaline to push through the numbness before the pain comes. But there is so little strength in that hand. Then it comes: a howling pain as my brain receives the messages. My right hand loosens of its own accord as bones pierce tissue and muscle and maybe even skin.

I swing my elbows now and pin his neck between them, my weight on his chest, my face against his, my knee in his stomach to control the roll of his body. It is my last chance. I try frantically to puncture his neck with my elbows, twist his head with my other hand, snap it to the side. Then I try with both hands again, but there is only that terrible pain as the bones and muscles refuse to obey.

With a cry Vaal shoves hard against my weight. Our positions reverse. I see those intense blue eyes as he hesitates long enough to take two gasps of air, looking down at me as if I am a fool, as if I have misunderstood everything. Then one hit with his right fist, crushing the bridge of my nose. Then another hit. And another.

32

MY BIRTHDAY

I can't see if a bone is sticking through my skin. But the pain in my hand is nothing. It is nothing. I pull against the tape. The pain is nothing. Nothing.

I force my thoughts to Torpakai. I imagine her still alive now with the Soviets gone from her country. With the Soviet Union gone, period. What would she be doing? Would she be struggling against the new government? Would she still be in the hills carrying on? Or perhaps with a family now, and a child, and a peaceful smile. Perhaps her biggest problem would be turning the crank to draw water from the well. Or making sure every last cow was in. Or satisfying her husband. Or something else. No more bandoliers and rockets and helicopters. I know she would be happy.

Mind over matter. The pain is nothing.

My hands are bound to the arms of a chair. I pull harder against the heavy gray tape. For some reason one wrist slides just a little. A quarter inch. The pain is nothing.

Anna. I try to picture her life in Seoul. Smoggy air, high-rise buildings, a million restaurants. But she has probably moved on from Seoul, taking her demons somewhere else. Or maybe she has subdued them. Maybe she is content now. Maybe she has found somebody who can hold Plato together with the hungers of the body.

I pull harder on my wrists. The tape slips a little more this time, but it is tight everywhere else. Tight across my eyes. Tight around my legs and ankles. Tight across my chest, where it binds me to some kind of chair. Only my wrists are able to move, as if the tape is somehow wet and slippery there.

Then I taste it, slippery and salty and thick. The blood streams over the lower half of my face, from my nose and cheek down over my lips and spilling into my mouth. I can feel it dripping down on my shirt. I can direct the blood. I lean my head to the left and wait for it to run down my arm to my wrist. Then I pull again. The pain is nothing. I try the other side. The wrist slides a full inch this time, but the tape is caught on something, maybe a piece of broken bone pushing up against the skin.

There is no nail I can tear the tape on, no pocketknife cleverly hidden in my pants, no sharp corner of a table, or anything else. My own blood is all. Blessed blood. I am afraid the blessing will stop.

I tilt my head, and the blood falls on my arm, running faster as I continue to work my wrist back and forth, trying to ride the tape over the bump. I think of the fantasies. Not just Japanese fantasies. Fantasies everywhere. Not just in me. Not just in Bangkok. A planet filled with fantasies British and German and Greek and Chinese fantasies. The common denominator. The real United Nations.

I pull against the tape. The saying "No pain, no gain" pops into my mind, and I want to laugh. I pull my wrist again, and the tape finally rides over the bump. No pain, no gain. The tape slides a little farther, up to my fingers, which are oily wet.

No pain. No pain. I focus my thoughts on Song and try to imagine what she looks like now. I cannot find her in my mind. Then she comes into view. But her eyes are now iced with too much knowledge of life. Her face is beaten down. An exhaustion all about her. She is defeated. No longer the smiling youth, everything replaced by a hardness, an irrevocable fear, a mistrust of life. She is like everyone else now. She is like me.

Then I realize that today is my birthday. My birthday. I want to cry. I came into the world forty-six years ago. A year older than yesterday. Or maybe just a day older. I remember the precise moment some years ago when it sank in that I wouldn't go on indefinitely, that sooner or later everything would come to a grinding halt, maybe even a slow, grinding halt as my body just wore out, and my mind would be helpless to change anything. At best I would just lie in bed listening to the raspy sound of my breath on the respirator. Unlike Torpakai, who did not wait for that slow deterioration. She plunged in, leaped from the edge, thinking it an indulgence to worry about who or what was going to kill her, thinking it plain pride to be concerned with how long she might stretch out her life. Better a sudden, clean death, even if it was violent.

And me. Maybe for the first time in my life I am unafraid. I am a dead man already. That is what Vaal said as he looped the heavy gray tape around me. He was not angry or disgusted. Just matter-of-fact. Everything in stride. Everything in control. Detached. Completely steady. His options funneled down, he said. That is all.

I pull my wrist. No pain.

Then the wrist slides out. I reach up and try to grip the tape covering my eyes, and I feel the point of a wrist bone trying to push through my skin. No pain. I manage to peel the tape back from one eye, and the overhead light floods into it. I squint, waiting for the eye to adjust, waiting for the pain to subside so I can pull the tape further. I use my sleeve to wipe the blood from my face, and I feel my nose crushed all the way to the left side, numb and still spilling with blood. The blessed blood.

Now I can make out a form in front of me. His face is close as he leans forward in a chair, watching me struggle. My eye tries to focus. I reach up again and pull back the tape from the other eye, and now there are two forms in front of me and two doors, and everything else is doubled. I blink again and again. My eyes start to clear. The form continues to watch me, and I look into his penetrating eyes.

"I have never seen an American struggle so hard," he says.

I hold up my free hand and see the wrist bone pushing against the skin and the thumb broken backward. "I think my other hand is broken too," I say. "Can you cut the tape loose?"

Dr. Kenji Yanaga rises. He looks the same as in the video, a slender man, middle-aged and tall for a Japanese, with a perfectly trimmed mustache. His eyes are red and strained, but he is immaculately dressed in a clean suit and tie. Dr. Yanaga holds the old Japanese pistol awkwardly in his hands, which are delicate and well kept. He does not cut the tape.

"You've heard of Iwo Jima and Saipan," he says in a voice that is gentle and unchallenging. "And you've heard of all the places where the Japanese mistreated the Americans. But I think you have never heard of Tarawa Island. Am I right, Mr. Gaines?"

"Please. Can you cut the tape?"

He continues, with a pained smile. "My father was defending Tarawa when the Americans landed. It was a defeat for your country, Mr. Gaines, so it's not in your history books, just as hardly any of the war is in ours. On Tarawa Island the Americans were forced back into the sea. My father told me he killed twenty soldiers in one hour. He counted them. Not as a kind of victory but so that he would never forget how many lives he was responsible for taking. He could have killed more. He should have killed more. But he told his commanding officer that his gun malfunctioned. He hated war. He hated every kind of killing."

"I couldn't have known that. They tricked me, Dr. Yanaga. They used me."

"They use everybody, Mr. Gaines, including me. And they used my father to get at me."

"I am sorry," I say, and the words sound hollow and meaningless.

"Your nose is bad, Mr. Gaines." Dr. Yanaga goes to a sink and comes back with a wet rag. He dabs gently around my nose with cold water, cleaning off some of the blood. He steps back. The blood continues to stream down my face.

"After the war, when I was growing up, my father told me stories about the Americans who landed on Tarawa. About their uniforms and funny helmets, their large noses and stubble beards, how big they were. And how they struggled, lying there on the sand."

"Everyone wants to live, Dr. Yanaga."

"My father even wanted the Americans to live. He let others escape. Twenty dead was too much for him. Even one was too many. He had been against the war from the beginning, but no one could speak about such things. And then came August ninth. They were going to bomb Kokura. But Kokura was obscured by a cloud. Nagasaki was the alternative. Not just twenty deaths, but fifty thousand in a second. My father lost two brothers on that morning."

"But you and your Trinity Two," I counter, "would be responsible for more than just fifty thousand deaths."

Dr. Yanaga goes over to the sink. I try to pull on the tape around my chest. He comes back and sits down again.

"Your organization," he says, shaking his head with exasperation. "Little men with little ideas. Trinity Two may fail, but not because of your organization. Obliteration of millions in a second, for what? The pointless game of political seesaw? I have done everything I can to stop it."

My head still pounds from Vaal's blows, and now my mind spins. One more person claiming to save the world. Yanaga is playing with me. A joke. A little game of his own before he kills me. I shut my eyes to blink back the pain that rivets my face and hands. I can only stall for time. "If you want to stop it," I say, "then tell DeForest. You two are on the same side."

"I did tell him. But your people are not interested in facts. They are interested in fantasies—their own as well as everyone else's. But it is because of me that Trinity

Two has progressed so slowly. Data has been lost. Deadlines pushed back. Tests misfired. None of it traceable to me. I have scattered the culpability throughout the entire network. If my own organization doesn't know I have done this, I promise you that yours could not either. DeForest is a buffoon, like everyone else in your organization. His childish antics have only interrupted the delays I put in place. He wants to destroy me. When he blackmailed me, I realized I had to destroy him and his little fantasy business or I would have no chance of stopping Trinity Two."

"No, you're here for personal revenge, Yanaga. To kill me and the girl and the child."

"What else could I tell DeForest? But if that's what I wanted, I would have killed you already, yes? We would not be having this discussion, Mr. Gaines." He smiles at me patiently. "DeForest got you here, not me. He's the one who wants you dead because you are a threat to his program. But all I want is to stop DeForest and his hag mistress Rennard."

Yanaga is lying, of course. Everyone is lying. To each other and to me. "You're no better than the rest of them, Yanaga. A middle-aged man possessed by fantasies, who bought a seventeen-year-old to rape at his will. You used her, and broke her, and now—"

"Is that what DeForest told you?"

"I saw the videotape!"

"But you know nothing of the facts. Yes, I went to the Fantasy Store with colleagues, Dr. Inoki and some others. They frolicked. But I couldn't be part of it. I waited in the lobby, looking at that selection of sly prostitutes. I did not feel any pity for them, everyone using each other. I have never liked such business, even in Japan, and I told the hostess that. I came with my colleagues once again, and this time the hostess said she had someone special for me. When I saw her, I knew she wasn't a prostitute. I paid money, and we just talked. I was so drawn to her. I knew they would destroy her. Someone would destroy her."

"So you forced Songkha before someone else could."

Dr. Yanaga looks away. "At the time I did not see it that way. I reasoned away my actions. But the truth is I could not resist her."

"You mean you could not resist yourself."

"I am just a man, Mr. Gaines. I have never married. I was lonely and hungry. Yes, I used her, the way my colleagues bought their cheap whores, but on the condition that she be mine alone and nobody else's. That, I rationalized, was a way of protecting her. That is my shame."

My mind runs to my own desires to protect Song and possess her for myself.

"Is there something in your life you would take back if you could, Mr. Gaines?" he asks sadly. "No, perhaps you cannot understand."

"DeForest said that you're married and that you hid your wife and children to protect them."

"Then DeForest is a liar as well as a buffoon." Yanaga stands and comes closer again; his dark, narrow eyes stare into mine. "I need your help," he says, "to destroy De-Forest and his fantasy business." Yanaga rips the tape from my chest and frees my ankles and then my other hand. I examine it. It is only bruised, not broken. He helps me stand and steadies me until I gain my balance. Then he holds out the Japanese gun solemnly, as if passing me an honorary sword. "We have to eliminate DeForest and Rennard," he says.

"Then you do it," I say, refusing the weapon.

"I am not a murderer," he says. "I have spent my life preventing deaths."

"I'm not a murderer either."

"Yes, you are, Mr. Gaines. You have killed twice. My father, who you thought was a leader of the Yakuza, and that butcher Dr. Inoki. But you still have a thread of humanity. You kill only when you believe it is necessary."

"How do you know I won't kill you?" I say.

"Because we both want to stop the insanity. And if you do not see the necessity of their deaths in order to stop their fantasy business, then you will have to kill them anyway in order to escape from here.''

Yanaga tries to force the gun into my good hand, but I push it away. It is a trick. "I won't kill them," I say. "I can't kill again.''

"But you can, and you will, or they will kill you.''

He is right. The options funnel down. "What about Songkha and her child?''

"I cannot hurt them either. I never would. That was just my way of getting here, inside DeForest's fantasy business. I think of Songkha often. I care for her. And I am ashamed of my actions.''

So many saviors. So many lies. My head is pounding, and I am too bruised to command a focused thought. Yet Dr. Yanaga seems straightforward. No dogma or political rhetoric. Even his honesty about using Songkha.

"I ask you again," he says, still holding out the weapon. "If only for an atonement for killing my father.''

There is a click of the door latch behind me. Automatically I grab the gun in my good hand and spin around, my eyes still blurry, the revolver aimed. I am surprised that already I am prepared to kill again.

Steven Vaal enters. He closes the door, then looks up and sees me with the gun.

"Come in, Steven," I say. "Welcome to the meeting of the saviors.''

33

SAVIORS

Vaal steps forward hesitantly, his eyes going from me to Yanaga, then back to me. He holds out his hands to show me he has no weapon. "I was hoping this would be over, Peter," he says. "It's not easy for me. But you know I had no choice."

"Yes, everything funnels down, doesn't it?"

"Except now you're the one in control. So the decision funnels down for you, Peter. What will you do? Kill me and let the rearming continue? Can you live with the consequences of that? Or maybe you will kill both of us, and the rearming still continues. Same results, isn't it? So what does the funnel tell you, Peter? Now it's all in your hands."

I try to focus. Get past the pain and understand what is happening. "You used Songkha," I say, "to blackmail Yanaga. But Yanaga wants to use me to kill you and stop the Fantasy Plan."

"He's lying," Dr. Yanaga breaks in. "He fought me for the gun."

"You two have a lot in common," I say. "You both want to end the rearming. You're both liars. And you're fools for trusting each other."

"I never trusted him," Vaal says. "And you shouldn't either."

"Shouldn't I? Did he tell you he's been trying to stop the rearming?"

"We have no proof of that. Just his word. We got him by the balls, Gaines, and I'm not letting go till he follows through. You and I can work together on it."

"Old times' sake, Steven?"

"No, it's practical now. You have to join us or there's no way out of here for you."

"And where's Songkha and the child?" I say. "Are they here?"

"No, they're both in Bangkok. If he killed them, we needed to get it on tape. But that's not necessary now. We'll make the case for street rape. We still have him by the balls."

I motion Vaal toward the chair. "Have a seat, Steven," I say. "Dr. Yanaga, tape him up tight." Vaal doesn't move. I raise the Japanese gun in my left hand and sight down the barrel at his face. "I will kill you if I have to, Steven."

Vaal goes to the chair and sits. "This is a mistake, Peter. You can't trust him."

"And I can't trust you."

Dr. Yanaga takes the roll of thick gray tape and quickly circles it around Vaal's chest and around the back of the chair, then around his hands and ankles.

I pull up the other chair and push the gun against Dr. Yanaga's forehead. "Sit," I say, "and tape your ankles first, tight." I move behind him as he does it. "Now tear off a long piece of tape," I command. With the gun against the back of his head, I struggle to hold the long piece in my broken hand, which is blue and palsied and swollen like a small balloon. But there is still a little motion in the fingers. I try to push through the pain and grip the tape, but my hand is slick red with blood. I raise my wrist above my head to let the blood drain and reduce the throbbing. I lower it and grab the tape, grimacing as I loop it around Yanaga once. Then I take the roll of tape and wrap it around him several times.

"You two deserve each other," I say. "You're both trying to save the world. But you can't. If it's not the Fantasy Plan or Trinity Two, it'll be something else, some other horror, great or small. The insanity won't stop. It never fucking stops."

I look at the two men. They can finish each other off. Or they can stop their games. But I won't kill anyone. I am leaving. I am leaving. I came here because I thought I could do one thing, and now I realize that everything has funneled down. There is only one choice left. And that is no choice at all.

I tuck the gun under my arm and open the door with my left hand. I step outside onto the porch. The sky is dimming, pink and turning purplish, but the perimeter lights have not yet switched on. I want to live. And I want Song and her child to live. That is what is right. But right causes wrong. Many deaths. And wrong causes right. Many others can live if they die.

There is a silent howl in my head. And with it an overwhelming sense of absurdity. It is all laughable. A man with a broken hand, who wanted to save a girl who resided largely in his head. Coming here was a mistake. I was led here not by my truest self but by my weaknesses, my unconquered desires, my pitiful fantasies, a sentimental sickness. That is why my face is smashed and my hand broken. It is symbolic. Punishment for a man who should leave the world alone, let it slide its own way, let it be taken care of by those who understand it better.

So my choices funnel down. To the only right possibility.

I will save myself. Only myself. Me. I can escape. There is no reason for me to die here. I have tried, and there is only so much I can do and no more, and then I must save myself. I have done my best. No one can accuse me now.

I feel an immense relief. The funnel has decided for me, and now the world seems beautiful again, and magnified. I look up. The pink and purplish sky is hiding stars that I know are there, stars that will be invisible until darkness. I am alive. I will make my way back to Ohio, to my mother and my sister. Maybe Song and her child will die, must die, and maybe that will be enough for Vaal and Yanaga, if that is what they arrange. Maybe the Organization will leave me alone, and maybe I can get a job, and maybe take vacations, and maybe meet someone, and maybe have children, and maybe and maybe.

Amkha can stay or follow me, whichever she wants. Amkha. I have forgotten Amkha. Where is she? Where have they put her? Perhaps there really is a truck coming to take her back to Bangkok. Perhaps she will be all right. No, that is absurd. I have to find her. But I may have only minutes before Rennard or someone else finds Vaal. It is useless. Even trying to save Amkha. But if I move quickly, I can make it to the gate and cross the path through the perimeter, and at least I will live.

With the gun in my left hand, I move quickly through the quadrangle to the stone wall, hugging the wall as I head for the front gate. At times my double vision returns, and I have to slow to determine which tree and which rock are real. My face still aches terribly from the broken nose. The ground is overgrown with vines and moss, cushioning the sounds of my steps.

The wall turns at a bend, and in the dimness I make out four people at the gate with Uzi-type automatics slung over their shoulders. Guards. I crouch and strain to see them clearly. No, it is two people, not four. The burly dentist. And standing next to him is the young man who was in the clothing store and then on the bus. Vaal was right. I was escorted all the way.

The choices funnel down again. Two people. Five bullets against them. I don't want to kill them. And I won't kill them. But if I can get close enough, I can take them out with bullets to the legs or knees. Five bullets.

If the gun will fire.

34

There is a strange sound behind me. More feathery than a whisper. Gentle, it reminds me of Song's soft chanting when I went to her cell that night. Except this is different. It is a sigh and a murmur and a gentle cry all at once, as if all three sounds are coming from the same mouth. Seductive and luring. Without notes but somehow musical. It resonates in me like a sympathetic string, something I can't remember, something before words, before memory.

I lean back against the wall and listen. The sound comes again. It lasts a few seconds longer. Then I know what it is: It is order in the chaos; it is a good that is good. Yes, a good that is totally good.

I turn back. I follow the feathery sound. It stops.

I go to the closest stucco hut and peer through the window into the dim room. It is a kind of barracks. There is a tiny light like a muted candle or flashlight. One long table. Mats on the floor. Hooks for clothes. I smell marijuana smoke drifting out.

Seven young women sit cross-legged on the mats, each of them in a shapeless white nightie like kids at a slumber party. One of them pinches a joint between her fingers, makes a face, and stifles a cough as she holds her breath, then exhales with a long sigh. She passes the joint along. They all have faraway looks in their eyes and seem to be visibly drifting. Five are Asian. The youngest is Caucasian. The other is either black or Indian. Some of them have their eyes closed, while others stare off at nothing, each of them escaping to the resort of their choice.

The Caucasian girl rises and moves unsteadily to a corner where there is a large pail. She lifts the lid and squats over it. There is a rush of water for nearly a minute. None of the others takes notice. She replaces the lid and returns to her seat. I hear the soft movements of their bodies, the swish of the nighties, their occasional giggling at nothing, and the exhaling of smoke-filled lungs. But the feathery sound is not here.

I turn back toward the gate. Then the sound again. I cannot resist it. I move toward the next stucco building. There are no lights inside, but the room is lit dimly by the glare of the perimeter lights outside. It is another barracks, and I see bodies inside. Five or six small bodies, naked and partially covered with a single sheet. I am prepared for the worst. But they are only large dolls, three to five feet, plastic, fleshlike dolls, naked, lying side by side with a sheet partially tossed over them, arms bent, their faces turned away from me. One doll has longer hair than the others, and it drapes across another doll's shoulder. Discarded dolls. Dolls bothered by flies. I do not need to go closer. There is no one there. They are not my dolls. There is only one word in my mind: *No*.

My mind switches back. Escape. I will head for the gate and take out the two men and escape from Wonderful Place. I will make my way home. I am so hungry and tired. Then tears cover my face, tears that I don't understand, tears for dolls.

One doll stirs. Then another. I hear a sigh, and one of them rolls over, her hand flopping across another doll and resting there. There is a soft cough and then a stirring that causes each of them in turn to silently readjust their arms and legs.

A door opens from another room, and a form comes

closer, a form that is larger than the dolls. It is Amkha, also in a white nightie. Behind her comes another form. She is still in the shadows, but I recognize her by the way she moves. There is a fleeting rush in the valves of my heart, and I am breathing faster. Wearing a cotton nightie, she steps into the reflected orange light, holding something in front of her. She lowers herself and sits cross-legged. She looks different. Her hair is longer and tangled, and she seems older, her face stretched a little, a young woman who has not been able to take care of herself. But she is still beautiful. I realize that the picture I had of her in my mind all these months was so simplified, but there she is, and now I remember more of the living details: her eyes, the length of her neck, the slope of her shoulders. There is also something different, a kind of sorrow and exhaustion covering her.

She shifts to the side, and in the yellow light I see what she is holding. She lowers a strap on her nightie, bares her breast, and holds the infant against it.

It is a version of Song I have never imagined. It was nowhere in any of my fantasies. And then that feathery sound again, a whimper, a cry, and a gurgle all at once. It is coming from her arms. There is a mysterious smile on Song's face as she gazes down at the naked infant.

I must have made a noise because Song's eyes dart to the window. Startled, she draws back toward a corner. I quickly go to the door and nudge it open. Inside, it is hot and smelly with the stink of sweat and feces. The dolls do not stir. Amkha says something to Song, something about who I am, but Song continues to slide away from me on the floor, frightened by the gun or maybe by my smashed nose and the blood that has dried on my two-day beard like a scabby mask.

One of the naked dolls awakens and sits up quickly. She wipes her eyes and stares at me, then pulls part of the sheet over her. She is Caucasian and blond and moon-faced with sleepy, squinting eyes and thin arms. Maybe nine or ten years old. I stare at the moon-faced girl. Something familiar about her, pulling at my memory. Where have I seen her before? An abduction I read about? A photo in the paper? Then an image comes into focus. A picture. On a table. With a smiling man who has his arm around her. The picture was in Arlington, in Penny O'Hara's apartment. The picture must have been stolen along with the girl and then used as a prop at the apartment.

Still covering herself, the moon-faced girl tilts her head and looks at me curiously, as if I am part of her dream, or maybe she has already seen everything in the world, and even this man with a broken face cannot surprise her.

I move toward them and kneel before Song, keeping to the side so that the yellow light lies evenly across her. Her skin is darker than I remember, and she seems a matron now. Perspiration pearls on her forehead and nose, and there are sweat rings under her arms. Her body, like her face, is a little wider, and there is a sore at the corner of her mouth. Her eyes are a woman's eyes now, yet at every instant they change to a girl's eyes. They look at me with fear, but in them I also see the same innocence as before. She has not really changed. She has not lost her earlier self. Though soiled by this place, something about her has remained untouchable, or at least this place has not penetrated her irrevocably. Or maybe all of this is in my mind.

There is that feathery noise again, a sound so familiar yet so out of place. Soft and oddly seductive. The mouth of the infant holds fast to Song's nipple, pulling at it gently but rhythmically. Her breast is no longer a sex object, no longer a fleshy mound to be discovered and fingered and played with. It is a link in that child's first nakedness, as if there are two bodies here but only one life, or two lives but only one body. I hear the sound again as the infant releases her nipple and takes a breath and yawns, and the sight of this transports me interiorly. I feel the hinges go, detaching me from the world around me, from any world I have known. And I feel eyes watching. They are Song's eyes, afraid of my bloody face and my broken and crippled hand.

I want to touch the infant. I inch closer, but Song draws back, clutching the naked bundle tighter.

I set the Japanese gun down on the floor and wait, both arms extended and motionless while she studies me. Finally Song leans forward and places her child in the crook of my elbow. Her bottom is wrapped loosely in a cloth. It is a girl. I search over her tiny face. Every infant looks the same to me, the way chipmunks and sparrows look the same to other people. Every child is a vague form waiting to become something definite, a fleshy soft mystery preparing to elongate and grow into something nobody can imagine.

I search her tiny face again and hold her against me. I can smell her, the helpless smell of infancy. Part Thai and part Japanese and part everyone, yet all herself too. Though she is not my child, I begin to feel something spread inside me, a tenderness, a kind of glow, a protective urge. I have experienced every other emotion, every kind of disappointment and anger and love, but this is so completely new and shocking to my system that it seems that what I took to be the world before is only slime, and I am crawling out of it for the first time. This is not my child. And yet I realize that in some way this is my child. My child.

I roll her back and forth in my arms, cradling her bottom. Her eyes are enormous and clear. I remember hearing that it takes weeks—or is it months?—for eyes to focus. But these eyes seem focused on me, as if I am being watched by a tiny god. My child. My child.

A voice startles me from behind. "There will be no more games, Peter. It is all over now."

35

VAAL

He is stronger than I am, and unbruised, and unafraid of me. He steps toward the old Japanese gun on the floor and picks it up. Yanaga stands behind him, staring at Song and the child.

"Give me the child, Peter," Vaal says in a cold voice, with anger behind it.

The infant coughs in my arms and gurgles up some spit onto my shirt. This tiny *konketsuji*. This mongrel. This mutt. An infant of no importance. Song moves closer on all fours. Amkha stands against the wall, trying to disappear in the dim light.

I point at Yanaga. "He will kill her," I say to Vaal.

"That's the least of your problems," he answers.

"Yes, everything has funneled down, Vaal," I say just as coldly.

"That's right. For what we get, the costs are small. A tiny cost, really. Unfortunately you're part of it. You're dead already, Peter. All three of you. There's no way past us, and no way out of here. Accept it. I would if I were in your shoes. How many soldiers have died for lesser causes?"

I feel my mind pulling apart, yanking in different direc-

tions, and I am going to break down completely. I should
have left when I had the chance. I should have kept going
at the gate, risked it there. I should have saved myself.
Lose-lose is all that is left. And now it is final.

Song reaches up for her child, but I push her away with
my body. My eyes are blurry, and my head is dizzy. I
cannot attack Vaal with either strength or reason. There is
no middle ground in this war, no way to protect both a
million families on the globe and myself and Song and
this infant in my arms. Painfully I adjust the infant so that
she rests in the crook of my arm. I cradle her head with
my other arm. There is no other choice. I take a step
toward Vaal and hold out the child. Song cries out, stands,
and grabs at my hands, screaming. With a twist of my
body I throw her off.

''Now you're making sense, Peter. There's no other
way.''

I look from Vaal to Yanaga, then down at the tiny
beginning in my arms. The baby girl coughs again. It is
the cough of life. Innocent spittle comes from her mouth,
warm, velvety drool that I feel on my skin. This is Song's
child. The promise of a person. And I am the only guard-
ian there is. And now that all is final, and the three of us
will die, everything funnels down for me even further. My
mind quiets, and in the quiet I can hear that small, uncon-
fused place in my heart, that undisturbed place that is not
caught up in fantasies about anyone or trapped by hopes
and imaginings of a better world. The silence of my heart
is loud, like a roar or a shout that has always been there,
so clear and close that I never noticed it; and it is declaring
that the logic of the Fantasy Plan is ungrounded and that
the mathematics of saving so many is irrelevant, because
what is happening here is evil, pure evil.

''What is her name?'' I ask Vaal as I hold her out to
him. My voice sounds calm, so much outside myself that
I don't recognize it.

''I don't know,'' he answers. ''It probably hasn't got a
name yet.''

''What is her name?'' I ask again as I hold out the

child and take a half step closer. Vaal reaches for her with
one hand, the gun in the other. With a sudden kick I catch
Vaal where every man is vulnerable. He doubles over,
putting one hand on his knee but still managing to keep
the gun trained on me. He shakes his head slowly and
smirks at me, as if I am unbelievably stupid and it is all
so useless.

"There's no way out, Peter. You can gain nothing."

I clutch the infant tighter, protecting her from the gun,
and swiftly kick again—this time to Vaal's face—so hard
that I nearly lose my balance. He swings his body to the
side to soften the blow, but it is enough to jar the old
Japanese gun from his hand. Yanaga does not go for it,
but continues to stand there, watching. Amkha springs forward and grabs the gun with two hands, raises it and
points it at Vaal.

He ignores her. His nose is bleeding, and he is holding
his hand to his eye. "Just three, Peter, in exchange for
so many," he growls angrily. He comes for me again,
staggering, determined.

Still clutching the child, I turn and from the side I kick
at his knee, snapping it backward. He goes down with a
groan but is up again. Amkha still has the gun on him,
her arms tense and shaking. Then Song springs forward.
She leaps at Vaal and kicks hard, her foot finding his
stomach. I know how strong fear can be and what it can
do, its mysterious primitive force. Song's face is a hard
mask as she kicks Vaal again and again. But her blows
have little effect. Vaal just bats her away. She springs
back, clawing at him, a wild overflow of tension and fear.
He shoves her to the floor. As he turns toward me I kick
one more time, the crotch again, and he doubles over
again, groaning.

"What is her name?" I shout at Vaal.

He lowers himself to his knees and after a few seconds
vomits on the floor. The smirk is gone, and there is only
grimacing and a throaty growl coming from him, like a
cornered animal.

"What is her name?" I demand. I kick again, and the

toe of my foot catches the side of his head, and he goes down. I stomp wildly on his head and neck. There are cries around me now as all the dolls awaken in confusion and terror. I stomp again and Song screams at him and follows with her own kick. Yanaga backs away toward the door. Maybe he is on my side after all, but will not take part in any killing, any violence.

An explosion. Part of the ceiling falls. Catherine Rennard stands at the door with the pistol she has fired, holding it in two hands, a 9mm CZ-75 with black finish and a ten-round magazine. Keeping the pistol and her eyes on me, she steps past Yanaga and kneels over Vaal. She sees Amkha aiming the old Japanese revolver at her and starts to turn.

Amkha pulls the trigger. There is a dull sound of the hammer hitting metal, but that is all.

Rennard swings her gun back at me. The infant screams in my arms. "What is her name?" I demand of Rennard. "What is her name!"

Catherine Rennard understands what I mean. There is a sadness in her voice. "I don't know," she says. She bites her lip hard. She understands that she has to choose. This child or a thousand, maybe a million other lives. There are two goods, and she cannot have them both, or maybe there are two evils. But I don't care. I do not wait for her to decide. There is no time. Bracing the child against me with my swollen right hand, I spring and grab at the barrel of the pistol with my left hand, fumbling to get it away from her. The infant screams louder, and Song claws at both of us to get to her child and finally pulls the infant away. I twist the gun in her hand and it fires over my shoulder. I twist again, and finally jerk the gun away and curl a finger around the trigger, steadying the gun with my right arm.

Yanaga recedes to a corner now, just watching, maybe waiting for us to kill each other off. Rennard's eyes move from the gun to me and then to the wailing child, who is now in Song's arms. Rennard's lips quiver, and her face collapses in pain. She begins to cry bitterly, her shoulders shaking, as if something caring and motherly has finally surfaced in her.

It is an act, of course.

No, it is real.

No, it is an act.

"What is *your* name?" I shout at her. "What is *your* name?"

My swollen fist flies forward against Rennard's face, crunching something delicate in her cheek and cracking something more in my wrist. The pain shoots all the way to my neck. She tumbles to the ground, motionless.

There is chaos now. A screaming baby, the crying dolls, Amkha and Song terrified, and Vaal curled on the floor, groaning and coughing. Still, Yanaga doesn't move.

Using my legs and my left hand, I try to push the dolls to their feet. But they cringe and hide under their sheets. Amkha claps her hands, shouts, and motions wildly to them. They leap up, the sheets falling away, revealing their small nakednesses. There is a boy mixed in among them. They were using their nighties as a cushion on the wood floor, and Amkha quickly helps them slide the nighties on.

I still hold the gun in my left hand, trying to steady it with my right. I stand over Vaal and Rennard. I will pull the trigger and kill them both. There is no other choice. They would follow us or contact others. They have to be put out of the scene altogether.

Song watches me intently, clutching her child to protect the little ears from the impending explosion. Amkha too waits for the explosion. I look back to Song, and she cringes, but her eyes are wide open and eager. She wants the evil act that is good.

But I will not do it. My hand falls to my side.

Amkha rushes me and grabs at the gun, shouting something I can't understand, except that I know she will finish them off now. She will perform the good evil. The evil goodness.

I shove Amkha away, shouting, "No more!" I fling the gun through the door, out into the night, and I hear it slide somewhere across the dirt. I push Amkha toward the door, and turn to see Yanaga encouraging the children, hurrying them outside in a confusion. He stays behind. Our eyes meet and he points to Vaal and Rennard on the floor.

"You should have killed them," he says.

I shout to Song, and she too hurries out and into the darkness, her arms covering her child. My child. Everyone's child.

36

THE WALL

We can't go to the gate. After Rennard's shot the guards will be alerted, maybe even one of them coming. The wall is our only chance. And it must be now, before the perimeter lights are turned on.

Then a soft whirring sound in the distance as the generator starts. The purplish night slowly turns orange around the edges of the compound. But we have no choice. The perimeter lights grow brighter as Amkha hurries the children toward the low place in the stone wall. In their flowing nighties they look like angels or small ghosts chasing each other in the night. Song and I move slowly as she cradles her child, trying to hush her.

When we reach the wall, Amkha and the children are huddled together and kneeling. The yellow lights color their nighties and their terrified faces.

In the yellow glow I assess our group. Ten in all. Six dolls, Amkha, Song, the baby and I. Some of the children have brown faces, some white. Round faces, and narrow. Eyes blue. Eyes brown. Eyes wide. All eyes teary and frightened. Two girls, including the moon-faced blonde, are Caucasian. A chubby girl, about nine or ten years old, is probably Chinese. The two other girls are Thai, each about twelve years old. The boy is taller and thinner than the girls and looks the oldest, maybe twelve or thirteen. He appears to be Indonesian.

The presence of children always surprises me. The seriousness of the world has left me little time to think about things so uninvolved. They are neither friend nor foe. Usually they are just *there*. But now they are *here,* in front of me. Children from around the world. Fugitive children. Castoffs and kidnapped children. Exiles from their species. Children of no importance.

They continue to kneel, trembling. I realize there may be no common language among them and no way I can talk to all of them.

"Who speaks English?" I ask, keeping my voice low, not wanting to make them more afraid than they already are.

"I can," the moon-faced girl answers in a meek and frightened voice. Her accent is American. She begins to sob and shifts herself inside her nightie, drawing her knees up to her chin and burying her eyes in the soft cotton.

"What is your name?" I say quietly.

"Florie," she answers through the cloth.

"What's her name?" I ask, pointing to the other Caucasian, brown hair with large, sad eyes.

Florie glances up. "I don't know. I don't know anybody's name. I think she's from France." She points to the two girls who look Thai. "Those two talk to each other."

I turn to Amkha and point to the two Thai girls, who are staring at me in shock. "Are they going to be okay?" Amkha says something to them, but they don't reply. I turn to the young Indonesian boy, who is so thin, with a beautiful angular face. Embarrassed to be in girl's clothes, he pulls at his short nightie. Then he stands straight and stiff and steps apart from the girls, trying to tell me he is a man.

"What is your name?" I ask him. He shakes his head as he answers, replying in some language—perhaps Bahasa Indonesian—that he doesn't understand. He has a wide mouth that reminds me of a friend I had in fifth grade,

Sammy Baldwin. In my head I give him that name, Sammy. I want to show him that I know he's a man, but I cannot even extend my hand to shake his. I pat him clumsily on the shoulder and then try to salute him. He salutes back.

I turn to the others. I want to know all their names, and then I wonder how long some of them have been here and if they even know their own names. I want to hold them all and talk to them all, and it occurs to me that some of them, or maybe all of them, may not be alive a few minutes from now: the plump Chinese girl with puffy red cheeks, the dark-haired French girl with the sad eyes, the two Thai girls who stare with a vacant terror, and Sammy.

I am responsible for them. Is this just another mistake, another of my many? It is such a long shot, and it would be better if they stayed. But it is too late to rethink it now.

We don't need language. They know they must get over the wall and across the perimeter, and they know the terrible danger whether they go or stay. I reach out and huddle them closer, feeling them quiver like nervous bunnies. I shepherd them to the wall. Amkha bravely takes the lead and climbs up the stones first. She straddles the top and reaches down. The little Chinese girl puts her hand up, and Amkha hoists her over to the other side. Next Amkha lifts one of the Thai girls up and over, then the other Thai girl, and then Florie. The French girl goes next. Then it is Sammy's turn. He refuses Amkha's hand, grabs at the rocks himself, and feels with his bare feet until he finds a foothold. Sammy struggles to the top and falls to the other side with a loud crash.

Now it is just Song and her child who are left with me. I hold out my arms, and Song hesitates again before handing the baby to me. The infant's bottom is wet, and she is starting to cry again. One thought is in my mind.

"What is her name?" I ask Song.

"Songkha," she answers quietly, and strokes the child's cheeks with the back of her hand, soothing her.

But Song doesn't step toward the wall. She points in the direction of the other cottage where the older girls are, the ones escaping through marijuana. She wants to run there and get them. I shake my head, blocking her way and forcing her to the wall. This is the real world, vulgar and low and unfair, and the other girls will have to wait or fend for themselves. If we make it out, I can come back for them. Yes, I will come back. Definitely I will come back.

There are noises behind us, footsteps. A flashlight cuts the air in the distance. I should have killed Vaal and Rennard. But the light seems to be moving away from where we are, and I can only hope they will expect us to try to go out through the gate.

Song sees the light too and reaches up to Amkha, who helps her over the wall. Then Amkha leans down and takes little Songkha and passes her over the other side to Song. I can't grip with my broken right hand. I grab with my left hand and reach with my right elbow. Amkha grabs my shirt and pulls. I swing a leg up and roll over and crash down next to Sammy. The yellow lights glare in my eyes.

There are still noises from the other side, but no shouting, so I doubt we've been spotted. The children are flattened against the wall, braced and too frightened to move. Together we face the eerily lit perimeter. It is the moon's surface, but with evenly raked lines, an attempt to smooth out the soil. An attempt to conceal the places where things have been buried.

But we will have to cross here. We will have to cross now. And if we make it, we will hide in the jungle until morning, then navigate away the best we can.

But who will start? If I go first and don't make it, it is the end for all of them as well. They will be captured or they will get lost in the jungle. But I cannot tell anyone else to go first.

Amkha helps me take off my shoes and socks. I step forward to show the others how to do it, not by sliding their feet sideways to search for a safe spot. I step straight out, touching lightly in one place with my toes, feeling for the tip of any device. If I detect something, I will lift my foot to the side and step there. But I feel nothing except grains of dirt. I slowly plant my right foot. No explosion.

There is wetness falling to my shirt again, and at first I think it is more blood from my face. But it is a sudden flood of perspiration. I look around and listen. With death facing me, everything seems so close. Reality is a blaring horn. I am aware of the eyes behind me, the mosquitoes above me, the pain in my wrist and my throbbing fingers, and I'm aware of each particle of dirt under my toes. I balance my weight on the safe spot and reach with the other bare foot for the next spot. Every place looks the same. I put the toes down lightly, then a little more weight. Nothing.

I look back to see if they understand: *Step straight. Don't sweep your feet sideways.*

They are already barefoot but still frozen in fear, their backs against the wall except for Florie, who is turned away and crying with her forehead on the stones. The Chinese girl and French girl are looking down with their eyes closed. I motion to Sammy, who is looking at me. He starts to step, then draws back again.

"Come on, Sammy," I call out in a low voice. "Come on, Sammy, show them how."

He understands. He stiffens, and his eyes open up wide. He glances at me. Then he braces himself, and I know what he's going to do. I put up both hands to shout no. But he thrusts himself from the wall and with long, gliding steps starts racing across the yellow dirt, his head down, as if he might be able to outrun the explosion.

37

SAMMY

*H*e leaps, sailing in a long arc over the last six feet of dirt, and plunges headlong into a growth of broad leaves and ferns on the other side. There is a rustle, and after a moment leaves part and his head emerges. Panting and smiling, he squints at us through the bright perimeter light.

The Chinese girl giggles with relief. Sammy's success will give them heart, help us to move boldly. There is no more time.

I retrace my footprints to the wall and move to Sammy's smaller footprints. I motion to the others, and I think they understand. We will go step by step in his prints, playing an exact game of follow the leader. My feet are larger, and I have to be careful as I plant them in case he missed a mine by a fraction. I take eight steps, and I am in the middle of the perimeter.

I turn and face them, willing myself to be calm so that they will be calm. I point at Florie and motion her forward. She draws back. I wave urgently, and she finally steps onto the dirt, her blond hair matted to her forehead and shining in the yellow light. She has to stretch to reach Sammy's wide-running prints. As she focuses on one foot-print at a time, her steps seem very slow, and her hands are out at her sides like a tightrope walker's. She takes six steps and is only a few feet from me now. I reach with the crooks of my arms and lift her toward me. She is such a light weight. I swing her past me and set her down on the next footprint. She continues on her tightrope for another six steps and then falls forward into the bushes, safe.

I point to one of the Thai girls who was in shock before. Still in a kind of daze, she moves as if she's walking on air, barely looking down. Behind her the other Thai girl starts out on her own. The first one reaches me, and I lift her to the next footprint behind me. She continues on, and I watch until she reaches the other side.

The second Thai girl follows close behind and is only two steps away from me. I reach for her, lift, and swing her past me and plant her down. She is trembling terribly. She takes one more step, then freezes, balancing on one foot, afraid to put the other one down. She holds her arms out for balance, but it doesn't help. I try to snatch her, but my hand won't grip her nightie. She falls heavily on her side.

No explosion.

The little French girl is almost to me, but she sees the Thai girl sprawled on the dirt, struggling, and she freezes. I reach for the French girl and lift her under her arms, pulling her to me and cradling her like a baby. She cries, hugging me desperately, and I squeeze her close to calm her.

There is a rustling noise. Sammy is coming back for the Thai girl who has fallen. I wave him away, but he is focused on her. Four long steps, and then he moves off the path just inches and puts out his hand.

An explosion.

Not the big one I expected, but something smaller, disabling. Sammy does a funny little half step, part hop, then leans to the side, putting out his hand as if he's afraid he might fall on another mine. He does not cry. He does not even mumble. His mouth is open, and his lips curl in.

Blood comes in quick spurts from where his foot used to be. The bottom of his white nightie is splattered.

The explosion was soft, but the sound will carry, pinpointing where we are. Frantic, the little French girl pushes out of my arms and runs wildly to the other side and falls into the leaves. Now there is so little time. I rip my shirt off, grip it with my teeth and pull with my good hand. I tear a strip, then step off the path to Sammy and tie a tourniquet just below his knee. The spurting doesn't slow from his jagged shinbone, which dangles out into nothing. I push my hand against his wound, cupping the muscle, which splays out around my fingers, desperately trying to hold the blood back. It is no use.

I cradle him in my arms. He is so quiet and brave. A little man. Braver than I am. They all are braver than I am. He does not smile or speak but looks up at me. Then he says a few words that I can't understand and can't answer, and I can't help him at all. There is a gurgling of some liquid deep in his chest. His eyes are still open when his body begins to soften. He is spiraling away from me, a weightless fall, spiraling away from everything into a blank darkness. He seems so small in death, even smaller than he was in life. I lay him gently down and carefully adjust his head as if he will somehow be more comfortable.

I stand. I thought I could change something. Make amends. Undo something. Add a little good to the world. Take away a little of the bad. But I have only made things worse. Vaal had said only three would die, and now there is already one, not even one of the three.

I must stop it all now. Go no farther. I will call out for Vaal. Song, Amkha, and the Chinese girl have not yet crossed. They are still safe. And Vaal can help the others get back into the compound safely. Then I will beg him to spare Song and her little child.

I look over as the Chinese girl starts out without my command. I shout and wave my arms, warning her to go back. But she won't stop. Her eyes are bleary with tears as she steps carelessly. She misses all the footprints but also misses any devices. I sweep her into my arms when she reaches me in the middle, and I carry her the rest of the way.

No sooner do I set her down than Amkha is beside me, having crossed quickly and noiselessly. Now only Song and little Songkha stand on the other side. I look across and into the glare of the yellow lights and see her rocking her child gently in her arms, hushing her, waiting, maybe wondering which is the greater risk to her child, crossing or staying. I can still call everything off. But before I can speak, she steps out.

38

There are so many footprints now, and slide marks and scrapes in the dirt. Song steps slowly, her head leaning over her child as she peers down at the strange yellow dirt. She is a ghost walking, an eerie apparition wrapped in a flowing nightie that falls between her knees and drags along the ground, a nightie that reminds me now of a yellow flower dress in the amber light. One step. Another. Another. Another. I remember the spiraling dream, how she came toward that spot as if God had put it there, or maybe the devil, and as if the whole universe had mapped it out long ago, planning to get even with me or with her, or maybe just declaring the immense meaninglessness of it all.

One more step. Then Song stops with one bare foot awkwardly in front of the other. She is halfway across, only a few inches from where I had stood. She is not looking down, but up at me now, completely motionless, not even rocking little Songkha, who is crying.

Has Song stopped because she felt something? Have her toes touched something? Or does she just want me to come and get the child?

As in the dream, she stands there waiting for me, except

266

she is not smiling at all. Everything about her is frozen. She even seems to be holding her breath.

Quick, careful steps, and I am almost to her. As I get closer, I see she is terribly frightened and silently crying. I reach out and touch the small bundle in her arms. At first she does not offer the infant to me but waits, still frozen, still holding her breath. Then, slowly, she hands me Songkha. The infant immediately struggles and cries louder, knowing it is not her mother's arms. Song stands, not moving an inch, balancing herself, one foot still in front of the other. But now that I have the child, Song's body starts to relax. She exhales and smiles with immense relief, and I realize she was just scared, just asking me for help. I wonder if maybe she remembers me now, if maybe she is smiling at me too.

I turn and start back, realizing that I have also been holding my breath. I exhale, panting and sweating. Little Songkha and I are almost there. I reach the far side again and go down on one knee in the tall grass and leaves. I close my eyes with relief, holding her against me, muffling her infant cries. Then I pivot slowly to check on Song. She is still balancing herself, her feet apart. Trembling, and with her eyes fixed on her child in my arms, she seems to wait an unearthly minute.

She lifts her rear foot. There is a quiet popping noise, a primer detonating, followed by an explosion. Not like the other one. A glaring blue and white light that blossoms upward. And then thunder shakes the earth.

A blast of wind hits my body, plastering my shirt tight to my chest and tossing me on my back. At the same instant a cloud of red mist, and unrecognizable bits fly toward me. It is dirt but wet like mud. Pieces of it in my face. Red speckles on my shoulders. But little Songkha is covered in my arms. She is safe. Yellow lights glare down into my face. I put up a hand to shield my eyes and feel tiny fragments in my forehead, rough shards like glass.

Somewhere there is an echo, then another, and then a terrible ringing in my ears. I roll to my knees and elbows, still clutching little Songkha. The dirt below me sprinkles with red droplets. It is red everywhere. So much red. Red is life. Is it my redness? Is my life spurting away?

My pants are ripped, and my legs exposed, a pox of red speckles everywhere. I close my eyes and try to think. Song, I must find her. I must find her.

There is heat against my body. I open my eyes to see grass fires on both sides of me, and white smoke. I kneel and look across the perimeter. No one is there. Only a small crater where she stood and a mound of something, a heap, a twisted mass. There is a sound, a shout, and I spin around on my knees. More shouts. But they are all my shouts, followed by a whimpering, and it is mine too. She is dead. No, the white smoke is hiding her.

White smoke. The heat is stronger. Song is caught in the fires. Or she has run clear altogether. I scan through the smoke to catch her movements. But she has escaped. I push myself up, tottering as I stand with little Songkha tight against my chest. I turn in every direction. Behind me are the trees. Song must have lost sight of me and passed beyond me and headed through them, running wildly. I must find her and hide her.

The grass fire is closer, and I shout for her, but now the ringing in my ears drowns out my own sounds. The grass fire turns to black smoke, and flesh is burning. I fall to my knees again, rocking back and forth with little Song-kha. Her mouth is open, but I can't hear her screams. Pain spreads through my legs, my chest, my arms and head, but I must concentrate on Song. I must find her before they do. There is a voice speaking. It is my own voice, a voice inside me, and I am not really hearing it but feeling it. It says, *Oh, God, no,* and it accuses me, saying, *It is too late, too late to redeem yourself. Everything is lost. Everything is your fault, from the very beginning.*

39

A STILL POINT

The noise level rises, but it is only in my ears. In its center is a terrible pounding, the cosmic clock of my pulse.

My hands are pale yellow in the light but spotted with red. I look at the thumb broken backward and my broken wrist like a small balloon. The splintered bone is pushing through the skin now, and I try to push it back in, but it won't go. I have to ignore it. I have to ignore every distraction. I have to move boldly, through the jungle growth and up out of the valley. I can't even worry about Song. She has escaped. Yes, she has escaped and is running wildly in fear. When she calms down, she will find us, or she will be waiting for us somewhere.

The noise in my ears begins to subside, and there are other noises now, shouts and high-pitched screams of little voices. I rise to my feet, cradling the bundle which screams. I turn and face the other screams, which are coming from behind, screaming dolls coming toward me. The screams stop when the children see me. The horror on their faces. My broken nose and bloody face. Clothes torn and splattered with red pocks. Singed hair. Bone protruding. Staggering and grotesque, I take a step toward them. They back away. The chubby Chinese girl covers her eyes. Even Amkha backs away from me.

Barefoot, I step sideways along the outer edge of the perimeter, looking for a space between trees and the leaves that jut out. I glance back. They are following, Amkha first, then Florie, then the two Thai girls and the others holding on to each other in single file. They are sobbing. After about twenty yards the lights reveal a narrow break in the growth, not a trail, just a groove into the jungle that circles the outside of the perimeter. I push through some leaves, cradling little Songkha who still screams in my arms.

The perimeter lights fade behind me, and now there is only the black wall of trees and night. This ring of jungle is only thirty or forty yards deep, but I am a blind man holding a screaming child with one arm and brushing back invisible branches with the other as I try to move forward. Mosquitoes rush up into my face, covering me. I try to wipe them away, but they stick to the blood on my cheeks and chin. I hear the children coughing out mosquitoes behind me. Something reaches out from behind. It must be Amkha, grabbing the waist of my pants. I imagine them all behind me now in a line, holding to each other, and I am careful to walk slowly so that no one will get lost.

Then my bare feet find cold mud, and I stop. Except for the whir of mosquitoes, every jungle noise stops with me. The brush of leaves, the rustle of branches, the whimper of tall grasses: They are all mute. Even little Songkha's screaming has stopped. An edgy silence. I fight to listen for any other human noise, running feet or whispers, but there is only the drumming in my own ears and the quiet sobs and raspy coughs of the children. I reach out in the utter blackness to feel their heads to make sure they are really there. Yes, there are six of them. They are in the mud too and now struggle to lift their feet. They huddle around me, crying, and then we continue on, a monkey chain of hand holding hand.

Finally there is the faintest light ahead and to the left. I push toward it. There is a natural sloping downward, and the mud gets deeper. Then we brush through some leaves, and the world opens to us again.

The mud is thinner now, watery and cold, and our feet sink deeper. It is dark, stench-filled mud, alive with bacteria and algae. It is the smell of the world rotting. There is a damp clump wriggling on my ankle, shiny black. Before it can fasten, I flick it off with my other foot and push it back into its subterranean world.

The faint light I saw before was from the sky above us, a canopy of stars, their light reaching us from a billion miles away. It reflects in the water at our feet, shining on the children, revealing their faces, swollen by mosquito bites.

I encourage them forward, out of the last few yards of sucking mud, and we begin our climb from the valley floor, zigzagging back and forth in a line. Song must be on another trail, making her own way up. There is no commotion from the compound. Perhaps they have decided to leave us to the wilderness or to wait until morning to find us.

At the top of the hill I look back at the villa ringed in yellow and can just make out the footprints where we crossed. The children cry as they stare down at the distant and tiny form of Sammy, who seems pasted to the ground. And the empty crater. And the heap, the twisted mass. It is not Song. It is not Song. I try to calm the children by pointing up at the clear cathedral sky. But they don't care about the stars. They just continue to stare down at Sammy and claw at the bites on their faces.

We sit a moment to rest beneath the grand sky. Quietly a memory seeps through all the pain: of how as a boy I spent hours at a science museum staring up the long wire of a pendulum that swung lazily from one side to the other. I could not see where the wire was attached ten stories high, but I knew that somewhere up there was an unmoving center, a geometric point, a place that was motionless.

Gazing up at the stars now, I wish there were an invisible wire connecting me to a still point somewhere that is free from the earth's confusion, where there are no justifications for evil, no bargaining for right. A place where there is no orphanage or perimeter or blue and white flash of light and a silent heap and crater. A placc whcrc thcrc is only goodness. A place for children.

Which way to go now? The universe offers no opinion.

A breeze brushes against my cheek, and with it comes the faint sound of running water. Amkha hears it too and hushes the children.

"Pra puttaroop sirung," she whispers to them.

Little Songkha's face is swollen with bites, and she is beginning to cry again in my arms. I stand and then point in the direction of the trickling water. *"Pra puttaroop sirung,"* I repeat in a whisper. Rainbow Buddha.

40

SHADOWS

We move in single file, a thin line of the world's people, as we approach the back of the marble Buddha. The statue is like a huge shadow against the starry sky.

I am first, cradling little Songkha while trying to keep my broken hand as high as I can to minimize the throbbing. Behind me Florie clutches my shirt, followed by the two Thai girls, then the Chinese girl and the French girl, and finally Amkha. We are a sad parade.

At the base of the statue a man sits cross-legged in a golden robe. In front of him two candles flicker. He must hear the baby screaming, but he does not move or even open his eyes. His hands rest delicately in his lap, palms up. His head is shaved. His back is straight, his chin raised and motionless.

The temperature has dropped quickly, and the mosquitoes have fled the cold air. A chilly gust crosses my cheeks as we approach him, and with it comes a fresh scent of wilderness, as if a cool trickle of oxygen has just escaped from a spring somewhere in the sky.

I glance at little Songkha and hope that her mother will find us soon. In that explosion of the bright blue and white flash, she jumped clear. Now she is climbing the hill to look for us. Certainly she can hear her child screaming. In a minute she will find us here at the base of the great marble Buddha.

We stand in front of the monk. The thin light of the candles illuminates the Buddha's marble sandals and marble ankles. The monk remains motionless, the folds of his golden robe splayed out around him in a circle. He does not acknowledge us. He is somewhere else. In some cosmic reverie. Here yet not here, deserting this place and us.

A moth finds the two candles and circles them wildly, beating itself against the glass, its paper wings sputtering in the air.

I know the moth. I know the beating of its wings. It is like Song and like every other frail and confused person who strives for a moment of clarity. The moth is Sammy, who will always be the same in my mind: a tiny young man saluting me; not a doll but a brave person who deserved more than a frightful life and a frightful death. In my mind I see the ants marching in columns toward Sammy's blood, tickling at his ear, forming a black line across his cheek, across his lips, and even into his open mouth.

I shake my mind free of the image. There is still so much that has to be done if we are to escape.

The children and Amkha face the monk, as if maybe he has the answers. In the chilly air there is a soft white vapor from his mouth. But he does not move. He does not help us. There are no answers anywhere.

I hand the tiny bundle to Amkha, and I step past the monk and the candles to the trickling water as it flows over the great Buddha's feet. I lower my broken hand into the black, mossy water. It is cold, very cold and at first seems to burn, but finally it is numbing, and I am grateful.

There is a rumble of thunder, slow and deep, from miles away. A storm somewhere. I look up, but the air is still clear and strewn with the radiance of stars.

We need warmth now. Amkha hands little Songkha back to me and quickly scrapes twigs and dried leaves into a pile. She motions the children to move some rocks into a circle to shelter the fire and hide the flames. Everyone works together. Then Amkha goes to the monk. His eyes are closed, and he does not see how she bows politely before removing a candle to light the fire, and then bows again when replacing it. The leaves burn quickly, but the twigs and reeds are green and at first resist. She adds more leaves until the flames tear a little hole in the night.

The children huddle together, opening their arms to the heat. The light flickers gold in their eyes as they scratch at their cheeks and foreheads. Amkha gets up and a few minutes later comes back with handfuls of mud. She spreads the mud over their swollen faces, one by one. Now, in the firelight, the children are nearly black-faced, with circles around their eyes. They look hideous, like deformed flies. I don't know whether to laugh or cry. But tomorrow the mud will be useful as camouflage when we escape out of this place the same way Amkha and I came in.

I want to make them understand that we are stepping toward freedom, not toward death, that we are doing this together. I speak first to the two Thai girls, asking them to tell me their names. *"Khoon chur a-rai?"* I say to them.

"Chrai," replies one behind her tearful mud mask. She looks to the other Thai girl.

"Dorais," she says meekly.

I try to smile at them, a reassuring smile. But the pain is excruciating, and I am aware of how grotesque my face must look against the flickering flames.

I nod to the French girl. *"Comment t'appelles?"* I say.

"Je m'appelle Ellie," she responds.

"Ellie, tu es parisienne?"

"Non, je ne suis pas française. J'habite Québec."

"Québec?" I say, trying not to sound surprised. *"On est très loin de Québec. Mais n'ais pas peur. Tu es sûre. Je vais t'emmener chez toi, à ton papa et ta maman."*

She trembles a smile.

The Chinese girl scratches at her face through the mud. *"Bu yao chua tse chi de lien,"* I say, telling her not to scratch, that it will only get worse. I am aware that of all my years of language learning, this moment is the most rewarding moment. I ask the Chinese girl her name. *"Ni ming ma?"*

"Yi Ping," she answers softly, still scratching at her face. *"Ni neng di wo huy chia?"*

She wants to know if I will take her home. "Yes," I say in English. Then I look at all of them. "I will make sure all of you get home."

They seem to understand. Their eyes are on me. Little Florie speaks up. "How? I think it is very far."

"Where do you live?" I ask gently.

"In Los Angeles. In a big house. Four-four-two-three Oak Drive."

I nod. "I will make sure you get there."

Yi Ping yawns a gigantic yawn, and soon the others follow. So cold and frightened, yet they cannot stop the sleep. Ellie leans her head against Yi Ping and closes her eyes. The two Thai girls hug each other as their eyes flutter closed.

The fire is winking out. Amkha goes hunting again for sticks and leaves. Little Songkha is almost asleep in my arms, her skin brown in this light, her eyes unfocused. She does not know me. She does not know friend from foe. She is not really one of us yet, her world still so simple. The weight of her in my arms is comforting. She is the future, a secret that no one can guess. I lie down and place her on my stomach, drawing my knees up, holding her against me in the dark.

I doze too and then awaken at the sound of thunder. But the storm passes in the distance. Amkha is curled beside me, her arm across my stomach and her hand touching little Songkha. The fire is out, and the children are nestled around us, dolls again, everyone sharing their warmth. The candles have burned out, but the monk is still there, still visiting some place I do not know.

The sky is a little lighter. In moments the stars will fade behind the morning veil. Ahead of me lies the longest day of my life. I must rouse the children and set out. We must be ready as soon as it is light enough to walk.

Then a shadow shifts in the corner of my eye. I turn

my head sharply, and the shadow disappears, blending into other shadows as if sucked back into the darkness.

I can feel him out here. Death is in that direction. Shadows seem to hover, their edges moving, conspiring. It is not a trick of my imagination. Death is real. He was even my friend once. He does not have a bony finger as in the stories. He is a gentleman who has been to college and to the Branscomb Institute. He has blond hair and blue eyes that sparkle in a knowing way, as if he understands the world very well. And now he is looking for us because he knows what is best.

I roll over onto all fours, shielding little Songkha under me. I squint into the shadows but can see nothing more. I strain to listen. I concentrate, willing my heart to be calm so I can stop the pounding in my ears and hear where he is coming through the dimness. An infant is supposed to die. I am supposed to die. Maybe we all will die now.

41

THE LAST PERSON

I try to gather all my vision into one spark, my eyes fixed and unblinking at the spot where the shadow had moved.

Two forms separate themselves from the shadows, a man and a woman, nearly as dark as the shadows themselves. I try to anticipate where the others will be, sort out their assignments as they attempt to outguess my moves. Maybe a handful are circling. Others are cutting off our escape. And one or two remain back at Wonderful Place in case we try to trick them and return. Maybe they believe that this artist at operations is also an artist at escape and evasion. But it is too late to worry about the others, too late to think of anything now except these two shadows.

The sky lightens quickly. The man and woman are under the overhanging trees, only thirty yards away. They must be able to see us spread out here on the ground, the children still asleep.

They step toward us slowly, inches at a time, their eyes sweeping left and right as if anticipating an ambush. Or maybe they are looking for others in their search party. I can see Vaal's clothes are torn, and there is disgust on his face. I can even see the coarse blond stubble around his angry frown. He looks like a ghost, his blond hair so whitish. He holds some kind of automatic rifle, thick, black, and compact, carrying it in two hands like an experienced infantryman. Rennard stays half a step behind, her hands at her side, and in her right hand is a pistol, probably the same CZ-75 that I tossed away. She looks like a witch now, her face dark and incensed, her hair tangled from branches and vines.

A ghost and a witch are coming for me. They are coming to get their dolls back.

I feel all of the last four days crashing in my head. The struggle to get here. The confusion, the lies. And then I didn't kill Vaal and Rennard. I should have done the difficult thing, the terrible but necessary thing, the evil that was good.

I rise to my knees, leaving little Songkha curled on the ground near Amkha. Vaal turns directly toward me. With an easy motion his hands move, and I hear the action of the bolt engage.

Let them come toward me. Let them deal with *me*. Let them have *me* if they want, and maybe somehow a few of the others can get away. That is the most I can hope for now.

I stand, and my head and my hand throb as if a hammer is hitting them every second. Around me bodies are spread in a circle. Dolls. Not moving. Not crying. Not knowing what is about to happen. And the statue—it too is unmoving, except for its colors, which are now taking on the whitish pink of the new day. The old monk is also unmoving. His candles burned down. He is my last chance. If there is good in the world, then the monk will rise suddenly and with a single gesture demand that they stop. His years of spiritual equilibrium will pour forth with holy authority that no one, not even a ghost and a witch, would dare question, and in an instant they will be brought to their knees, and the monk will lead us to one of the caves in the hills, to feed and shelter us.

Except he does not move. He sits straight, silent. The world will go on, and there is no way out of it. That is why he does not help. There is no help. There is no heaven to make everything right. There are only this ghost and witch with their guns. The good that is evil. And Ellie and Florie, the Thai girls, and baby Songkha—the good that is good. Yes, the good that is good.

Everything happens so fast that I can't rely on my memory anymore. The picture that I see in my mind is clear, but I am not in the frame. It is all happening around me and to me. Vaal steps toward me, quicker now. I am surprised by his animal eyes and the depth of revulsion in his face, a revulsion that says this time there will be no leniency, no arguments, no appeals. I have become more than just a nuisance. I have refused to understand. Something *must* be done now because they are going to save the world.

He raises the automatic rifle to his shoulder as he walks, pointing it directly at me. I raise my hands and step away from the children, who are still asleep. There will be one shot through my heart or through my head, and it will all be over. The children will be led back. Amkha will be beaten. Little Songkha will be given to Yanaga, who will kill her to protect his lineage. Trinity Two will be stopped. The world will go on just as before.

My hands still in the air, I try to get distance from the children in case I can dive into a bush or scramble somewhere and make them come after me. Or maybe Song will arrive just in time and she will have a gun and spray bullets at them to stop this. But my mind sees the explosion at the perimeter again and the crater where she stood, the mangled mass, and the blood splattered across my face and hair, and I know that Song will not be coming.

Vaal moves quickly now, past the children, sighting down the barrel.

My hands involuntarily go out to protect my face, as if flesh and bone might deflect a bullet. I can feel all at once the strange sensation of my life: the Work, the years of loneliness and isolation, and the slow transformation of my mind and body from its youthful energy to this tired form. And I feel that all along everything has been neatly unfolding to lead me to this place and this moment, step by step through the course of my own choices. But in some final way I have not failed. I *did* try. I *did* come back here. I *did* attempt to change everything.

Vaal takes aim, and I see just the small mouth of the barrel. The world is magnified frame by frame, the spectrum of my mind becoming wider but the focus narrower. The smallest thing fills an eternity. A leaf crunches loudly under my feet. The cry of a hawk somewhere overhead. The great Buddha's head, its pink hue changing to orange as the sun rises and the light creeps down his shoulders in millimeters.

Vaal turns to Rennard and nods. Suddenly I know what is happening. It will be her test. *I* will be her test. Just as the man in Kyoto was *my* test. But there is no sympathy or reluctance in her face. It is as Vaal said: She is totally committed.

She takes three steps forward and raises the handgun. I want to shout, "*Don't!*" but I am resolved not to beg. Yet in my head is an enormous *No!* It grows louder. *No, I will not die standing here. No, I will not leave this world passively. No, I will not be dead before I can comprehend the finality of all this. No! No!*

I begin to move. So slowly, it seems. A middle-aged fullback, clumsy and heaving but intensely alive, feet slipping on the dewy ground, but every thready little nerve wide-awake, my arms and torso lunging, hands held up to protect my face. The explosion, so loud it is beyond understanding, and a bullet splits the side of my left hand and grazes my scalp, but there is no pain, only a splatter of red across my face. Another explosion, and something grooves my neck. No pause for conscious thought. Now my steps are not small and slow, but a dead run. I leap, hearing shouts of confusion from the children. I fall hard, onto nothing.

She has jumped to the side and spun to the ground, now in the prone firing position. From my knees I leap at her again and roll over and over and over toward her, hugging my arms against myself to protect my bloodied hands. An order is shouted to Rennard, a command of some sort. Yes, kill me. But I will kill you too, Rennard. You will be the last person I will ever kill. You will be the last person I will ever see. I think of the slaughter of the infant she is willing to undertake. Sheer evil. Sheer evil.

Another explosion, but I cannot feel it. Another, and I cannot feel it. I scramble along the ground and plunge wildly at her. I feel her hands and then the barrel of the gun, cold and hard and serious, and I try to twist the metal back and forth. I have never felt such pain. And then another explosion. The gun recoils from her grip, and I lunge at it, lifting its thick weight with splintered hands.

More cries from the children, and I hear them scrambling somewhere. Vaal is out of my vision, but he does not fire at me. Rennard jumps to her feet and scrambles away, then turns. I hold the gun between my hands and raise it, but I cannot grip it. For some reason Vaal does not fire. I am alive. Still alive. Why doesn't Vaal fire? Why doesn't he fire? Has Yanaga come across the perimeter and grabbed him? Is he the Savior we need?

I have no time to think. I sandwich the gun between my swollen and bloody hands, and point it at Rennard. She stands frozen now, or she is studying the gun as if she does not believe I will do it, or believe that I *can* do it, my hands so slippery and swollen and broken that I cannot even pull the trigger.

Sometimes people make pacts with God, telling Him that if He'll come through just this once, they will be different or give Him some special payback. Usually they want something big. But what I want is small. I just want to pull this trigger. God, help me pull this trigger, please.

But the God of heaven is not the god of this world or of fantasies and screaming babies. Perhaps I should pray to the devil. He is the god who makes fantasies come true. I will pray to anyone—Jesus, Buddha, God, the devil— whoever will pull the trigger. Him I will worship. *Pull the goddamn trigger.*

42

SCREAMS

Something slides in. A bone. A finger. Rennard gives a strangled little cry. She is not hit, only surprised, stunned by the noise from my hand. Then I see the small hole in her blouse, low on her breast. Her mouth opens as in a dream, trying to shout, trying to tell me to stop. I fire again, and this time her hair leaps and her head takes on a strange, distorted form. Her legs go out from under her, and she crumples backward.

Spots in my eyes, and I fight them off, fight off the dizziness, the growing darkness. There is a soft roar of unconsciousness coming on, oblivion, a swelling roar that is trying to overtake me. For an instant darkness grips my mind. Then I swim up again to a whiteness, a brightness, and it hurts my eyes, and then I can see the world again as I fight off the pain to stay conscious and not go into shock. The world looks orange and blood-red, or it is only the great statue of the Buddha alchemizing the colors of the morning light. I expect Vaal to be standing over me, grinning, ready to fire, and it will all be over.

But he is not there.

Spots are still in my eyes, and through them I see Amkha and a swarm of children pulling at Vaal, leaping and punching. Little Songkha lies on the ground alone, kicking and crying. By the Buddha the monk still sits, not hearing little Songkha's cries or not caring. Vaal tries to twist from the grip of the children, swatting them away; they are dwarfs, little people of no importance, the lowest rung on the human food chain. Then Amkha has him by the shoulders. He pushes her back and swings the butt of his weapon, a crushing blow against her face, and she crumples.

I have no hands that I can fight with. But the time is now. Indisputably now. I stagger to my feet and run at him, a curdling yell escaping my throat, the frustration of a lifetime. He turns, trying to level the gun as my body slams his. I clutch him hard to keep him from raising the weapon, and we go down together, rolling and rolling for position. A single word struggles from his mouth: *sonofabitch*. I am on top, his arms to his side now, and there is an instant that we see each other's eyes, locked together in a perfect understanding. We know what we are doing, what each is trying to do. Everything comes to me at once, the bright light of the future reaching me through a narrow tunnel, and I have a knowledge of what may happen if I kill him. People from every nation have a stake in what is happening now, here on this backside of a hill in this backland of a half-backward nation. Every human being. And I think they all would want Vaal to stop me. But it does not matter. What matters is this one evil, this evil here, now, the screams of little children swarming, kicking, and a baby crying.

I have only one weapon left. I slam my forehead downward against his head and up again and then another slam down. And another. There is blood on his face and scalp, but it is mine, and I slam down again, holding his arms down with my elbows, the gun forced into the dirt, pinning his body with my weight, smashing, smashing. All of this for the dolls. All of this for little Songkha.

He tries to buck me off, and I am winded, unable to breathe, and feel as if I am drowning, and with all my remaining strength I smash him again. I start to drift, to pass out, and I fight it off, trying to focus on the screams around me to keep me awake or maybe alive, smashing him again, each blow more painful, but each blow rendering him more helpless, a little less struggle from him each time. I can feel him, but barely see him, my eyes smeared with liquid. I smash downward one more time. He is motionless. Unconscious or dead. The color seems to wash out of him, and then he is a red blur, and then he is lost behind the blur.

There are sounds inside my head now, and I hear every word in the world, every language, and they all are speaking of the huge mushroom clouds and condemning me, all of them saying the same thing: that these children are just a handful among the millions. I am just one, and little Songkha is just one among the millions. Just one. Just one.

I roll off Vaal's body onto my back. Above me is the statue, blood-red but still serene. Part of me seems paralyzed, and all I can do is sweep my hand across the dirt, groping for little Songkha. I feel children around me, above me, touching me gently, brave children, the world's children telling me that they will make a difference, that they will make the world good and safe.

I sweep my hand across the dirt again and find a tiny leg. I cannot grip it. I cannot pull her to me. I crawl toward her blindly. My ears open, and I hear the screaming, the wonderful screaming. And I curl in a ball around her, enveloping the screams, and she is warm and wet against me, and safe, and I don't want to hush the screams because they are loud and urgent and sweet and strong. They are screams of life.

It is finally over. I begin to weep with happiness and feel the tears on my face flowing over the blood. I lie on my back again. I wipe away my eyes and look up, longing to see a clear sky. A new day.

Dr. Kenji Yanaga stands over me.

"They are dead," I say. "I did what you asked." Then

I see that he is holding Vaal's automatic rifle, pointing it at me.

"My father's name was Takeo," he says over little Songkha's screams. "He was the little man, Mr. Gaines, who was walking home to my mother that night."

43

"**I** waited two years to meet you," he says, pushing the barrel against my cheek. "I thought you might look like one of those murderers in your movies. That you would have scars and speak with a growl."

The pain in my hands is so great that it is numbing, or I am going into shock. I look up the barrel to Yanaga's eyes. "What about the child?" I say.

"Just a child," he answers.

"But your child. A mongrel. A *konketsuji*."

"Then she is everyone's child," he says. "She is innocent. I will take her to a real orphanage. Nothing bad will happen to her. I promise. All children are innocent. Songkha was innocent."

Yanaga turns to Amkha and nods. She rushes over and lifts the baby from my arms, then steps back.

"I identified my father for the police, by his suit and shoes," he continues. "There was not enough left of his face when you were finished with him."

"You know they tricked me."

"It doesn't matter. You did it. You did it for your organization, but you are guilty. They tricked me also. And I am guilty too. Of using Songkha. I hated the fantasy business, yet I played into its hands. I always tried to be a good man, but when I saw Songkha, I could not help myself. Do you have fantasies too, Mr. Gaines?''

"Others will be coming, Yanaga. We don't have time.''

"You don't have time,'' he replies. "I have all the time in the world. Your fantasy business still needs me to stop the rearming. I am their only hope.''

"But they will take the children and force them. There are others like Dr. Inoki waiting out there.''

"I am not a man of vengeance, Mr. Gaines. But I am a man of justice. My father made me swear I would never kill. But I must break that oath now. Just once. And without remorse. For my mother and my family's honor.''

"Let me stand up, Dr. Yanaga.''

"Yes, I will let you stand before I kill you. And I will shoot you in your face, the same way you shot my father, except you will know why. Maybe when I am finished, your mother will identify you by your clothes and shoes. You have a family, I understand.''

"Yes.''

"Good.''

He moves back and motions for me to stand. I go to my elbows and slowly struggle to my feet.

"DeForest and Rennard were fools to think I would try to stop Trinity Two only if they trapped me. Now they are both dead, and that is no loss. I thank you for your help. You have my word that if it is possible, I will stop the rearming. But I must finish this first, for my father.''

The rainbow Buddha changes to blue. The monk does not move. An owl lifts from the trees. Then, from off to the side, a little voice speaks shakily but with determination.

"*Je vais vous tuer, monsieur.*'' Ellie, the Canadian girl, stands unblinking, holding Rennard's pistol in two hands, pointing it at Yanaga.

"She says she will kill you,'' I translate.

"Then there will be no one to stop the rearming. Tell her that.''

"She's only a child, Yanaga. She won't understand.

And you will make her kill you. You will make her live with that.''

The children move closer to Yanaga. "Get back!" he shouts, unnerved, swinging the weapon around at them. They stop. He turns back to me to take aim.

Then Florie steps toward me. "No!" I scream. "Stay back!" But she keeps coming, unfazed. She wraps her arms around my leg, half hiding from Yanaga, her face filled with tears. Then Dorais and Chrai, the two Thai children, step forward and huddle against me on the other side, both facing Yanaga. Then chubby Yi Ping comes and stands behind me, peeking out under my legs. Amkha last, and she boldly stands in front of me with baby Songkha.

I look to Ellie. She faces Yanaga and steadies the gun. He faces me and steadies his weapon. We are a triangle of the world's hopes and fears and mistrusts, each of us making choices. All the intrigue, all the lies, all the debates of great nations and minds, and it funnels down to one little girl standing alone, deciding if the rearming will continue, and maybe deciding the future of the planet.

''*Pas plus de meurtres,*'' Ellie says firmly. There is no apology in her voice.

Yanaga looks to me. "No more murders," I translate.

Yanaga turns back to Ellie, then gazes upward at the clear sky. The sun is already high above the Buddha.

''*Pas plus de meurtres,*'' Ellie says again.

Dr. Yanaga tries to steady the gun on me, but the weapon trembles in his hands. He looks as if he will collapse. Then he lowers the weapon, and it falls from his hand.

EPILOGUE

I keep trying to think of ways I could have made it turn out differently, made it turn out better. But I can't. Everything has already turned out, except for the future. The strategic struggle for power continues, and I have no idea if Yanaga will be successful in stopping the rearming.

My life goes on. We were able to make our way out through the jungle, taking the same route that Amkha and I had taken in, the children first washing me and bandaging me with their nighties and then Amkha leading the way as the children helped me across the valley and through the jungle and back to the road. The secrecy of the Fantasy Plan and the isolation of the orphanage worked to our advantage, and we were able to elude whatever guards or patrols were sent after us. Or perhaps Wonderful Place had no other guards at all—except the yellow lights, and the moon-surfaced perimeter, and the plastic detonator caps waiting beneath the dust like hundreds of little soldiers.

Once at the road, we flagged down a truck heading south to Lamphum and then caught another truck that took us through Phitsanulok and Mae Sa and finally to Bangkok, the perfect place to disappear. We rested for two

290

weeks in a shack along a back canal. Each day a doctor came to change my bandages and give me medication. I slept almost every hour of those days, and the children slept too. But each time they awakened, they did every little thing they could for me.

Then, on a Monday morning I took the children to the Bangkok branch of the United Nations, to the Division of Children's Welfare on the second floor. I left them behind a counter with a warm, matronly British woman who was teary-eyed when she saw how they hugged my waist and cried and then bravely said good-bye to me before I left. I gave no explanation to the woman, and none would have been believed. I just told her these were important children, and I was entrusting her to find their correct homes. I took her name, Lesley Turner, and told her I would check back every few days to see what progress was made.

From there I went back to the Fantasy Store. I knew I could not stop them, but I had to do something. I would walk in and smash the glass separating the women from the customers, let it fall in sheets so that the women were not looking into a mirror but into the eyes of the men who had come to rent them. Let the men be on display too. Let everyone be face-to-face.

But the Fantasy Store wasn't there. It was the same address and the same blue building with a yellow door on Thaniya Road near Lumphini Park. But it wasn't there. Transformed overnight into a boutique of some sort and a salon. At first I thought that maybe everything was just a dream, so incredible it all seemed, except that my hands and my head were still bandaged, and a group of Japanese men wandered the street with address cards and perplexed looks. No doubt they would get the new location soon enough. The name of the game is and always has been access.

Right now I am sitting in front of a cassette recorder, recording all this. I turn it on and off by punching a button with a pencil I hold in my mouth. I cannot change cassettes myself, but Amkha is here to help me.

We are no longer in Thailand. Amkha and little Songkha

have no future there, so we made the journey south into
Malaysia and to Kuala Lumpur, the capital city. Here it
is easier to bribe officials to obtain visas and a false
birth certificate.

And Song. I lost the picture of her, and that is okay. I
must forget. Because remembering makes everything present, makes everything happen again and again. But even
without the picture, the reel of her still plays in my mind,
how her very presence dared me to remember what goodness was and dared me to remember what *I* was like before
the numbness set in. In my mind Song steps again across
the perimeter so bravely and freezes, one foot in front of the
other, balancing as if on a high wire; the immense silence
as I cross to her and reach out for the small bundle, and
she hands me her child, and the relief on her face, even
a soft smile, knowing that little Songkha is safe. I step
away, and then I hear it again, the quiet popping noise,
and I see the glaring blue and white light. Rewind, replay:
She steps bravely, she freezes, the silence as I cross, she
hands me little Songkha. Rewind, replay: Over and over
she hands me Songkha, she hands me Songkha, she hands
me Songkha.

I want it to have happened some other way, that the
small crater where she stood, and the twisted pile, were
just a mistake in my vision, a trick of the lights. I want
to believe that in the confusion she made it safely to the
other side and then on to a small town where someone
nice gave her food and work, and later she will meet
someone gentle, a nice Thai man to care for her, and she
for him. But Song is not in some small town, and she will
not meet a nice Thai man.

I ask Amkha to change cassettes for me. She is sleepy
because it is early morning. The sun is just now beginning
to stream in through the window. Lovely in the golden
light, Amkha rises from the bed. She brings me a fresh
cup of coffee, then checks the bandages on my hands,
concerned that I have stayed up through the night. She
replaces the cassette with a new one, the last one I will

need. She pushes the play button and kisses me gently on the cheek, then on the neck and returns to bed.

My story is almost finished.

Things rarely end the way we think they will, the way we hope they will. In this case they have not yet ended at all. I still need to make my way home, and there may be more incidents on the way. But I am so tired of it all. So very tired. Tomorrow I will mail these cassettes to *The Times* of London and a copy to *The New York Times*. It is my hope that the world will know about the Fantasy Plan and the young women. It is my hope that the world will care. But I understand how the Organization works. Files disappear. Headlines disappear. Cassettes disappear. Children disappear. Even agent handlers disappear. In the event that something happens to me before I get back, I will also send a copy to my mother and my sister in Ohio.

And if I make it back to Ohio, my mother and sister will be surprised that I am not alone for once, that I arrive with a woman and a child. And not just a woman, but someone beside me who is simple and comfortable and true, someone who has already begun to fill in the lonely spaces of my life.

I will tell my mother and Beth that little Songkha is my child. That's not the truth. But sometimes the truth doesn't make sense. Still, the fact is that little Songkha is already my child, more than anyone else's.

If I make it back, if *we* make it back, and the Fantasy Plan is revealed, I will then have a chance to begin my life again. I will use my real name. I will work a forty-hour week. I will look my co-workers in the eye. I will explore the one country I have seen the least, taking Amkha and little Songkha with me to Yellowstone Park, and to see the great stone faces on Mount Rushmore, and to stand with me in the tall bluegrasses of Kentucky. On weekends I will go by myself to a major-league park and relax in the bleachers with the sun in my face and delight in the freedom of the people around me, people who are laughing and shouting and unconcerned with any international games, any ultimate outcomes.

And in the end perhaps my father was right. The world will not change. It will always go on as before. But I can change. And I am changing my life. With Amkha and little Songkha my own world is wide open again, spacious and good.

We are coming home.

I am coming home.

ACKNOWLEDGMENTS

My thanks go to my mother, Jane Collins Gilboy, who first taught me to love words and who has been supportive of my writing and never hesitant to offer criticism when needed.

Occasionally an author will have an extraordinary editor who is also a collaborator. That was my good fortune in the case of *Operation Fantasy Plan*.

Susan Dane worked extensively with me on this manuscript from its first draft. Her editorial insights and her extraordinary sense of "story" and story structure have contributed to each page. I want to thank her for challenging me when I needed it, for giving each line and phrase her thorough attention, and for helping guide the project over the two years of our work.

Electrifying Thrillers by
Ryne Douglas Pearson

"A gifted high-tech specialist . . .
with mind-boggling expertise"
Kirkus Reviews

CAPITOL PUNISHMENT
72228-3/$5.99 US/$7.99 Can

Bodies litter the street in L.A.—victims of a lethal
chemical killer unleashed by an American monster
who has decreed that the government, too, must die.

OCTOBER'S GHOST
72227-5/$5.99 US/$7.99 Can

Thirty-five years after the Cuban Missile Crisis, an
attempted coup breaks out against an aging Castro.
He aims a nuclear missile at a major city to force the
United States to become his ally against his enemies.

MERCURY RISING
80294-5/$6.50 US/$8.50 Can

What is locked in his mind will rock the world. . .